SOLO

Book Four of The Siren Series

By Alisa K. Michaels

a Y.A. Novel

For permission, contact **Belen Books, LLC**.

This is a work of fiction. Names, characters, businesses, places, events, locales, and incidents are either the products of the author's imagination or used in a fictitious manner. Any resemblance to actual persons, living or dead, spiteful Mermaids or Merfolk, Greek Mythological deities (benign or malevolent), conspiring high school socialites, or actual events or places is purely coincidental.

ISBN: 978-1-959715-40-5

Library of Congress Control Number: **2024933420**
Published by **Belen Books, LLC**
St. Petersburg, FL | Winter Park, FL | Chicago, IL USA
Belenbookspublishing.com

Edited by H.M. Fortalices and Beverly R. Waalewyn
Cover by Paul Hight and the Belen Media Group

10 9 8 7 6 5 4 3 2 1

18.3527° N, 65.0406° W

Printed in the United States of America

In Loving Memory of

Jasamine, Desmond & Anita

"if
the ocean can calm itself,
so can you.
we
are both salt water
mixed with
air."

— Nayyirah Waheed

SOLO

PREFACE

Every night since being back on Isla Flora, I dream.

Some mornings I wake and the dreams are foggy, hard to remember. Other times, they come to me in vivid technicolor; crimson reds, burnished golds, burnt umber, cool cucumber, iceberg blue, deep onyx… all of it shockingly beautiful and overwhelming.

There are scents I remember as well. Intense fragrances of wet wild grasses sprinkled with earthy mushrooms combined with heady mossy notes. Of course, my mind lingers over the flowery balm that combines with all of these elements to create the loveliest of natural perfumes. I breathe it all in, into my heart… into my soul… into my memory.

Around me, songbirds sing and chirp their greeting to Gaia's creatures and to a world just waking, just stretching… and it is heavenly. I close my eyes and let it wash away my doubt and fear…

As I take all of it in, a new smell slithers its way into my wonderland. It is the stench of emptiness and cold, of despair and hopelessness, of ruination and death. Then I understand why.

We cannot escape.

They are here...

CHAPTER ONE

Before *the Calling*, the sea was my master, and I was its bitch. I lived and breathed for it. No doubt, I would kill for it… enslave souls for it. The sea was my sanctuary, my fortress of solitude, my *sanctum sanctorum*. It was my home, but alas, now, it is just something lovely to look at, to admire—

I can't hold my breath much longer!

The churning sea ceases for a moment, and I take the opportunity to fight my way topside and take several quick, necessary breaths.

"Ando! Mom! *Somebody!*" I scream as another furious wave whips me around like a *Raggedy Ann* doll.

'Don't panic! Don't panic!' I keep reassuring myself as I hold my breath and tread water as if my life depends on it, which it does.

Refusing to give up, I duel against the waves and breach the surface again so to inhale a quick breath, but as soon as I do, another watery sledgehammer bashes me back under. With invisible hands, the undertow starts to pull me out towards open ocean, an ocean where there are no rules of engagement and no mercy. There is only fight or die, and right now, I do not wish to do either.

Dread engulfs me as my body slips farther down until I land on the sandy bottom below. Deciding that I want to live, I kick my feet and paddle my arms as I battle my way back to the surface, but still I feel like I am strapped with heavy weights. The aqueous embrace devours me, and without thought I inadvertently gulp causing my lungs to fill with salty liquid.

I'm a damn Siren! I can't die by drowning! It's too ironic!

Rapidly, this limpid world begins to fade as I drift into the abyss, and in the distance, swimming toward me is more of nothing. Logically, I know the seas are home to creatures that no longer see me as an equal, instead now view me as food. Sadly, with this epiphany, I realize there are no beautiful creatures with aquamarine eyes racing to save me.

Exhausted from treading water, I let my body go limp, knowing that this is my end. Wanting the peace that comes with oblivion, I close my eyes and listen to the muffled roar of the sea and pray that I will leave this plane of existence quickly, courageously.

Hopefully on the other side, I will see Grandpa Theo singing Greek folksongs as he dances. Or perhaps I will meet Grandfather Marcus, my mother's biological father, who once sailed the world on a fierce Roman battleship. In my brief existence, I have learned that anything is possible and in my heart, I know that Heaven is waiting for me.

Then, as if by divine providence, my brother's voice calls to me from somewhere beyond.

"Lena!" I hear Ando shouting. "Don't die! I'm sorry for being mean to you! Wake up!"

Multiple times, I feel something hit me on the chest followed by the sensation of hot air being blown into my mouth. Hot air flavored by… *Crackleberry Crisps*?

"I'm sorry, Lena!" Ando wails, and this time I feel my lungs expand then contract, filling and emptying like bellows over an ironsmith's forge. "You can't leave me alone!"

Hearing that plea, I bolt upright; sputtering and gagging as saltwater expels from my lungs, through my mouth and lands on my soaked bathing suit. Right next to me sits my brother, panting and crying at the same time. Uncaring of how he appears, he throws his arms around my neck and squeezes me tight. All I can do is gently hug back.

"What happened?" he begs, wiping his runny nose with the back of his hand as he slowly releases me.

I sit for a moment or two thinking about what happened, or, more accurately, what *did not* happen. Everything is foggy and difficult to remember. Needing to formulate an answer, I replay the events in my head and painstakingly explain them to my brother.

In true Ando form, he listens intently and then replies.

"Wow!"

I nod.

"I know, right?" I manage to squeak as my lungs and limbs slowly lose their strange burning sensation.

"Why wouldn't your gills work?" he asks with a confused frown.

Slowly I shrug, trying to figure out what went wrong.

"Do you feel sick?" he questions, touching my forehead as if he were a doctor and I was his ailing patient.

"I feel fine," I confess weakly. "But—"

Ando glares questioningly at me.

"But... what?" he probes with deep concern.

"Ever since Dad passed away... I mean after *the Calling*—" I stop abruptly as the memory floods into my mind again. For the past few weeks, I have tried my hardest to block it, but it refuses to leave me alone.

"C'mon, Lena," Ando urges, bright eyes glistening tearfully. "Tell me."

Taking a deep breath, I begin again.

"Since then, I haven't heard the call of the sea," I answer flatly. "At all."

My brother's eyebrows hitch.

"Not even a little bit?" he exclaims with bewilderment.

Sadly, I shake my head.

"Are you sure?" His eyes narrow.

"Of course I'm sure," I huff, trying to rise to my feet, but floundering back down.

"Stop, Lena!" Ando orders, holding me down without any effort. "You need to rest."

Suddenly, my body begins to shiver. Goosebumps cover my skin to the point that it hurts to touch. My throat also feels icky.

"I-I'm f-freezing," I stammer, rubbing my hands over my arms and legs in order to heat them.

"Take my hands," Ando commands like he is the older sibling.

"Okay," I whisper, letting him help me to my feet.

Gallantly, he places my arm around his small shoulders and takes my weight as we slowly walk up the rocky steps. With every step, my muscles tighten, and my limbs feel heavier. Truthfully, I have not felt this worn out in a very long time.

As we enter the house, Mom spots us from the top of the staircase. In her hands are a stack of neatly folded bath towels which she drops as she runs toward us, not caring that they spill onto the floor. The fear in her aquamarine eyes is both blinding and comforting at the same time.

"What happened?" she shouts, taking me from my brother's embrace.

"Lena's gills wouldn't start!" Ando cries, his eyes tearing.

"That's not possible," Mom denies under her breath.

"It's true," I confess with a sore throat.

"I found her!" he exclaims. "She wasn't breathing!"

Mom hugs him tightly then does the same to me.

"I'm c-cold," I tell over my chattering teeth.

"Sit down," the distraught woman instructs gently. "I'll be right back."

Quest driven, she disappears into the kitchen leaving Ando and me alone.

"I'll get a blanket," my brother notifies as he runs upstairs to the linen closet.

Within a few seconds he is back carrying a light gray fleece that we often used during the frigid Ohio winters. As if I will break, he carefully wraps it around my shivering shoulders making sure to tuck it around my body to hold in the precious heat. Intently, he studies me as if answers will come to him by just gazing at my face.

"Is that better?" he asks, looking up at me with those adorable puppy-dog eyes.

I nod my answer; finding it difficult to speak through quivering lips.

"Here you go, sweetheart," Mom announces as she exits the kitchen carrying a steaming bowl of canned chicken noodle soup and a mug of hot cocoa.

Eagerly, I reach out to take the items from her, but the air outside of the confines of the fleece feels like shards of icicles against my skin.

"I'll help you, Lena," my brother says with a sad little smile. "You just stay still."

"Thank you," I blush, feeling like an invalid, but enjoying all of the fuss.

With great care, Ando feeds me spoonfuls of the delicious soup as our mother asks me questions about my accident. As detailed as I can in my tired state, I repeat all that I had said to Ando.

"And that's when Ando saved my life," I utter, sipping the chocolaty beverage with the slightly dissolving mini marshmallows.

With great determination, Ando feeds me the last of the soup then hurries into the kitchen. He returns shortly holding a plate with a ham and cheese sandwich and a granny-smith apple. Grinning, he hands it to me.

"No thanks," I grimace. "I can't eat anything else right now."

Quizzically, my mother and brother glance at each other, then at me, then back to each other. Their mouths gape with surprise at my dismissal of more to eat. Normally, I could finish an entire stack of sandwiches plus a gallon of soup before feeling satisfied, but whatever is affecting my Siren abilities is also messing with my appetite.

"You should take a nice hot shower," Mom suggests, gently touching my shoulder as she tries to comfort me.

Still needing to warm-up, I nod.

"I will," I agree, standing slowly so as not to lose my balance, fall, and damage my body even further.

"Lena, be careful," Ando sighs as he notices my wobbly legs.

"I'm trying to," I smirk, not wanting him or our mother to worry any more than necessary.

Completely concerned, they continue to glower at me. Frankly, it makes me feel horribly uncomfortable and a bit like a baby who needs a great deal of care. I am a badass Siren chick who can kick the butts of slimy sea goddesses and stop an unstoppable God of War. I make myself smile with that image.

"May I go to bed?" I ask to the room in general. "I'm drained."

"Of course," Mom replies, giving a distressed smile. "Do you need some help getting upstairs?"

With as much strength as I can muster, I shake my head, wanting some solitude.

"No," I answer weakly. "I'll be fine."

"If you need anything… anything at all—" she reminds sincerely.

"I will call if I need you," I interrupt, tightening the blanket around my shoulders as I laboriously trudge to the upstairs bathroom that Ando and I share. "I promise."

Painfully, and with great effort, I undress then carefully examine my body for any strange bumps or bruises, but there is nothing remotely unusual anywhere on me. That is when I realize not even the pin-sized bruises between my fingers and toes can be seen anymore. Unfortunately, my skin is no longer blemish free either. There are a couple of pimples on my forehead I am positive were not there this morning.

Just great!

"I haven't had a pimple since before we moved to Isla Flora," I grumble to myself as I turn on the shower to its hottest setting.

When the water is at the perfect temperature, I step beneath the spray. The heated liquid feels incredible against my chilled epidermis. With my eyes closed, I stand immobile; listening to the sounds outside, enjoying the warmth of the shower when a soft knock at the door startles me.

"Everything alright in there?" Mom queries.

"Yes," I sputter, wiping my face with a fluffy white washcloth hanging on the towel bar. "Everything is fine."

From outside the bathroom door, I hear her slippers shuffle away then swiftly return.

"Do you need anything?" my mother's voice lowers.

I grin to myself at her sincere concern.

"No, I've got it all under control," I giggle, loving all of the attention.

"Would you like me to make you another sandwich?" she tempts in her maternal way. "Your brother ate the last one."

Her revelation makes me smirk.

"I can make you a tuna sandwich," she offers sweetly.

Just the thought of tuna or any kind of seafood grosses me out to the point that my stomach violently lurches. Involuntarily, my esophagus tightens, and I suddenly lose control of my gag reflex. Foamy soup-like particles with a brown hue suddenly come rushing out. Thank goodness I am still standing in the shower.

Huh? It's been a while since that happened.

"Selena!" Mom gasps, rushing into the washroom and yanking the shower curtain aside in a frenzy, revealing my nakedness.

"Mom!" I huff, using my hands to cover as much of my body as possible. "May I have some privacy please?"

"I'm sorry!" she apologizes with beet-red cheeks.

"I'm okay." I steady my voice.

"Can I fix you something else?" Mom continues, trying to appeal to my now empty stomach.

"I just want to sleep," I reveal, putting the semi-frosted shower curtain back in its original place.

She glances at the wall clock to check the time.

"But it's only a few minutes past nine in the morning," she enlightens with worry.

"Believe me, I need the rest after what I've been through," I chuckle half-heartedly.

I really do.

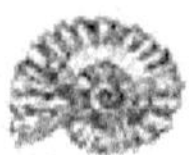

The orange-hued sun is setting when I finally wake. Outside the waves pound against the stony shoreline, warning of an imminent storm heading our way. To my relief, there are still a few seagulls trying to catch a meal before bad weather sets in. Somehow, that makes me feel better.

Then, as if answering an unspoken biological need, my stomach growls ravenously at the thought of food. Another good sign. Sniffing the air, my nose detects the faint hint of something cooking downstairs. Fueled by my desire to eat, I grab my robe, covering my *Betty Boop* night shirt.

On steady feet, I race down to the first floor and into the kitchen where the tantalizing aroma is escaping. Mom is busy at the stove, stirring something in a large pot while Ando sits at the dining table playing with his toy cars and *G. I. Joe* action figures. Both look up when I enter the room.

"What smells so amazing?" I beam, coming around the counter to see what is cooking.

Mom grins.

"What's in the pot?" I enquire with a grumbling tummy.

"Mommy is making seafood stew," Ando informs, then licks his lips.

Then just like that, my hunger magically disappears.

"Oh," I reply, filled with disappointment. "I thought you were making your famous beef stew."

My mother's face saddens.

"But the last time I made beef stew you said you preferred seafood instead," she reminds, wiping her damp hands on a kitchen towel decorated with pictures of tomatoes, onions and carrots.

"I thought I did," I confirm with a frown. "But now I'm not so sure."

Feeling guilty at her distress, I fake a smile.

"The stew smells really great, Mom," I praise, hoping she will believe me.

Ando chimes in.

"*I* can't wait to eat it, Mommy." He expertly sucks up to our parent.

"Me too." I grin as I open the refrigerator door and immediately spy the orange juice, which looks sweet and refreshing.

Extremely thirsty, I pour myself a glass and chug the entire thing down in one long gulp. Licking my lips, I pour a second serving, and this time drink it more slowly as my family members stare at me with confused expressions.

Embarrassed and feeling like a bug under a microscope, I plop down on the chair beside my brother at the table. My starving stomach growls another complaint.

"Here we go." Our mother brings two bowls of stew and places one in front of me and the other in front of Ando. Next, she returns with a dish for herself. Gracefully, she sits to my left where David would have sat.

Glancing up, she notices the red swollen bumps on my forehead. Feeling awkward, I quickly cover them with my left hand, but it is too late. Ando has noticed them as well.

Terrific!

In true Ando form, he scrunches up his face as if he has eaten something rotten.

"What are those things?" he scowls.

"What things?" I question, playing it off.

Boldly, he points to the obvious blemishes.

"Those puffy bumps on your forehead," he replies, continuing to point to the red beacons on my face.

"Are those *pimples*?" Mom gasps, squinting to get a better look at the annoying objects of hatred and disgust.

"Yes," I sulk, wanting to hide under the table. "They are revolting. I know."

Ando beams.

"Can I pop 'em?" he asks with all seriousness.

My eyes widen in horror at the thought of him even suggesting something so nasty.

"You cannot pop them!" I exclaim, emphasizing each word so that there is no mistaking my wishes.

"How long have you had them?" Mom interrogates, changing the subject.

Casually, I shrug before answering.

"They were there since this morning," I notify with a sigh. "Can we please talk about something else? Something that doesn't deal with my zits?"

"Sure," the half-human responds as she appears to be in deep thought but then returns to my blemishes. "When was the last time you got a pimple?"

"Back in Columbus," I apprise, feeling like all of my business is out for everyone to poke at. "Why?"

"No reason," she replies flatly without elaborating. "I'm sure it's just a fluke, but if you need me to buy some acne medicine let me know."

"It's probably a fluke, like you said," I agree. "I'm sure they'll disappear on their own. I don't need any pimple medication."

At that thought, my stomach twists and contorts into a tightly wound ball of knots. Suppose I am being cursed with epic-sized pimples as part of my punishment for what happened to David…

Instantly, I lose my appetite, but this time my guardian is not accepting my queasy expression as a conclusion to the tense conversation. She simply stares at me, using her mother's intuition to decipher my nonverbal cues. No telepathy required.

"You have to eat something," Mom states emphatically, shifting the conversation once more as she takes her first bite of seafood stew, but instead of looking pleased, she frowns and pushes her bowl away.

"What's wrong?" I ask, hoping she is alright.

"I've been feeling a bit queasy lately," she mopes, appearing a tad bit sallow.

Ando, needless to say, is busy devouring his stew. He wastes no time talking and goes directly to stuffing his face with chunks of clams, cod, mussels, shrimp, plus an array of fresh vegetables. Without looking up from his bowl, his small hand reaches for the breadbasket and removes two slices of white bread which he uses to sop up the tangy broth.

Our mother forces herself to take a few more bites but is unable to finish. Instead of wasting it, she reaches for a slice of bread, and following her son's lead, rips it into smaller pieces which she uses to daintily dunk into the well-seasoned liquid. After a few bites of the moist morsels, she smiles and returns to eating with gusto.

I, on the other hand, sit quietly as they consume the hot meal, all the while contemplating what I should eat. At last, it comes to me. The thing I have not wanted in months.

"I'm going to make a peanut butter and jelly sandwich," I announce, leaving the table to construct my dinner.

Momentarily they stop, smile at me, then return to their bowls.

Devoted to my task, I go to the cupboard that holds the plates then to the pantry where I get the extra-chunky peanut butter. With nimble fingers, I rummage through the fridge for the seedless raspberry jelly and the loaf of white bread. Finally, I go to the drawer that contains the silverware to retrieve a knife. With complete focus, I assemble my sandwich. When it is completed, I take a huge bite. To my astonishment, my taste buds explode with delight at the simple combination of peanutty goodness mingling with ripe raspberry perfection.

"Mmm," I moan, suddenly craving a glass of milk which I quickly obtain from the fridge. Still standing in front of the appliance, I gulp down an entire eight-ounce glass of the creamy white substance. "Does this milk have something else in it?"

Mom and Ando do not speak, only stare at me.

"I'm not being funny," I admit, blushing. "It tastes incredible!"

Mom clears her throat.

"Umm," she hums. "It's the same milk I always buy."

Interested in knowing the ingredients, I begin reading the label.

"Hmm," I sound, tapping my bottom lip with my index finger. "Vitamin D, calcium… "

"Is there a special ingredient?" Ando inquiries as he glares at me with a stupefied expression.

"Nope." I giggle, putting the plastic gallon bottle back in the fridge. "Just regular old milk."

Without further chitchat, I ravenously devour the entire sandwich and make another. It takes less than two minutes to build and eat the delicious concoction. I chase that with another full glass of milk. Still my mom and brother sit ignoring their food as they study my actions.

"Do we have any more Crackleberry Crisps?" I query, walking to the pantry where the boxed cereals are located. Usually, I like cereals with less sugar, but for some reason I want… no… I need a bowlful of that particular cereal.

"Lena?" Ando whispers with saucer-like eyes. "What's wrong with you?"

"Nothing." I blush, ignoring his tone.

On my tiptoes, I retrieve the cereal box along with a bowl and dump as much of the container out that can fit into the white porcelain vessel. Next, a generous portion of moo-juice gets poured over the multigrain flakes until it turns a lovely shade of pink. Grabbing a spoon from the dishrack, I begin eating with enthusiasm.

"I thought you didn't like Crackleberry Crisps?" Ando questions with a confused gaze.

Shrugging, I continue stuffing my face, enjoying the intense strawberry flavor and the crunchy texture. I used to like these before we moved to Isla Flora, but for some reason I no longer wanted them once here. Maybe my taste is reverting to when I was a kid.

With gaping mouths, Mom and Ando watch as I empty the entire bowl of delicious cereal before they return to their now lukewarm dinner. When they finish their meals, and because I feel so wonderfully full, I volunteer to wash, dry and put away the rest of the dinner dishes. This earns me a kiss and a hug from my mother.

As I do this task, Mom wipes the table while Ando returns his toys to his room leaving us alone for the moment. As if an unseen switch is thrown, my mother glances up at me and the tension returns. Suddenly, it is like there is a great divide of emotion keeping us apart. I can understand why.

My mother is angry because she let David, my stepfather, volunteer to be my savior during 'the Calling' on Paradiso. I am guilt-ridden because they allowed him to volunteer and have access to the strength of *The Three* and it was too much for his heart to take.

It was my fault. I know this. If I had not gone power-hungry, none of this would be happening and David would be with us right now.

"What are you thinking?" Mom inquires, glaring at me strangely.

For some reason, the question throws me for a loop. Why would she be asking me this? As Sirens we are linked. We can hear each other's thoughts, even when we do not want to.

"I was just thinking about what happened during *the Calling*," I reveal without subterfuge.

Mom still studies my mannerisms.

"Think something else," she requests, taking a step towards me.

Curiously, I stare at her.

"Why?" I manage, cracking a nervous smile.

"Please," she begs. "Think about something else, anything else."

"Alright," I mumble under my breath, wondering if this is some sort of colossal joke.

I wait for her to make a sassy comment about my thinking that she is playing a prank on me, but instead she continues staring at me with a dumbfounded expression.

"Selena!" she snaps making me jump like a scared cat. "I asked you to think about something!"

My eyes widen and my mouth gapes.

"I did!" I snap back, temporarily forgetting my place in the hierarchy of the family.

"Please," she states more calmly. "Do it again."

"But Mom—" I begin.

"Again, Selena," she interrupts, clenching her hands and tapping her right foot.

Before I can do as she requests, Ando comes rushing in. His brow is sweaty, and he is panting like a hot dog. Immediately, I notice the panic in his bright eyes.

"What's wrong?" he blurts, out of breath. "Why are you yelling at each other?"

Trying her hardest to keep still, Mom clasps her hands in front of her but keeps tapping her right foot.

"I can't hear your sister's thoughts," she finally admits after an extremely long pause.

"No way!" he exclaims, looking at me then at our mother.

"Try reading her thoughts," Mom commands with a shaky voice.

Being a good son, Ando obeys, but almost immediately frowns. Shaking his head like he just walked through a cobweb, he tries again. I simply stand waiting to hear him poking around in my brain at my personal ideas without any concern for my privacy.

"Well?" the exasperated Siren questions in her *Sherlock Holmes* detective mode. "Anything?"

Ando shakes his head.

"Try again," Mom urges forcefully as she leans her weight against the kitchen cabinet, looking as if she will faint.

Unrelenting, my brother puts on his determined face and attempts to enter my mind once again. He looks like he is constipated as he fights against an unseen barrier. After several minutes, he stops.

"What did you hear?" Mom interrogates, waiting on pins and needles.

Ando sighs, long and heavy.

"Nothing," he whispers solemnly. "Nothing at all."

CHAPTER TWO

During the mental *'examination'* that my mother and brother performed, things just kept getting stranger and stranger. Overly zealous and resolute to find the cause of my lack of thought or rather their inability to probe my innermost feelings, they actually took turns hypothesizing about my condition. Mom even contemplated calling Tia Ligeia and Tia Leukosia for guidance but then decided against it. When I asked why not call, all she could do was shrug. Even Ando found that weird, especially since our mother hates when people shrug their shoulders. It makes her hostile.

"How do you feel right now?" Mom questions like my pediatrician.

"Are you feeling hot or cold?" Ando interjects, making me want to pinch him hard.

"I feel fine… I guess," I inform, wanting to escape to my room.

"Is your tummy upset?" my brother adds.

"No, not at the moment," I reply, giving a disappointed glare.

"Do you have a headache?" Mom continues.

"No, but I'm getting one," I say sarcastically, rolling my eyes.

"Tell us how you feel," she encourages, sounding desperate.

"I'm tired," I respond, making them feel guilty.

It was only then that they allowed me to go back to my room.

I have been hiding out here for over an hour listening to the sea through the open window, taking immense pleasure in watching the rhythmic motion of the sheer curtains as they slither to and fro, back and forth. Their hem delicately caressing the smooth hardwood floors as they dance. Even the music of the palm tree fronds brings me joy as they are jostled by the gentle evening breeze.

Ahh! Serenity! I have not felt this in a very long time.

As I lay on my bed, counting the divots in the ceiling my cell phone rings. The screen shows a picture I took of Nicole making an outlandish expression. I smile at her photo and happily answer.

"Thank goodness you called," I say softly into the device.

Nicole giggles.

"Is Ando driving you crazy?" the teenager probes, and I can hear the smile in her voice.

"Actually, both Mom and Ando are going to send me to the loony bin," I whisper into my cellphone.

"What are they doing?" Nicole demands, her interest on high alert. "Is it *Sireny-things* that I'm not supposed to know about? Will I get brain-sucked if you reveal too many secrets?"

Quickly, I remove the phone from my ear to snicker and give it a roll of the eyes.

I love my friends. I truly do. I would do anything for them, but some of their speculations about Sirens are downright ridiculous.

Obviously, they consider Sirens the same as Mermaids, which is completely inaccurate. I am not sure what the truth about *'Merpeople'* is, but I do know that they have tails and we do not. Other than that, all I know about the species is that there is a long hatred between *them* and *us*.

Unfortunately, the aunts and Mom never want to discuss the matter, so for now, I will let sleeping dogs lie.

Not wanting my best friend to think that I hung up, I put the phone back to my ear.

"Moving right along," I playfully jibe. "What are you doing?"

Nicole thinks for a few seconds.

"I was calling to find out if you want to spend the night?" she interjects, hopefully.

Thank heavens! Some good news at last!

"I thought you might need a break with the whole *David-thing*," my friend announces in her motherly way.

"I would love to spend the night." I sigh, exhaling the built-up frustration lingering in my system.

"Do you think your mother will let you?" Nicole queries. "We can come get you."

"You mean… you and your brothers?" I fish for details with growing anticipation along with a growing smile.

The teen lightheartedly chuckles.

"Yes," she finally whines. "Jordan and Justin will be with me since I only have a learner's permit."

I actually hear myself *Eeee!*

"Let me ask my mom," I tell, grinning from ear to ear like a Stepford Wife. "Don't go away! I'll be right back!"

Nicole laughs at my overexuberance.

"No worries, silly bean," she replies. "I'm not going anywhere."

"Okay!" I exclaim loudly. "I'll be quick!"

Throwing the cell carelessly onto the mattress, I race downstairs to my parents'—I mean Mom's—room to ask if I can sleep over at Nicole's house. The overprotective Siren loves Nicole and her parents, Mr. and Mrs. Wong, so I do not think she will have any problems with me spending the night.

"Mom!" I exclaim as I burst into the room without knocking. "Are you in here?"

There is no answer.

"Mom?" I glance around the neatly kept bedroom. "I need to ask you a question."

Slowly, I study the space. My parents' room is simply furnished, yet elegant. Neutrally painted in a muted khaki and decorated with espresso-colored modern, clean-lined furniture. There is not a lot of stuff either, which is the way I like it.

Along the far wall is a dresser and mirror with just a few family pictures and an antique silver jewelry box that once belonged to Grandfather Marcus' mother. According to my mom, the small object is worth over a quarter-of-a-million dollars in this day. In the far corner is a large, ornately carved cedar trunk that also belonged to Mom's father that he kept his belongings in while out on missions at sea. My mother calls it her most prized possession.

That is worth a small fortune too, but she loves it for its sentimental value.

"Marina Marquez?" I announce a tad louder. "Are you in here?"

It is then I hear sniffling coming from the walk-in closet to my left.

"Mom?" I say again as I walk to the closet and slowly open it.

Inside, my mother is sitting on the hard floor thumbing through old photo albums and crying. Surrounding her is a sea of crumpled tissues and the now empty box that they came from. Her aquamarine eyes are dark and now a murky sapphire. Seeing her like this makes my heart clench and instantly I lose my jovial attitude.

This might not go as expected. I brace for a negative outcome but promise to not make a big deal of it. After all, the woman has been through enough.

"Mom? Are you okay?" I quiz, wanting her to feel better. "Why are you on the floor?"

Sadly, she looks at me. Her onyx curls are pulled back into a messy ponytail making her look like a teenager and draped around her shoulders is David's favorite blue flannel shirt. The one he was wearing the first time she ever saw him off the coast of Anchorage, Alaska.

"I was missing your father and decided to go through our family pictures." She sniffles while wiping her nose in a tissue she has clenched in her hand. "Did you need something?"

Nervously, I debate if I should ask. It would probably be better if I just stayed home. I decide to forget about the whole sleepover thing. Mom needs me.

"I miss him too," I confess, feeling the tears welling in my eyes.

The emotionally fragile Siren takes my hand in hers and gives a squeeze.

"Ouch!" I complain as I pull my hand out of hers. "I know you're strong Mom, but Jeez!"

Finally, she giggles.

"That hurt?" My parent interrogates. "I'm sorry, sweetheart. Sometimes I don't know my own strength."

Gingerly, I massage the injured area wondering why my mother's touch is so unusually steely. Sirens are naturally strong creatures, especially when they are angry or extremely happy. Tia Ligeia and Tia Leukosia are the most powerful of all of us since they are of the original three. Once, I witnessed Ligeia wrestle a whale shark with an abscessed tooth into submission so they could treat him. She used only one hand and did not even break a sweat.

"It's alright," I reply, sitting on the floor beside her, still rubbing my hand.

"C'mon, Selena," she chastises without heat. "What did you need to ask? I know it deals with Nicole."

"You read my mind!" I gasped loudly.

Mom giggles once more.

"No, I heard her ringtone when your cell phone rang." She snickers, dabbing the edges of her tear-filled eyes. "I gave birth to you, pushed your big head out. I know when you are fishing for something."

I blush at how smart moms are, especially how smart my mom is.

"Oh!" I snort then decide to get straight to the point. "May I spend the night at Nicole's?"

She sits straighter but remains seated.

"Tonight?" The word rushes past her lips.

"If that's okay," I reply meekly.

"Well—"

"I don't need to go—" I start to say, but I cut myself off. "I can tell Nicole that we can do it another time."

Mom debates silently.

"You may go," she agrees without persuasion, bribe, or whining. "You need to spend time with your friends."

Ecstatic, I hug her tightly almost toppling her over onto her side.

"Thanks, Mom!" I squeal like a piglet that just escaped its pen. "You're the best!"

Mom laughs.

"I know," she smirks. "I know."

Thirty minutes later, Nicole and her older twin brothers arrive at the house. Mom greets them at the front door and ushers them inside as she asks if they want anything to drink. They cordially refuse but make small talk instead.

Nicole's brothers, Jordan and Justin, are back on the island for the summer and are too cute for words. Both are over six feet with dark hair, athletic frames and flawless honey complexions. Their hair is cut low, neat and simple, but the style perfectly highlights their chiseled cheekbones and almond-shaped, hazel eyes. If Andrew did not exist, I would gladly —

"How's college?" Mom questions the twins.

Justin and Jordan will be sophomores at *The University of Miami* in sunny Florida this fall. It so happens to be the college that Dwayne *'The Rock'* Johnson also attended. *What a stud!* But I digress. Justin, the elder by five minutes, is majoring in marine science while Jordan is studying occupational therapy. For a couple of *'hotties'* they are also quite intelligent, so intelligent in fact that they received full scholarships to attend *U of M.* The boys are also on the university's varsity swim team.

"It's a lot of work," Jordan, I think, speaks first. "Between the swim team and studying, there isn't any time to have fun."

"Yeah," Justin continues. "We both have full class loads and work part-time on campus."

"I'm impressed," Mom responds with a bright smile. "I know your parents are very proud of both of you. Keep up the great work."

They both blush at my mom's sincere compliment.

"Thank you, Mrs. Marquez!" They both answer, and for a brief moment I can see them as Sirens.

"You are very welcome." Mom nods.

"Oh, by the way, Mrs. Marquez," Jordan (possibly Justin) adds. "While we're home for summer break, if you need anything fixed around the house we can help."

"Thank you, boys!" She beams. "I'll remember that."

Mom seems so natural around males. I grin. It must be a Siren thing.

"Are you ready, Selena?" Nicole jogs over to where I am waiting at the base of the staircase.

Ando rushes down the stairs and gives the pretty brunette a big hug around her waist.

"Hey Andover!" she teases just like Andrew would.

Ando giggles and blushes at the same time. *That little carp!* I still cannot believe he has a severe case of puppy love for one of my best friends. Not only is she ten years older than him, but she already has a crush on Mike Taylor, Andrew's best friend.

"Only Andrew can call me that." The boy smirks, trying to hide his obsession for my friend.

"I forgot," Nicole teases, tussling his dark hair, but for some reason my brother does not get upset with her. When anyone else does it, he practically bites their head off.

Turning to me, Ando examines my bag.

"Can I come too?" he pleads with a wistful expression.

"Not this time squirt." Nicole smiles. "We're going to have a girl's night."

"A girl's night?" he repeats with a frown. "What's that?"

"We're going to style each other's hair, talk about boys, eat junk food, and maybe watch a scary movie," Nicole tells with enthusiasm.

Ando grimaces.

"I don't like scary movies." He pouts until Nicole tickles him.

"Ready girls?" the twins ask in unison.

"Yes," I answer without looking at their handsome faces for fear I will stick my foot in my mouth.

"We'll take good care of her," Nicole promises hugging my mother. "No need to worry, Mrs. Marquez."

"I'll call in the morning," Mom informs with a small smile. "Don't stay up all night."

"We won't," Nicole and I respond together, knowing we probably will be awake all night.

Then I turn to my pouting sibling.

"See you tomorrow night." I give him a hug and a quick kiss on the cheek.

"Fine," Ando broods, staring at his bare feet.

"I'll be back before you know it," I sooth, easing my own guilt.

Eagar to leave, Nicole takes my duffle bag and hands it to Justin, I think it is Justin… it might be Jordan, I am not sure. After all, they are identical. Only the Wong family members can tell them apart, and for some reason Mom and Ando. I used to be able to discern between the guys, but now… not so much.

So strange.

"Have fun, but use good judgement," Mom reminds knowingly.

"We will," my female counterpart replies before I can, then takes my hand and leads me outside.

"Bye! See you later, Lena!" Ando shouts as he runs back upstairs as if he is on a mission. "Have fun!"

I grin at his sense of urgency as well as his swift mood changes.

"Later, baby bro!" I call after him, ecstatic to be heading to my best friend's house.

CHAPTER THREE

Nicole's home is stunning. Like ours, their house is on a mountain that overlooks the ocean. The only difference is theirs is not built directly into the side of it. They also have a two-story house, but instead of being more traditional it leans to the modern side, especially with its butterfly roofline and long rectangular windows. Someday, I hope to have a home just like it.

"C'mon, slowpoke," Nicole teases good-naturedly. "Mom is making us snacks."

"You better share those snacks," one of the twins calls from behind us.

"Maybe, we will… maybe, we won't," Nicole fires back then sticks out her tongue.

"That's it!" the twin yells as he runs after his younger sister. "You've been itching for a big-brother-slap-down since we got back to Isla Flora for summer break!"

"Lay a hand on me and I'm telling Dad!" Nicole shouts as she starts running toward the house, pulling me along with her.

"Having Selena here isn't going to save you, lil sis!" he yells mischievously.

"Leave her alone!" the other twin scolds while grinning. "Or I'm going to give *you* a slap-down!"

"I'm telling!" Nicole squeals like a kid on the playground.

"Go ahead!" her brother encourages, obviously getting a kick out of chasing us. "Dad's not here to save you this time!"

"Justin! Help me!" Nicole grunts out of breath.

"Stay out of this, Justin!" Jordan laughs, still chasing Nicole and me around the beautifully kept front yard.

"Be cool, brah!" Justin laughs loudly as his siblings act like toddlers.

"Nah, man!" Jordan shouts defiantly. "She put shaving cream in my shoes yesterday!"

"That's because you used my expensive hair conditioner on the dog!" Nicole huffs indignantly.

"Well, you're a dog and you use it, so I figured it was okay," Jordan teases.

Nicole suddenly stops dead in her tracks. Slowly, she turns with a look that would freeze water. Jordan immediately stops too, seeing his sister's expression warns him that there is about to be a brother-sister-smack-down. Being an intelligent person, I step a few feet aside just in case things get brutal. Having a brother of my own, I know firsthand what destruction can occur when relatives go at it.

"Now, Nicole." Jordan's voice is a bit shaky. "I was only teasing. Don't get upset."

"You...called...me...a...*dog*," his sister replies in a monotonous tone that sends shivers down my spine. Apparently, it has the same effect on Jordan.

"I'm s—"

Unfortunately, he does not get the opportunity to apologize because Nicole suddenly runs at him, hits him square in the chest with her right shoulder which sends her older brother a few feet into the air. He lands flat on his back with a deafening thud. Then with lightning speed, Nicole pins him to the grass with her body where he lays panting for breath.

"Get off of me, crazy chick!" Jordan pleads through short choppy breaths.

"If you call me a dog again, I'll have to do *this* again," Nicole cautions without humor.

"Nicole!" Justin yells, seeing that things have spiraled out of control. "You've made your point. You're a badass. Let him up."

"Not until he apologizes," Nicole growls, refusing to get off her brother.

"I was trying to apologize before you Sumo-wrestled me," Jordan wheezes, face sweaty and contorted with pain.

His sister only grins: a maniacal grin that makes my skin crawl and my palms itch, and for a second, I swear her bright amber irises flash a hellish onyx then return to normal.

"What the—" I gasp but immediately convince myself that it was a trick of the light or a passing cloud casting a shadow. Even though there is not a cloud to be seen.

Then, as if enjoying his agony, the petite teen adjusts her position so that more of her body weight is pressing against her squirming brother.

"We should have never taught you how to play football when you were a kid," Jordan groans, holding his chest with one hand while attempting to pry his sister off with the other.

"Or karate… or kickboxing… or boxing," Nicole adds with a justified smirk.

"I'm sorry!" Jordan winces. "Please get off me, Nicole! You're freakin' heavy!"

But instead of relinquishing her hold on him, Nicole's face darkens, her right hand curls into a fist, cocks back, and just as she is about to lay a beating on him, Mr. Wong rushes out of the house. Without hesitation all three stand as if they are inmates at a federal prison and their father is the warden.

However, I know better. Mr. Wong is one of the sweetest men I have ever known. He is thoughtful, caring, and a devoted husband and father. It makes me smile that just like Ando and me, the Wong children feel differently about the strictness of their parents.

"Hey!" The deep voice of their father booms from the doorway of the house. "Get in here! Leave your sister alone!"

"She hit me!" Jordan complains as his dad stares at all of them.

"We'll talk about this later," Mr. Wong informs without humor.

"But Dad—" Jordan whines with heated cheeks.

The handsome, middle-aged Asian man gives him a look that leads to the young man's silence.

"You can harass your sister tomorrow," Mr. Wong finally chuckles. "Nicole, no more beating-up your brother."

"Yes, Dad," Nicole concedes with an innocent smile.

"Brat!" Jordan mumbles as he passes us and hip-checks his sister.

"Goober!" Nicole counters with a smirk, knowing that her place as the baby of the family along with being the only girl gives her certain inherent advantages. However, all of her friends know that the twins hold a special place in Mrs. Wong's heart. Ando and I have the same relationship with our parents—

I guess I should start using the past tense.

"Come inside," Mr. Wong implores, waving us in. "Your Mom has some goodies for you."

"Yes, Dad," the Wong children reply in unison making me smile.

"Follow me," my best friend requests, returning to her pre-*Terminator* personality, takes my hand once more, and then ushers me inside.

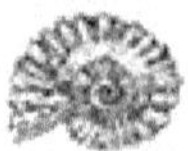

As soon as we enter the house, the tantalizing aroma of Chinese food tickles our noses. Mrs. Wong is from the island of Trinidad and happens to be an amazing cook. It has been said by her family members that she can take five ingredients of absolutely anything and turn it into a gourmet meal. I have had firsthand experience witnessing this phenomenon.

Last Christmas, Jenny and I spent a couple of nights hanging out with Nicole's family during winter break. Mrs. Wong had not gone to their family-owned grocery store for food and all that remained in the kitchen was half of a box of corn flakes, a small bag of shredded coconut, a bottle of hot sauce, a bag of white rice, two eggs, two whole frozen chickens, and a few bottles of spices. Within a short period of time, the beautiful mother of three created an Asian coconut chicken dish that rivaled *James Beard Award* winners.

"Whatever your mom is cooking smells delicious," I reveal, following Nicole upstairs to her room to put my bag away. "Do you know what she's making?"

My friend enthusiastically nods.

"The entire family helped make egg rolls, wontons, and teriyaki chicken wings for tonight," Nicole tells with a broad grin. "Mom wanted to make something special for you."

My heart clenches from the thought of having a second mom as great as Mrs. Wong. I know that my mother loves me, but recently she has been incredibly standoffish and quiet. Feeling the same pain of losing David hurts me too, but in my case, I would rather talk about it than keep it bottled up inside.

Marina Marquez, on the other hand, holds the patent on being closed-lipped. Ando also keeps a lot of things to himself now. Before, he would talk to me about everything. These days, he shares most of his troubles with his sea life confidants. Recently, I have seen him hanging out with his old dolphin friend, Whistler. At least he has someone to confide in.

Several times I have tried talking to Nicole about what happened in Capri, but every time I bring it up, she changes the subject. I cannot tell if she is afraid of me having an emotional breakdown or just does not know how to handle the topic. She respected my stepfather, even thought of him as a second dad, so I would understand if she was hurting too much to deal with it as well.

"Nicole! Selena!" Mrs. Wong calls from downstairs. *"Time to eat!"*

Not needing to be told twice, we both race down to the first floor where the rest of the Wong's are gathered in the family room on the massive black leather sectional sofa around the huge seventy-inch flat screen television set. The space has towering ceilings and is decorated with a mixture of contemporary furnishings and Asian accents. It is elegant and comfortable all at the same time. In front of the couch, there is an Asian-style coffee table that is currently draped with a tablecloth and laden with dishes of golden-brown appetizers along with chips, dip and sodas. A stack of paper napkins and bottled water are there too.

"Find a spot to sit, girls," Mr. Wong, a California native, encourages.

His wife stands to greet me with a long tight bear hug. She smells like a hybrid of scrumptious fried foods and dainty floral-scented perfume. It is a scent that fits her well.

"Nice to see you, my dear," Mrs. Wong addresses lovingly in her sing-song Trinidadian accent.

"Thank you for having me over," I respond sincerely, enjoying the tender embrace.

"How's your mum?" she questions in a whispered tone.

"I think she's better," I mutter, feeling put on the spot. "The food looks great!"

"Please, have a seat," my best friend's mother kindly urges. "The movie is about to start."

"What movie did we decide on?" her daughter questions as she sits beside her mom and pats the space beside her for me to be seated. Following her nonverbal request, I take my place beside her.

Robotically, she hands me a plate and tells me to help myself as she does the same. Hungrily, I fill my plate with a variety of finger food including several wontons, chicken wings, an egg roll, and a little bit of tortilla chips and homemade salsa with a dollop of sour cream. I decide to eat one of the teriyaki wings first.

"Mmm." I cannot help the moan of delight that escapes my lips, making the others giggle and I turn red. Fortunately, my embarrassment does not last long. The Wong's are like my second family and Nicole is like a sister.

"Dad, what movie are we going to watch?" Nicole grills respectfully.

"Your brothers chose the movie," her father replies then takes a bite of a chicken wing.

"A Nightmare on Elm Street," the twins answer as one.

So Sireny!

Nicole rubs her hands together and grins evilly. This is going to be interesting. I know for a fact that the teen girl hates horror movies. She was terrified when she, Jenny and I watched *The Little Vampire* before summer vacation. She is definitely going to have bad dreams tonight.

That reminds me.

"When's Jenny coming back from Ireland?" I question Nicole as she wipes a glob of sour cream from her mouth with a napkin.

The teen thinks for a moment before answering.

"I think she flies back next Friday." Nicole smiles, excitement causing her eyes to sparkle. "I can't wait to see her! She always brings gifts. Last year, we got specialty Irish cheese and fruit preserves."

"They were delicious," Mr. Wong states, rubbing his belly.

I wince remembering that I was supposed to bring back souvenirs from Italy, but because of what happened with David, I completely forgot. Another rush of despair overwhelms me, and I excuse myself to escape to the washroom.

Uncontrollable tears blur my vision as I speed-walk to the first-floor powder room. Not wanting anyone to see me crying, I lock the door and sob into the hand towel. A moment or two later, a soft knock makes me jump out of my skin. Quickly I wash my face and perk myself up. When I open the door, Nicole is waiting outside wearing a melancholy expression.

"I know you're not alright, so don't say that you are," She pulls me down to the floor to sit beside her.

At least her house is carpeted except for the kitchen, bathrooms and formal dining room. Because of this, Nicole's parents make you take your shoes off when you enter. It is a custom my family does too.

"Of course I am," I fib, wiping my nose with a balled-up wad of toilet paper.

Nicole frowns.

"You're right, I'm not fine." I burst into a fresh outbreak of tears. "Everything reminds me of David. Do you know that he and your dad wear the same aftershave?"

Sympathetically, Nicole puts her arm around me.

"I'll ask him not to wear it anymore, if that helps." She smiles, hoping to comfort me. "Or I can hide it."

I chuckle feeling better.

"You'd do that for me?" I sniffle, catching my breath as I rest my head on her shoulder.

Nicole nods and wipes a stray tear away with her palm.

"You're my *sistah* from a half-fish *muddah*," she replies playfully, making me laugh.

"I appreciate you saying that," I admit, more at ease.

"If we don't go back now, the boys will eat all of the snacks," my comrade explains with a wink and a grin.

"We wouldn't want that," I counter, getting to my feet and helping her up as well. "Those wings are ridiculous!"

And ridiculous is good!

Around eleven we finish watching *A Nightmare on Elm Street* but decide to stay up and play *Monopoly* with the twins. Nicole keeps making excuses because she does not want to go to bed due to flashbacks of *Freddy Kruger* disemboweling multiple people in their dreams.

Honestly, I do not blame her. He is pretty hideous.

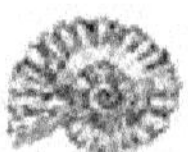

At three in the morning, I finally convince her that it is safe to go to bed. As we are about to fall asleep, Jordan has his revenge by sneaking into the room wearing a *'Scream'* mask and black cloak he wore for a college Halloween party. I swear, Nicole's howl almost shattered my eardrums, and she punched him so hard that she almost broke his perfectly shaped nose.

So, Mr. Wong was forced to ground both kids. On top of that, he also was not thrilled that Nicole's bloodcurdling cries woke him up from a dream that his recipe for egg foo young won a culinary prize, which was being awarded by *Iron Chef Morimoto*. All I could do was comfort Nicole until she fell asleep, clutching my arm in one hand and a baseball bat in the other.

Brothers!

After the commotion dies down, the room is quiet except for the filter in the fishtank that hums steadily. Somehow, I manage to fall asleep shortly after she does. I have always found the sound of bubbling water comforting, and I quickly begin to dream.

In my dream, Nicole and I are at the beach, the one near my house. We are building sandcastles near the shoreline while Ando and Mom go for a quick swim. Nicole decides to go swimming as well, but I want to stay on land. Being a good swimmer, she swims out several yards into the deep and gets a leg cramp.

"Help me, Selena!" my friend screams and flails as she goes under then bobs back up again.

Nervously, I look around, but the beach is deserted.

"Save me!" Nicole shrieks at the top of her lungs. *"Don't let me die!"*

Hearing those words, I dive into the calm sea and freestyle swim as fast as I can out to her location, but when I get there, I cannot see her anywhere. Panicking, I dive under, but as soon as I do, Nicole reappears and pulls me down to the seabed. Instead of beautiful amber, her eyes are black as a sharks, and instead of feet she has a *Tail!* A shimmering, fish-like tail rimmed with sharp protruding barbs, barbs that slice into my flesh as she flicks it at me. Suddenly, the water around us turns blood red and my limbs grow tired from the struggle.

"You are mine, Siren!" she hisses, and scratches my face with her three-inch talons.

"Get away from me!" I yell under the water, but my mouth fills and I start to suffocate.

"Stupid Siren!" Nicole barks like a furious seal. *"You think that you're better than us! You think that we won't win this war?! Well, wake-up, sistah!"*

And I do! Just as Nicole is about to bite off my face with her razor-like teeth, I bolt upright, completely awake.

Almost hyperventilating, I stare outside at the rising sun, which slowly transforms the dark horizon. Unlike in my dream, the sea is choppy and menacing. For a long time, I sit admiring it, wondering if any of my sea-friends are hiding beneath the rough surface. Beside me, Nicole is fast asleep wearing a big smile on her peaceful face.

Before I can wake her, she slowly opens her eyes and for a moment her irises appear black… just like in my dream!

"Holy crap!" I shout, rolling away, but forgetting we are several feet above the floor. With flailing arms and a loud crash, I fall between the mattress and bedroom wall.

Fully awake now, Nicole springs forward to my rescue.

"Selena!" she blurts, offering me her hand. "Are you alright?"

But instead of taking it, I hop to a standing position, pretending that I am unhurt. Apprehensively, I examine her eyes again, but this time they appear to be fine. No sign of anything unusual.

"What's wrong?" the teen questions with a bewildered expression. "Why are you so jumpy?"

"I don't know," I lie, rubbing my throbbing elbow. "I shouldn't have watched that horror movie last night. I hate those things."

Satisfied with that explanation, Nicole yawns, and heads to the door. I decipher that she must use the bathroom. I do too, but for the moment, I stay where I am.

"I'll be right back," she groans sleepily. "Are you sure you didn't get hurt when you fell off of the bed?"

In denial, I shake my head.

"I'm sure," I smile falsely, wiping the sleep from my eyes.

"If you say so," Nicole replies with a shrug as she exits the room.

Something is not right here. Nicole hates it when people shrug their shoulders. It is one of her pet-peeves, just like my mother. Jenny did that in front of her once and Nicole pinched her arm so hard that it not only bruised but also developed a painful lump. For Nicole to shrug her own shoulders is absolutely unheard of.

Instantly, my stomach twists into a ball of knots.

"Wait," I whisper to myself. "You're seeing things that aren't there and now you think that one of your best friends is some strange creature."

Shaking my head, I sit on the edge of the bed waiting for Nicole to return. It takes several more minutes, but when she does, she seems completely normal. Content for the moment, I exhale the breath I was holding.

"You don't look well," the teenager states bluntly, also not her usual manner. Again, I chase the disturbing thought out of my brain.

"How do you mean?" I respond, looking at my reflection in the window.

"Your complexion is pale instead of olive," she replies with a wave of the hand.

"I'm okay," I reveal, feeling like I have done something wrong.

Again, she shrugs, and this time her eyes flash blue. Closing my eyes, I whisper a quick prayer to help me keep my sanity. When I open them, Nicole is only a foot away, staring at me with a hateful look.

"Did I do something wrong, Nicole?" I quiz, jumping to my feet and backing away, hoping I did not do or say anything inappropriate.

"I don't think so." She smiles warmly, completely throwing me off kilter. "Are you hungry?"

I nod.

"Me too," she grins. "Let's raid the fridge."

My tummy growls its agreement.

"Sounds good to me," I snicker, following Nicole out of the room, wiping all negative thoughts from my mind.

In the hallway, we run into Jordan or at least I think it is Jordan. Last night, Nicole told me that Justin has more flecks of green in his hazel eyes compared to Jordan, and of the two, Jordan has dimples on both cheeks whereas Justin only has a dimple on his right cheek.

"Good morning, Justin," Nicole greets sweetly.

"Justin?" the twin scoffs. "Don't insult me that way."

Nicole blushes.

"Sorry… Jordan." She plays off her mistake with an endearing smile. "It's dark in this stupid hallway."

"No, it's not," Jordan smirks as he shakes his head. "Sisters."

"Ignore him," Nicole says, turning to me. "I'm famished. I haven't eaten in forever."

Her comment makes me laugh.

"What are you talking about?" I snort. "Last night, we ate more than the guys."

Nicole stops suddenly and thinks for a moment.

"Oh yeah," she responds, using her hands to emphasize her words. "Silly me, I forgot."

Confused, I stay a few steps behind her.

All of sudden, I feel cold, but not a regular coldness; it is the kind that you feel in your bones, deeper than that, you feel it in your marrow. It is the sort of cold that I remember when I lived in Ohio. The freezing weather used to make my skin hurt.

Downstairs, Nicole's father is reading the newspaper in the kitchen. Beside him sits a mug of hot coffee and a bagel with cream cheese.

"Good morning, Mr. Wong," I greet as we enter the room.

"Good morning, Selena," he greets back, looking up from his article. "Sleep well?"

"I didn't," I giggle, sitting beside him. "But Nicole certainly did."

A few feet away, Nicole is currently rummaging through the refrigerator. I hear dishes being moved as she searches for last night's appetizers. She starts grumbling as her father and I listen to the ruckus she is making.

"Dad!" my bestie suddenly bellows.

Startled, Mr. Wong jumps out of his seat and rushes to his daughter's aid. At first, I search for a bug or spider. Nicole is deathly afraid of any type of creepy crawly, but to my surprise the area is insect free.

"What's the matter?" Mr. Wong exclaims, glancing around.

"Where are the leftovers?" Nicole whines, completely out of character.

"Is that why you're making a fuss?" her dad responds with an angry grimace.

"Answer the question," Nicole states disrespectfully, perching both hands on her hips.

"Young lady," Mr. Wong replies, just as shocked as I am. "What has gotten into you? Show some respect."

Nicole pauses, surprised by her father's harsh tone and does something I never thought I would see in the Wong household. She slams the fridge door and storms out of the room leaving her father and me staring after her in total and complete disbelief.

"What's gotten into her?" Mr. Wong interrogates, literally scratching his head. "I'm sorry, Selena, but I'm afraid I'm going to have to cut short your visit. Obviously, my daughter will not be seeing outside of these walls for at least a week."

"I understand," I reply, swallowing hard as if a large acorn is stuck in my throat. "I'll call my mom to pick me up."

"Don't bother your mother," he sighs. "She's been through enough. Losing your dad at sea… horrible."

I gulp rather loudly at his recollection. Mom had fabricated the lie, but it was the first time I had heard it said aloud. Hearing it makes my heart hurt.

"I'll have one of the boys take you home," Mr. Wong proclaims, his voice naturally kind.

Eeeee!

"Okay," I blush at the thought of being driven home by one of Nicole's cute brothers. "If you insist."

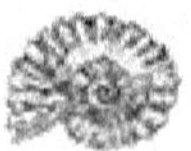

It takes only a few minutes for me to gather my belongings. This has been the shortest visit I have had at the Wong's in a long time. During my packing, Nicole is nowhere to be found. I even searched around the property looking inside her childhood hiding place, the treehouse. The treehouse is sturdily built and able to withstand even the strongest of storms, according to the Wong children. Unfortunately, she was not there.

"I hope we'll see you soon," Mrs. Wong says as she hugs me.

"Don't be a stranger," Mr. Wong encourages with a bright smile.

"I'll visit soon, I promise," I reply, hugging them both at the same time. "Thank you so much for having me! I had a great time."

"Are you ready to go?" one of the twins questions as he enters the living room holding my duffle bag.

Fortunately, he smiles, and I see two dimples, one on each cheek.

It's Jordan!

"Thanks, Jordan." I grin and blush at the same time. "I'm all set."

"Drive safely," both Mrs. Wong and her husband beseech at once. "Especially on the mountain pass."

Jordan nods in acknowledgement.

"I will, Mom," he vows, giving her a quick kiss on the top of the head. "Let's head out!"

"Okay," I say following behind like a puppy, still grinning like an imbecile.

Unlike Andrew, Jordan does not open the door for me or tend to look at me. Instead, the nineteen-year-old college sophomore throws my bag in the back of his Jeep and hops in the driver's seat. Patiently, he waits as I enter and fasten my seatbelt. Before I can thank him again for taking me home, he starts the vehicle and pulls out of the driveway.

Automatically, he switches on the radio and surfs the stations for something good to sing along to. *Oh no!* If something comes on and I am compelled to join-in, there could be problems.

"Could we leave the radio off?" I ask, getting flustered.

"Why?" is all the saucy sexy twin says.

"Umm," I hum, thinking on my feet. "I have a headache."

Jordan smiles.

Wow! He has the most incredible dimples! I mean... besides Andrew's.

Just as luck would have it, he finds a local station having an eighties music marathon. The first song that plays is *'Save A Prayer'* by Duran Duran; one of my all-time favorite songs from that band.

Immediately, Jordan starts singing along:

My heart starts beating wildly and my palms are dripping with sweat. I will have to throw myself out of this vehicle if he asks me to—

"Sing with me," Jordan urges with a blinding model-like smile.

Crap! What should I do?

"Don't leave me hangin' woman," he states pleasantly.

"I can't," I fib, clasping my hands together.

"Why not?" he asks as he turns up the volume so we can really hear the bass.

"I just… can't," I huff, turning away.

"Please," he begs.

"No," I deny, trying to be strong.

"Pretty please," he says with a playful twang to this voice.

Why is he so adorable?

"Ok," I reply, giving up the fight. "I'll sing, but don't say I never warned you."

The chorus drones in and I cannot help joining:

'… Don't say a prayer for me now
Save it til the morning after
No don't say a prayer for me now
Save it til the morning after… '

Preparing for the worse, I bolster myself for the rapidly approaching consequences of openly singing in front of a male, but nothing happens. Nothing at all.

Opening my eyes, I see Jordan jamming to the slow pop ballad and sounding really great.

"That was terrific! Keep singing!" He encourages, but something is different. Something is very different.

Jordan should be swooning over me by now. His hazel eyes should be dilated, and his gaze should be locked onto me. Right about now, his palms should be sweaty and itching to touch me, but he is not. He is just fine.

Confused and befuddled, I try again.

'… Don't say a prayer for me now
Save it 'til the morning after

No don't say a prayer for me now

Save it 'til the morning after

Save it 'til the morning after

Save it 'til the morning after… '

"I'm surprised you know the tune," he compliments in a brotherly manner.

"My Mom loves this band," I admit, smiling… really smiling, smiling from my head to my toes. I have no effect on him whatsoever! At all!

Zilch! Nada! Zippo!

CHAPTER FOUR

After Nicole's brother drops me off, I jog to my room. With even more determination than ever, I call for the aunts telepathically. It does not surprise me when I do not receive a response. They are notorious at not returning calls. Closing my eyes, I try again, but all I hear is the silence of my room.

Melody! That's who I need!

Melody will know what is happening to me. She knows everything. She is the beginning of our family line and is an all-powerful Muse. It does not get much better than that.

Grasping my volcanic glass charm to channel more power, I concentrate… but something feels different. Usually, the charm tingles when it touches my skin, but only I can feel it. Well, anyone who is a Siren can feel it since finite particles of it flow through our veins. This time, I feel nothing except the cool polished surface.

This can't be good!

Next, I try calling Ando, who is just a room away drawing on his sketch pad. My little brother is quite the artist. Mom says he inherited that from Grandma Parthenope who had inherited her natural artistic abilities from her mother, Melpomene the Muse, affectionately known as Melody. The nickname was given to her by Ando who said that every time he thinks of her, he hears music in his head.

'Ando!' I yell mentally, but of course he does not hear me.

This time, I try verbally.

"Fernando David Marquez!" I bellow. "I need you… *right now!"*

Within seconds, my door bursts open and my brother comes running inside. His eyes are wild, and he wears a look of a warrior about to start battling. He truly looks fierce.

"What's wrong?!" he shouts, fists in fighting position, thumbs back like our father taught us. "What happened? A snake?"

My brother knows I hate snakes. Anything that crawls on its belly and sticks its tongue out at you for no reason is bad news in my book. Ando, on the other hand, is not afraid of anything.

"I need a favor," I demand flatly.

"What kind of favor?" he asks with a suspicious look, fists still up.

"I need you to call Melody or the aunts, any of those would be good," I ramble as my mind races.

Slowly, his arms return to his sides.

"Why?" he frowns.

"Something is definitely wrong with me, Ando," I explain as I begin pacing the length of the bedroom, hands wringing all the while.

My brother just stares at me.

"Is it because you're not a Siren anymore?" he blurts casually like he is asking if I want to share a bowl of potato chips. His comment actually causes me to trip over my own feet and crash onto the area rug that my bed sits on.

"What did you say?" I query, rubbing my knees and shins.

"You're not a Siren anymore," he blankly informs, taking a seat at the foot of my unmade bed. Without a care, he swings his small feet as if he is on a swing-set.

"I'm not a Siren anymore," I repeat, feeling the words rolling around my mouth and feeling numb.

Ando nods.

"How is that possible?" I press the six-year-old genius.

"I'm not sure," he replies, rubbing the back of his neck like David often did when he was deep in thought.

"How did you come to this conclusion then?" I interrogate, losing patience.

He simply looks at me with those gorgeous eyes, and then he says the words that I thought I would never hear again.

"I had a dream… "

The entire world seems to have sped up. Mom is pacing the front porch, stopping every minute or so to look at me and shake her head. I feel rather inferior right now. Inferior, but somehow… *happier*? Although, I do not think I will say those words out loud for fear of jinxing myself back to the way I was before.

"Let me get this straight," Mom grumbles to herself. "Selena is no longer *'Of the Sea'*."

"Yup!" Ando exclaims as he balances on the railing like a tightrope walker at the circus.

"Ando, how did you come to this conclusion?" Mom probes using the same phrase I did, still pacing the length of the porch. It is the same porch that David varnished before we left for our summer vacation in the Mediterranean, the vacation that he did not return from.

"I had a dream that Selena was just a regular human being," he states blankly.

"Really?" Mom replies, dumbstruck.

"Uh huh," Ando responds as he jumps off of the porch railing as gracefully as a gymnast.

"Did I seem glad to be a human?" I blurt, holding back my enthusiasm.

"There's no way," Mom disagrees, shaking her head more aggressively. "Absolutely, no way."

"We need to talk to the aunts," Ando suggests as he sits on the top porch step. "They'll know what's going on. Won't they?"

"I hope so," Mom huffs and growls at the same time, then breaks into a wild Siren rant filled with colorful expletives and double-entendre. At the moment, our mother has the mouth of a well-seasoned, salty-sailor and it is not the sea that made her so.

Immediately, she closes her eyes. By the look of her facial expression, she has made the mental connection quickly and is currently in deep conversation with the aunts. Unfortunately, because of my current *condition* I am not privy to what is being relayed. As she communicates telepathically with them, she starts pacing again. Soon after, Ando joins her on the call. He laughs at first, then his smile turns into a frown. All I am capable of doing is watching and waiting.

"Other than being mortal, she's okay," my brother informs pensively, quite un-Ando-like. "Tia Ligeia says *'hi!'*"

"Hi!" I exclaim back. "Say *'hello'* to Tia Leukosia for me."

Mom stops pacing and begins tapping her right foot.

"Uh huh," she responds to the unheard voices of the aunts. "That's wonderful!"

Ando is smiling too.

Damn it! I wish I could hear what's being said!

"We'll do that," Mom responds to the voices in her head then turns to me. "Is everything going well on Paradiso?"

Then there is silence, the kind of silence that makes my mom cringe.

"Mommy?" Ando interrupts verbally. "Why are you blocking me from your conversation?"

Our mother does not answer, only waves him away like an annoying gnat. She smiles a bit but quickly realizes what she is doing and returns to a grumpy frown. Ando continues to pout but says nothing more.

"Thank you, Tia Leukosia, Tia Ligeia," she states lovingly. "I truly appreciate everything you are doing."

What are they doing? Why did she block Ando from the conversation? What is she and the aunts hiding?

Only Zeus knows.

"Well?" I ask, glaring at her.

"Well, what?" she responds with a faraway look.

"Me?" I huff. "Did they know what's wrong with me?"

"They have an idea," she reports offhandedly as she gazes out at the sea. Before our eyes the waves become more tranquil, more subdued. Mom is happy for some reason that she will not share with us. Then she smiles; truly smiles.

What is going on?

"Mommy, how did you do that?" Ando questions, studying the stillness of the water.

"How did I do… what?" she chuckles, playing coy.

"How did you make the sea so calm?"

Mom gives a serious belly laugh.

"I'm a Siren, sweetheart," she reminds.

"Yeah, but all you did was look at it," he states in awe.

Mom thinks for a moment then says something that I have never heard her say before.

"'If the ocean can calm itself, so can you. We are both salt water mixed with air.'"

"That's lovely," I gush, repeating it to myself. "What does it mean?"

"One day you will figure it out." The philosophical Siren gives an omniscient smile.

"It is nice," Ando agrees with a grin. "Will I figure it out too?"

"Most definitely," she gushes at her baby boy.

"Who said that, Mom?" I inquire, loving the sound of it.

"It's one of my favorite quotes from poet, Nayyirah Waheed." Mom beams, hugging herself like a young child would.

Then the unbelievable happens. Before my eyes, our mother, Marina Antonius Thermopolis Marquez, smiles brightly and for a brief moment, I swear her hair puffs and becomes bouncier and shinier. Her skin takes on a more polished radiance, and her aquamarine eyes glow brighter than the brightest star.

No matter how hard I try, I cannot take my eyes off of her.

Is this what Sirens look like to other beings?

No wonder they can charm anyone into loving them. Of course, it is even better when the object of your affection actually loves you and is not infatuated or obsessed with you. Tia Leukosia once told me that whosoever sees the *'true heart'* of a Siren is destined to find peace and contentment with her. She did not elaborate on what it all means, but she told me that Parthenope found true love twice. The first time was with Marcus and the second with Grandpa Theo.

"You're gorgeous!" I hear the words rush past my lips.

"Oh no!" my mother gasps.

"What Mommy?" Ando asks with wide eyes.

"Selena," Mom says, covering her eyes with her hands. "Go to your room."

"Why?" I question her random request.

"Ando, turn away from your sister," she orders my brother, who looks completely confused.

"But Mom," he pouts.

"No arguing!" she snaps as she physically turns him away from me herself. "Go now!"

"Momma, you're scaring me," I inform, hearing the terror in my own voice.

Not even when I first saw my mother strip naked and dive into the restless sea, I was not afraid. The first time I met the aunts, I was not afraid. However, this is not one of those times.

"Tonight, we'll perform the ritual and get some answers," she tells motioning me inside the house.

Ritual? What ritual?

"Until then stay in your room," she commands. "Do I make myself clear?"

"Y-yes ma'am," I stammer, racing indoors to the safety of my bedroom.

I suppose wishing for a happy ending is a waste of time.

Now I know I'm cursed!

The night is pleasant and warm with a hint of hibiscus in the air. Bright green palm fronds gently sway and as their leaves rub together it creates a relaxing tune. Even the softly lapping waves join in to create an evening lullaby.

"What exactly are we doing out here?" I question the judgement of my parent.

"We need to perform the ritual," Mom answers bluntly.

"What sort of ritual?" I continue to probe for more details.

After a moment of silence, my mother finally answers.

"We have to contact Gaia."

Why?

Then I realize they definitely cannot hear my thoughts anymore.

"Why?" I repeat, waiting for a response.

She pauses, obviously mulling over her response. I can see the gears in her mind working on a plausible answer, an answer that will not set me off. Her silence only makes my apprehension and fear grow until I can hardly take in air.

"Because only Gaia can explain this strange occurrence," she sighs, the sound is full of angst. "The aunts have no clue what is happening to you."

"What about Melody?" Ando speaks up.

"No one knows where Melody is," Mom admits sadly. "We hope she is alright."

"She's okay," Ando answers confidently. "Sometimes she visits me in my dreams."

"Do you know where she is?" I ask with my fingers crossed.

"No," he answers firmly. "She's not ready to be found, but she's always looking over us."

That knowledge makes me smile.

Our mother grins too. We all know that Melody can take care of herself. That was obvious when she kicked Amphitrite's butt. In all likelihood, one Muse is probably more powerful than all of the Sirens put together. She just never brags about it.

"Does she talk to you?" I question, my interest growing by leaps and bounds.

"She doesn't talk, but she gives me mental images and emotions," my younger brother tells with a content smile.

"That sounds nice," I sigh back.

His grin grows.

"It is," he blushes.

Our mother clears her throat to get us back on the topic at hand.

"It's time, kids," Mom informs as she draws an infinity sign in the dirt with her right foot. "I haven't done a summoning in centuries. Pray that this works."

Mom does not say a word, only motions for Ando to stand in the oval opposite to the one that she is currently standing in. Taking a few cleansing breaths, she readies herself, reminding me of how a boxer might 'ready' themselves for a high-stakes prize-fight.

When she is truly prepared, she speaks.

"Here goes nothing," Mom announces on an exhale.

"You can do this, Mommy," Ando encourages with a thumbs up.

Our mother smiles at the confidence he has in her ability to pull this summoning off.

"Una siempre externo los calibos... los terra... los Gaia... los infinite... " Mom chants in a language that is a mishmash of several languages together using a low, monotonous tone, over and over and over again. *"Una siempre externo los calibos... los terra... los Gaia... los infinite... "*

Almost thirty minutes goes by as we all wait, wondering if it will actually work, and when failure seems inevitable the earth starts to tremble, and the air around us crackles and hisses like a fire being doused by water. Just as I had experienced it on Paradiso. Thankfully, the tremors are not hard as a typical earthquake. Instead, it feels like when a bulldozer rolls over the ground.

At last, the soil at our feet begins stacking on top of itself creating a mound of dirt that is taller than my mother. As if time has sped up, the grass steadily begins to grow out of the heap then smoothly transforms into a long, olive-green gown dotted with unpolished shards of gold and jewels. The grass at the top of the mass continues to sprout until it resembles beautiful dark-brown tresses adorned with a wreath of vibrant magenta and deep violet hibiscus flowers with hints of lemongrass stalks. Before our wide-opened eyes, the entire thing becomes a woman. Without a doubt, the Goddess of Nature is the most stunning mocha-complexioned woman to have ever walked the Earth.

Why do I suddenly smell freshly baked bread?

Slowly, she opens her eyes, and sparkling amber irises specked with emerald blink at us.

Oh! My! Goddess!

"Hello, Gaia." I swallow the golf ball sized lump growing in my throat.

"Hello, my sweet Selena," the ageless goddess gives a perfect smile and the breeze fills with the glorious fragrance of lavender, even though lavender does not grow on Isla Flora.

"Thank you for coming here, great and loving Mother." Mom bows respectfully, her long curly locks grazing the ground. "Thank you for revealing yourself to us."

Thrilled to see the ancient goddess, I follow my mother's lead and bow as well. Ando, feeling left out, does the same. Gaia smiles at his polite display.

"You are of *The Three*," her voice flutters like delicate hummingbird wings. "It would be disrespectful of me not to answer when summoned. After all, you are the guardians of the Earth's waters."

In awe of her, I study her behavior. By all definitions, she does not remind me of a typical deity. She is not proud or boastful. The Nature Goddess exudes humility along with an unbreakable strength of character that never falters. I feel like a speck in her regal presence.

"How have you been?" Mom questions, attempting to make small talk.

Amiably, Gaia smiles brightly.

"Busy." Her smile suddenly turns into a frown. "Taking care of Terra has become more than a full-time job."

"Terra?" Ando repeats curiously.

"Terra is another name for the Earth," Gaia educates patiently.

"We are sorry, Gaia," I apologize, not liking the sound or the implications of that description.

The Mother of the Titans grins then holds her left arm out. Within seconds her arm is covered with native birds like charcoal-gray pewees, colorful male and subtly hued female Antillean Euphonia, even a couple of woodpeckers that not long before were high in the treetops fast asleep. With soft coos and whistles she communicates with them in a language very similar to Siren. Like the birds on Paradiso, they seem to be communicating back.

Nervously, I begin to shift my weight from my left leg to my right, and Gaia senses my apprehension and rests her hand on my shoulder. Immediately, I feel more at ease.

"Shall we sit and break bread together?" the goddess asks politely, gently moving her arm to dismiss her feathered subjects.

All of us nod our acceptance of her more than gracious invitation. Plus, remembering the spread we had on Paradiso, I know it will be delicious and memorable.

Glancing around, I admire the Isla Flora terrain and wonder what the goddess will serve us.

"Lena told me about the special way you make things come out of the ground," Ando reveals with a toothy grin.

"Has she?" Gaia chuckles and then blushes.

"May I see how you do it?" The six-year-old begs with an innocence that cannot be resisted.

Obviously under my brother's spell, Gaia smiles and with a nod of her head the ground begins to tremble again; however, this time it morphs into four throne-like chairs with cushions made of soft grass.

"Please, be seated," our host pleasantly requests, so we do.

"Wow!" Ando gasps, running his hands over the organic cushion.

"Now, we shall need some sustenance," Gaia suggests in her naturally royal manner.

Eager for the feast, all three of us nod, holding our respective breaths in anticipation. With a snap of her fingers, a tree trunk the size of a *Volkswagen Beetle* rises from the ground and as we watch, out of the stump grows a large bunch of dark-purple Concord grapes, several fuzzy peaches, and a large golden watermelon.

"Please, help yourselves," the goddess encourages, so we do.

Quickly, I gather a few grapes. Ando helps himself to one of the brightly colored peaches. Mom decides upon a wedge of sweet-smelling watermelon, of which she uses one of her talons to dissect. As she takes a bite of the juicy fruit, she moans her delight.

"It's so ripe and sweet," Mom compliments our host. "I've never had a piece of fruit that was so completely satisfying."

"Thank you, I am glad that you are enjoying it," Gaia grins from ear to ear.

Mom blushes, which is quite rare.

"It is the most delicious fruit I've ever tasted," she answers sincerely.

Then the goddess graciously offers her signature beverage.

"You must have some water," Gaia urges, and before our eyes a brook of clear spring water bursts from the Earth like a fountain. "I am sure you will remember this from the streams and rivers on Paradiso."

Ando goes first, cupping his hands to create a bowl-like shape. He takes a short sip… then another… and finally a long satisfying gulp.

"Oh wow!" he exclaims. "This tastes amazing!"

The Earth Goddess smiles that mysterious smile and all we can do is smile back.

"We have limited time," she admits, looking up into the night sky.

"Where are you going?" Ando asks in his usual way.

"Terra is expecting me," she frowns slightly, but even that expression makes her look even more stunning.

"Why?" He continues to probe.

"I am a physical part of the Earth," she explains. "When I am away for too long, it will start to whither and eventually it will die."

"Oh!" my brother sighs sadly. "We don't want that to happen."

Gaia nods in agreement.

"We have a slight problem," our mother informs the goddess. "Something is wrong with Selena."

Gaia frowns and touches my shoulder again, but this time she is waiting for something to happen. Whatever is expected to occur does not. This worries all of us.

"You are no longer of *The Three*." Gaia reveals a fact we already know.

"*Why* is she no longer a Siren?" Mom probes, her tone worry filled.

"The Earth is punishing her for her misuse of power," Gaia frowns and stiffens her posture, and for the first time I notice the grass around us wilts slightly as if it had not been watered for several days.

"But that has never happened before," Mom interjects, coming to a standing position.

Gaia shakes her head.

"Selena was told that tapping into the Earth's essence would lead to dire consequences," the goddess recalls, and her disappointment can be felt in the soft rain that begins to fall around us. Strangely, none of the raindrops land on us.

"That's true," I reply, bowing my head with shame. "Gaia warned me, but I didn't listen. *You* warned me too, remember? And I still didn't listen."

At this disclosure, Mom and Ando are silent. They will not look at me and who can blame them. I would not look at me either.

"I have explained to you, young one, when you channel the Earth, you tap into my strength... the strength that holds the world together, literally," Gaia repeats her previous warning.

At her displeasure, the ground beneath our feet rumbles, displacing tiny pebbles and fallen sticks. Above us, the shaking causes multiple palm fronds to detach from their trunk and slam down to the earth. Even the air loses its lovely lavender aroma.

Unable to defend my previous misuse of Siren *'magic'* I stare at her filled with self-loathing. Why did I think that I would be immune to punishment for wrongdoing? Of course, it would be me to become the first Siren ever to have her fish-card revoked.

"This is all my fault. Gaia warned me that power is addictive," I express my failure with several tears that escape. "She told me that it can lead you down a path that you do not wish to travel."

Ando and I both glance over at our mother, and then at the goddess. We can see that Mom is developing a migraine. She keeps pinching her nose bridge as if it will stop because of the action.

"Will she ever get her powers back?" Mom interrogates with teary eyes and a shakiness to her voice.

"The Earth will decide her fate," Gaia confirms, but her tone sounds bleak.

"Lena might be a human forever?" Ando pouts, looking at me with pity.

Mom puts her arm around Ando's shoulders, giving what little strength she has left to him. Me? I am not sure how to feel.

I am not a Siren. Not a weird mythological fish-girl with the ability to sway men with a mere flex of my vocal cords. No longer will I fight against my duality. My place is among people, eating hamburgers and spending time at the mall, window shopping with my friends.

Somehow, Gaia senses my relief, my elation at no longer walking a fine line between worlds. Not wanting to let my mother know of my real feelings, I frown, but inwardly, I am soaring through the heavens.

"Never forget who you really are, Selena," Gaia reminds with a reassuring hug. "You are a descendent of *The Three*. Your greatest strength is love."

"I will remember," I promise. "I will."

Maybe…

CHAPTER FIVE

Tonight, after Gaia disappeared back into the Earth, our family retired early. Filled with despair, Mom locked herself in her room. Ando, who eats when he is upset, ate two bowls of cereal and sent himself to his room. Feeling happier than I have in a long time, I made myself a grilled cheese sandwich, with a glass of ice-cold milk to go with it. It is not fancy, but it more than hits the spot.

Then, feeling rather upbeat, I clean the kitchen thoroughly, so Mom does not have to fuss at me. I even dry and put away the dishes in the dishrack. After sweeping and mopping the kitchen floor, I go outside and sit on the porch swing. The night is still pleasant and before I know it, I drift off into a light sleep.

Around two in the morning, I wake to the sound of soft crunching sounds in the front yard. Although it is faint, it has a distinct similarity to footsteps. Wiping the sleep from my eyes, I stretch myself partially awake but remain seated. Again, I hear that same crunching, but this time it is much closer.

"Who's there?" I call at a normal volume, not really expecting an answer.

Thankfully, I receive no response, unless you count a distant hooting owl.

Could it be… Belen?

Maybe Melody sent Belen to check on us? *Maybe* she is on the island to visit us? *Maybe*—

The sound of more footsteps through the grass alerts me once more. This time I know I am hearing it, and it is not a part of some dream sequence still playing in my head. Horror movies always start this way. The writer sets-up some poor, unsuspecting woman alone at night, minding her own business and through no fault of her own—

Whack! Snap! Blood! And… DeAtH!

What possessed me to watch *A Nightmare on Elm Street* with Nicole and her family? *Am I insane?* Probably.

It is then that I hear it.

"Se-leee-nah," it calls to me or so I think. It comes as a softly cooed whisper on the salty wind. The type of whisper that makes every hair on my body stand at attention and my blood run cold. It is the sound of something evil.

"Who's there?!" I question, not really wanting a response, and again only the answer of pained silence batters me. After several long, agonizing moments of trying desperately to quiet my thumping heart, I finally lean back against the swing. Ignoring my wild imagination, I start to drift off again. A minute later, the sound of scratching alerts me that something is amiss.

Why didn't I just go to bed in my room? Why?

"Selena," it whispers, the sound closer, and this time I am certain of it.

"Who-who's there?" I whimper.

"Selena," the soft voice replies, making me bolt upright. "Selena."

What the hell?

"T-Tia Ligeia?" I stutter, coming to a standing position. "Tia L-Leukosia? Is that y-you?"

"*Nooooooooooo*," whoever it is hisses vehemently, the sound making my upper lip perspire.

"You're on private property!" I educate soundly, reaching over for the rake that is leaning in the far corner. The one that my brother left when he cleaned up the yard debris after Mom mowed the lawn. "Get outta here or I'll call the police!"

"Are you afraid, little Siren?" the voice questions mockingly. "You don't have to answer. I can smell the fear oozing out of your pores. It smells yummy."

"Ha!" I provoke. "I'm not afraid of anything. My father owns a shotgun, and I know how to use it."

"Your father is dead… isn't he?" the person states knowingly. "Soon you will be too."

Unexpectedly, my survival instincts kick in. However, instead of confronting whatever it is, I bolt inside, slamming and locking the door behind me. The loud noise wakes both my mom and Ando.

"What's wrong?" the groggy Siren questions as she runs out of her bedroom wearing her favorite nightshirt. "What were you doing outside?"

"There's somebody outside!" I ramble, getting behind my brother.

"Lena, are you okay?" Ando asks, his eyes wide open.

Saying nothing else, Mom heads to the front door and opens it. Slowly, she looks around using her Siren-vision. Personally, I hope she does not see anything.

"I don't see anyone," she informs, stepping out onto the porch, as she does so, her talons break free of their hiding space under her fingernails.

"Maybe they left," Ando hopes out loud.

"You two stay here," our mother orders and no one argues with her. "I'm going to look around."

On cat-paws, Mom exits the porch area and goes hunting for her prey. Hopefully, she is in a better mood otherwise whoever it is might not ever leave our property. Mom may have lived with humans for a long time, but her heart and soul are those of a predator, those of an ancient Siren.

Several extremely long minutes pass before she returns. Her entire body is soaking wet and smells of wildflowers and salt water. She is also breathing heavily as if she has just completed a triathlon.

"Did you find the person?" I ask, hoping that she did.

"Not quite," she pants.

"What do you mean *not quite*?" I grill, getting a stomach cramp.

"Whoever it was moves fast… supernaturally fast," she tells as she strips down to her underwear. Ando runs to get her robe. Soon he returns with it, and we wait for her to slip it on.

"And what happened next?" I encourage her to continue.

"I chased it through the backyard then around to the side where it ran down the stone steps to the shoreline," she admits, looking agitated.

"How did it get away?" I blurt, clasping my sweaty palms together so my family will not see them shaking.

Mom pauses: her expression is one of confusion.

"It dove into the sea," she reveals with genuine surprise.

"But a normal person would be slammed against the rocks and killed." I do not have to remind, but I choose to anyway.

"Did you see its face?" Ando questions next.

"I did… sort of," she huffs as we follow her to her bedroom where she disappears behind the adjoining bathroom door. Next, we hear the shower turn on. Mom takes one of her quick military showers then comes out wearing a clean pair of pajamas. Her wet hair is still clinging to her face like long corkscrew tentacles.

"Mom?" I begin, trying to get her to return to the subject at hand. "Who was it?"

"I'm not sure," she confesses with bewilderment and surprise.

"How is that possible?" I grill without mercy, wanting answers. "Were you using your Siren-vision?"

Mom just glares at me.

"Of course I was using my enhanced vision," she answers flatly.

"What did it look like, Mommy?" Ando intervenes, knowing that our anxiety is growing.

"Its skin was like looking at harnessed moonlight, pale like alabaster," Mom describes painting the picture of a creature of the night like a vampire.

Wait! Are there such things as vampires?

After all, I never believed in Sirens, but I turned out to be one. I have learned that anything is possible. That is the scary part… *anything is possible.*

"Anything else stand out?" I question like I have seen on television detective shows.

"One thing stood out," Mom whispers nervously.

"What was that?" I ask, pushing her to keep speaking.

"Its face," she gulps.

"What about its face?" I probe inquisitively, my heartbeat filling my ears like a tribal drum of cannibals as they start the ritual feast.

Mom releases a held breath.

"It definitely *wasn't* human."

My luck sucks!

Unable to shake that gnawing feeling of dread, I convince Mom to let me sleep with her for the rest of the night, possibly the rest of my short human life. Ando, being a protective male, decides he will sleep on the couch just to make sure that no otherworldly prowlers breach our home. Armed with a water gun and a rope he found in the garage; he guards both our mom and me from harm.

"Are you sure you want to be by yourself out here?" I ask, not accustomed to being the damsel in distress. I am usually the cowgirl that rides into the thick of things and saves the day or causes the problems, depending on the day and circumstances and my level of Sireny-fury.

"I'm sure," Ando answers bravely, gripping the water gun tighter to his chest. "I'm the man of the house now."

Suddenly feeling proud, I kiss his forehead.

"Yes, you are," I compliment with a smile. "Goodnight, little brother."

"Goodnight, Lena," he says with a grin. "Sleep tight."

Quietly, I leave the room, turning off the light as I go. I glance over my shoulder just as Ando gives a big yawn. Another pang of guilt washes over me, but I push it aside.

"Is your brother alright?" Mom questions as I enter her room. She is already in bed, tucked under the covers, but this time she is wide awake.

"Aren't you tired?" I say, suppressing a yawn of my own.

"Not anymore," she smirks, patting the mattress beside her. "Why don't you lie down? You look exhausted."

"That's good advice," I reply, crawling under the covers beside her.

"How does it feel?" she questions.

I close my eyes, feeling safe beside my Siren mother. There is nothing in this world brave enough to face my mother when she is in full-on-momma-mode. She never backs down from a fight. I think that is where I must get it from.

Ligeia and Leukosia are the same. I have seen them battle killer whales and giant squids without batting an eyelash. There are stories online telling about ancient skirmishes where *The Three*—Ligeia, Leukosia, and Parthenope—were the prevailing warriors. Not only were they deadly on land, but in the water they were unbeatable.

Unfortunately, I am no longer of their kind. I am a vulnerable mortal who is neither deadly nor unbeatable. I am just me.

"How does *what* feel?" I snicker, attempting to be coy.

Mom laughs.

"How does it feel to be human again?" she clarifies anyway, even though she knows that I understand the question.

Clearing my head so that sleep can invade my mind, I sigh.

"It feels lovely," I respond, snuggling close to her, loving her warmth and protection.

"Sweet dreams, my girl," she replies, kissing the top of my head.

"See you in the morning, Mom," I state on a muffled yawn knowing that she will stay awake all night. "I love you."

My dream, at least I think it is a dream, is interrupted by a weird sensation I have of being watched. It bothers me so much that I wake up suddenly. Beside me is my mother, in a sitting position, fast asleep. On her lap is a fashion magazine and a bottle of *NoDoz*.

Apparently, non-sleep aid medicines have no effect on supernatural beings.

Not wanting to disturb her, I sluggishly maneuver off of the mattress to a standing position. Tiptoeing across the hardwood floor so as not to wake her. I get to the living room without any of the floorboards betraying me. On the sofa, also fast asleep, is Ando minus Alfredo. My brother without his furry companion is rare.

Wanting some water, I go to the kitchen and fill a glass from the tap. The water is cool and sweet. Not as delicious as the water on Paradiso, but still incredibly satisfying. Still in neat-mode, I wash and dry the glass and put it back into the cupboard with the others of its kind.

When I turn to leave the room, I feel that same sensation of someone or something watching me, stalking me. Boldly, I go to the window and look outside. There is a partially cloud-covered moon looking back at me from high above. To my dismay, the back and side yards are filled with shadows, which makes it almost impossible to see anything without special nighttime vision.

I am not certain what possesses me, but I go to the back door, quickly unlock it and step out onto the deck. The wooden planks are smooth under my feet, but I am guessing that it is due to David sanding and refinishing them when we first moved to the island. I smile as I remember how patient he had been when teaching Ando and me how to make it perfectly even.

The cool breeze is wonderful against my heated skin, so I stand letting it encircle me, caress me, envelop me. Down below, the sea still churns and slams against the rocky shoreline. I cannot believe that only a few weeks prior, I could have dived right in and never be harmed. However, times and circumstances change and for me, I no longer have the luxury of being a daredevil.

Being human is a balancing act of sorts. You have to be careful, but not overly careful where you are terrified of having any fun. You must be daring, yet not too daring that you lose good judgement. You are supposed to be adventurous but not cross the line of falling into danger. It is all enough to drive you to the brink of insanity, but somehow most humans manage to do it.

Needing to silence my own thoughts, I close my eyes.

"Your kind aren't very bright, are they?" The voice from earlier startles me as I feel my body being flung over the railing. Thankfully, it is toward the side yard and not over the side that overlooks the sea.

To my glee, I land on a clump of soft grass instead of the yard debris Ando raked into a large, neat pile. Knowing that I must get back inside, I stand, but as soon as I am upright another hard shove throws me on my back, knocking the wind out of me. Dizzy and disoriented, I stand again. This time I manage to wobble toward the back deck to the safety of the glass doors that lead into the house.

"Where are you going, *Siren*?" the thing hisses at me.

I can hear the grass crunching underneath its light steps.

What do I do now? I think to myself, not wanting it to get into the house.

"Come back, Selena." It laughs at my expense, and I feel its breath on the back of my neck, right before *it* pulls me backward away from the porch and dangles me over the edge of the cliff by my collar.

"*Stop!*" I scream as the tears start flowing. "Why are you doing this to me?"

It chuckles maniacally.

"Because I can," it says, loosening its grip, and my body drops several inches before it re-secures its hold.

"Do you want to feel the sensation of bones snapping as they crash against jagged rocks at hundreds of miles per second?" it questions like it is a cool thing to experience.

"*No!*" I screech. "Let me go! Wait! Don't let me go!"

"Let go of my sister, *Puta!*" Ando curses, but I do not care at the moment.

"Ando!" I yell. "Get Mom!"

I hear another set of heavier footsteps to my right.

"I'm here, baby!" my mother shouts as she grabs me with one hand and throws me to the safety of the side yard once again. With her free hand, she does a backhanded slap to the being that knocks it off balance. Screaming and swearing in Siren, Mom pushes her off of the edge, but the creature grabs ahold of my mother's pajama top and pulls her over with her.

"Mommy!" Ando bellows as he runs to the edge, looking over in despair. "I don't see them!"

As fast as I can manage, I hobble over to where he stands and join him looking down at the water below. All I see are crashing waves, but no sign of Mom or the intruder.

"Can you see them?" I entreat my brother, who looks as though he is at his wits end.

"No!" he shouts. "The water is too rough!"

"C'mon!" I yell, limping toward the stone steps. "We have to find her!"

"Lena, you're hurt!" Ando reminds, but I keep on course.

"I don't care!" I shout back. "I'm going with you!"

"Fine!" he concedes. "I'll meet you down there!"

Without another word, Ando does a graceful swan dive off of the balcony railing, falling past the rocky cliff side and finally piercing the choppy surface.

"Ando!" I yell.

I gotta get down there fast!

Hopping on one foot, I make my way down the rocky steps careful to avoid the slippery patches of moss. By this time, my left ankle is throbbing and swollen, but my mind is on Mom and Ando. Trying not to overthink, I reach the bottom without falling.

"Mom!" I bellow, scanning the area for signs of my family members. "Ando!"

Holding my breath, I limp to the edge. Carefully, I bend over to get a better look. In my current position, all I can see is seafoam and floating seaweed. Unfortunately, I still cannot see anything below the rough surface. Wanting a closer look, I get on to my knees; now my face is only a few inches away from the water.

"Mom, Ando!" I shout at the surface, praying for a response. "Can you hear me?"

"No." The contorted face of a half-fish woman pops out of the water in front of me. "But I can."

With long skinny fingers, she grabs me and pulls me under. Thankfully, I am able to take a deep breath before I plunge into the violent surf. My eyes immediately start to burn as they are assaulted with salt while the creature continues to hold me under.

To my distress, she wears a wicked grin on her slightly misshapen face.

"Baby Siren won't fight back," the creature smiles with gnarly teeth. "Baby Siren *can't* fight back."

Slowly, it leans closer to my face, so close I can see the particles of fish still clinging to its teeth.

"Poor, poor *dead* Siren," it hisses, eyes flashing ice blue.

Unable to communicate underwater, I begin thrashing around, hoping to wiggle enough to escape its tight grip, but it is hopeless.

"Squirmy baby Siren cannot escape," it snarls, then I guess she finds my demise not advancing fast enough, because she suddenly wraps her hands around my neck and squeezes hard.

Not wanting to die without causing any injury, with my free hand I rip the necklace from my neck. Gripping the glass charm with all my might, I slam it into the creature's left eye. There is a wet popping sound followed by the gushing splatter of marshmallow-like-goo. That is enough for the thing to let out an ear-piercing screech. Suddenly, it releases me, and I waste no time swimming back to the surface.

"*Mommy!*" I hear my brother's voice as I break through the surface into the dry world. "She's over here!"

"Selena!" our mother shouts, voice muffled with emotion. "We thought we lost you!"

"I thought you guys would save me," I gasp and wheeze as they pull me out of the pounding surf.

"We couldn't," Ando informs with a frown, heaving as they tug me onto land.

"Why not?" I demand, filling my lungs with air and wiping the salty liquid away from my burning eyes.

"Because…" Ando tries to explain then abruptly stops.

"Why didn't you get to me before I got chummed?" I assert, feeling my lungs returning to a normal breathing pattern. "There was only one."

"That's what we thought too," Mom declares with a loud exhale.

"I don't understand." I cough up some remaining water.

Mom and Ando both glance at each other then back at me.

"There were three," they answer as one.

My heart starts to pump faster until it almost deafens me.

Of course!

CHAPTER SIX

Morning arrives faster than expected. On the nightstand, the digital clock reads eight-thirty, but it feels much earlier than that. Too sore to get out of bed, I pull the cover over my head hoping to avoid the sun. Thankfully, it does not take long to fall back asleep. The next time I open my eyes, it is almost ten o'clock.

Making the mistake of swallowing my saliva, a harsh burning sensation starts in my throat and moves upward. It reminds me of the time I had strep throat and had to take antibiotics until the infection had gone away. All I know is that it was the most excruciating pain I have ever had.

Until now.

Then I notice something else. Next to my clock is a small bowl of clear broth. Hungry, I give it a sniff. *Ahh!* It is homemade chicken broth, the kind that Mom always makes when someone in the family is sick. Moving to a sitting position, I slowly sip the warm liquid until it is all gone. Even though my throat feels scratchy and tender, the soup makes my empty stomach feel less nauseous.

"Hi, Lena," Ando greets from the doorway. "Mommy and I saved you some pancakes."

I smile at him.

"I don't think I can eat those," I pout, getting a whiff of the cooking batter from the kitchen.

"They are blueberry." He smiles and wiggles his brows. "And they taste really yummy."

Sluggishly, I swing my legs over the edge of the mattress. It squeaks just a little. It always has, even when it was brand new.

"Thanks, little bro," I say with a thin smile.

"Is your throat hurting?" he probes, examining the finger-shaped bruises on my neck.

"Yeah," I answer, coming to a standing position and then falling back onto the mattress when I lose my balance.

Ando chuckles.

"Do you want some help?" he asks, coming around to stand in front of me.

I chuckle too.

"Would you mind helping your big sister up?" I question, holding both hands out towards him.

"Nope." He grins, then without any effort, pulls me to my feet.

"Ouch!" I yelp as my hurt ankle tries to take my full weight.

Ando glances down.

"It's swollen, Lena," he grimaces. "I'll get you some ice."

I nod my appreciation as he gives a shy grin.

"You're getting strong," I compliment, and he blushes.

"I'm growing up," he reminds. "I've got muscles now too."

Proudly, he flexes his mini muscles like he is a professional bodybuilder.

"They're small, but compact," I agree with a grin. "You should be proud."

"I am," he says with a shrug.

"I'm going to get cleaned up before breakfast," I state tensely, hoping that my ankle just needs a few days of rest.

"Do you want me to fix a plate of pancakes for you?" he asks thoughtfully.

"Maybe later," I say with a wink.

"Just one?" he insists.

Not wanting to hurt his feelings, I nod.

"Wait for fifteen minutes then heat it for me," I request, grabbing a pair of shorts, t-shirt and underwear.

"Got ya!" He grins happily. "Don't rush. Your ankle needs an icepack. I'll make one for you."

"Thank you," I say, giving him a hug before he turns to go downstairs.

"No worries," he replies, and for the life of me I swear he sounds just like David.

"Hey!" I blurt as he exits.

"Yeah?"

"What's Mom doing?" I question, taking a pained step toward the door.

He thinks for a moment.

"She had to go into the office for a few hours," Ando informs as he turns to leave once more.

"What for?" I grill, hopping to the door instead of attempting to walk.

"Her boss is working on a new advertising campaign, and she needs Mom to do the photo shoot," he relays.

"Sounds interesting," I reply with a wince. "I'll see you in a little bit."

"See ya." He waves. "Be careful in the shower. Don't slip."

I smile at him.

"I'll try not to."

I have never had this much trouble taking a shower. My ankle is throbbing, so I have to put all of my weight onto the opposite leg. As everyone knows, I am not the most graceful person on the planet, so hurting myself is inevitable. Accepting this, I cautiously manage to wash, shave my legs, and shampoo my hair. It takes a bit longer to get dressed and tidy up the bathroom when I am done.

Thirty minutes later, I finally arrive at the kitchen; my brother is waiting with one steaming pancake with syrup, a couple sausage links, and a tall glass of milk.

"I'm sorry that I took so long," I huff out of breath, gently plopping onto the nearest chair. "I didn't realize how much an injured ankle would slow me down."

"No worries," he replies with a great deal of understanding. "I waited a few minutes longer, just in case."

"How did you get this smart?" I joke.

"I've got a big brain." He giggles as he adjusts the chair for me.

I laugh.

"Yes, you do," I agree. "You really do."

Regaining my appetite, I eat while Ando sits and chats. Completely animated, he tells me about the latest antics with

Whistler and his dolphin pod members. With great enthusiasm, he reviews the new and improved school uniforms this year, but we soon realize that the only change is that we will have a choice of wearing long sleeves or our traditional polo shirt.

Confused, I look at my brother who looks at me.

"Why would we need long sleeves in the tropics?" I ask mockingly, taking another bite of the syrup covered pancake followed by a bite of the slightly spicy sausage link.

Ando shrugs and smirks.

"I don't know," he chirps, running to get me a napkin, trailing giggles all the way to the cupboard. "Maybe they're expecting snow and penguins."

Even on the coolest winter day, the temperature only drops to a mild seventy-five degrees. In Ohio, some winter days we had to face temperatures below zero with the wind-chill factor. Seventy-five degrees Fahrenheit is a walk in the park by comparison. One year, Dad forgot to turn off the automatic sprinkler system, and we came home to find a winter wonderland in our front yard. There were icicles hanging from all of the tree branches and on the white picket fence guarding the perimeter of our yard. It was gorgeous. Frigid, but gorgeous, nonetheless.

"What time is Mom coming home?" I query, almost finished consuming my food.

"Around three," he spills the information freely. "She's gotta go to the grocery store afterwards."

"Do you think we should make dinner as a surprise?" I question hopefully.

My brother's ears perk up.

"What should we make?" he asks, going to the pantry.

"What about lasagna?" I suggest. "Mom loves that dish."

Ando appears to be thinking.

"Do we have all of the ingredients?" I ask, hopping over to the refrigerator.

Quickly, I rummage through the freezer. It does not take long to find a large package of ground beef.

"I found some meat," I inform, resting the frozen package on the countertop.

Ando is still searching the pantry shelves.

"I got the lasagna noodles and a jar of sauce," he speaks louder so I can hear. "Do we have the cheeses?"

"I'll check," I inform, opening the lower door that leads to the fridge section.

It takes less than a minute to find a big tub of ricotta cheese, shredded parmesan and mozzarella cheese, and of course we always have eggs.

"I think I've got everything we need," I announce, feeling accomplished.

"What about spinach?" Ando adds. "Mom always puts spinach in her lasagna."

"Umm." I pause for a moment. "There might be a box of frozen spinach in the freezer hiding somewhere."

Determined to locate the green leafy vegetable, I search the entire freezer and right before my hope is dashed, I find the very last box hidden behind a whole frozen ham.

"I got it!" I reveal, pretending to cheer like a crowd.

"Daddy loved lasagna with spinach," Ando reminds with a sad frown.

"Yes, he did," I whisper, remembering the last time we ate lasagna as a family. It was in Capri at the vacation villa. I recall that it rained the entire day, and we were trapped indoors. That night we all played board games, Boys against Girls. The girls won, of course.

Shaking off the beautiful memory, I clear my sore throat.

"I'll put this ground beef in the sink with some cold water to defrost," I tell my brother who still stands smiling at the memory.

"What should I do?" he queries, wanting to help.

"Could you get me Dad's old crutches?"

He looks at me strangely.

"Why do you need those?"

I glance at my swollen ankle which is now much bigger and more painful.

"Oh!" he exclaims, now comprehending. "I'll get it out of the upstairs closet."

Ando rushes past me to retrieve the medical equipment. Carefully, I sit back down and prop my wounded leg on the seat of another chair. Underneath the skin, the veins are pulsing like bass drums. It hurts like crazy.

As I wait, I hear my cell phone ringing from my room upstairs. Unable to move quickly, I yell to Ando to pick it up. Without my Siren-hearing, I cannot tell if he has heard me. Shortly after, he comes sauntering into the kitchen with my cellular device to his ear and a broad grin on his face.

"That sounds like fun," he says to the person on the other end of the call. "I wish I could do that… no way… okay… here's Lena."

He hands me the phone.

"It's Andrew," he smiles, showing the gap where several front teeth are growing in. "I already told him you gotta hurt foot."

"Thanks a lot," I reply sarcastically, taking the phone from him.

"Just doing my job," he teases, skipping out of the room to do what, I have no idea.

Nervously, I take a few deep breaths. I am sure he will want to know how a Siren sprained her ankle. Hopefully, he does not freak out when I tell him the news.

"Hey, stranger!" I greet, trying to sound enthusiastic and not anxious. "How's the weather up there in Alaska?"

How's the weather? Really?

Andrew chuckles and the sound runs through my ear canal through my sternum and into my heart. Instantly, my heartbeat increases, and my mouth goes desert dry. I am glad that his effect on me has not changed. Especially since the whole Ares debacle over the summer.

"The weather is gorgeous," he replies with a smile in his voice. "How's the weather on Isla Flora?"

"Not too hot, thank goodness," I respond, getting tired of weather talk. "How's your father?"

"He's great!" Andrew discloses. "How's everyone in your family?"

I still have not told any of my friends about David except Nicole and her family, who were all sworn to secrecy. For some reason, Mom is keeping David's death top-secret. This I do not understand. People like his colleagues at Ocean World will be expecting him back at the end of next month. We were supposed to be in Greece right now, but because of circumstances we came back home a month early.

"Everything is… terrific!" I lie. "Couldn't be better."

Full of nervous energy, I stand and begin hobbling back and forth debating if I should tell him the bad news now or later, all the while my feet wear a path across the immaculate kitchen floor. But even if I do tell him the truth, what can he do from Sitka, Alaska?

Bound and determined to get it over with, I come up with a strategy. Clearing my throat in preparation, I begin to lay the foundation of my lie.

"Andrew?" I say with hesitancy.

"What's the matter?" he questions, knowing when something is wrong.

"There's something I need to tell you," I state with an accelerated exhale.

Silence bombards my ears.

"Is something going on?" He pauses then continues, adding: "With Ando?"

I choke back a cough as I swallow my spit the wrong way.

"No!" I exclaim. "No! Ando is… *Ando.*"

Andrew releases a held breath.

"Good to know." He snickers, and I hear shuffling followed by the sound of paper crinkling.

"What are you doing?" I interrogate with a curious grin, moving the cell away from my ear so as not to be deafened.

There is a short pause as he bids me to hold, and then I hear a raspy masculine voice in the background asking for his take-away order. I giggle as he requests: a fried cod sandwich with cheddar cheese, lettuce and tomato, a double order of French fries, and a slice of Mocha-Fudge Blackout Cake.

"I haven't eaten in a few hours." He defends himself with another smile that I can hear over the cell.

I suppress a snicker but roll my eyes.

"I've got a good appetite," he reminds with a chortle.

Clearing my throat, I tease with, "Yeah, I've heard that excuse before."

"Ha! Ha! Ha!" he jibes. "You're hilarious."

There is another halt in our conversation when his father calls and he has to switch over.

He returns after a minute and apologizes for all of the interruptions. I can imagine his dad teasing him about being in a good mood since getting to talk with me. Knowing this makes me blush.

"I'm sorry about that... what was I saying—"

My eyebrows hitch at his lack of focus. Normally, he is well-organized with perfect memory. Today, he seems slightly off-balance.

"You seem tired, Mister Barnett," I respond, feeling sorry for my... umm... *boyfriend?*

He releases a loud yawn just as I make my observation.

"Why are you so exhausted?" I probe wondering what he and the elder Mr. Barnett are doing for their extended stay in the wilderness.

"My father and I ran into a tribe of Inuit," his tiredness instantly dissipates.

"Inuit?" I pry, suddenly at attention. "What's that?"

"They are an indigenous tribe of Native Americans," Andrew educates. "This particular village has been estranged from the surrounding towns for hundreds of years."

My curiosity awakens.

"Really? That's amazing!" I exclaim, wanting to know more details about their trip, but he cuts me off.

"I'm sorry, Selena," he apologizes for no apparent reason. "I need to get back to the hotel. Dad wants to make another trip up to their village and it's really far away."

"Ok," I counter, understanding that our time is over for this call. "I guess we'll talk another time."

"I will call you back tomorrow," he adds sincerely. "If I can get a signal."

"I can't wait," I giggle at him being so flustered.

"Selena?"

"Yes?"

There is a long pause.

"I love you!" he proclaims and then hangs up, leaving me with my mouth hanging open.

I love you!

That's what he said!

Didn't he?

My device vibrates notifying me that I have received a text message.

It reads: *Yes, I did say I love you!*

Eeeee!

Immediately, I call Nicole to share the good news. Her cell rings until it goes to voice mail, but being all wound-up, I call again hoping that she will pick-up. On the seventh ring, she answers.

"Hello, Selena," Nicole welcomes, sounding distracted.

"Nicole!" I exclaim, my pulse racing. "Is that you?"

She chuckles.

"Of course it's me," she pauses. "You dialed my number."

"Oh yeah!" I blush, trying to calm my nerves.

"What do you want?" she asks, sounding a tad annoyed with me.

I pause wondering if I should share the news.

Yup! I should!

"Andrew told me that he loves me!" I actually *'Eee'* after divulging the information.

"Andrew actually told you that he loves you?" Nicole practically chokes on her own saliva.

"Uh huh!" I exclaim, unable to hold in my excitement. "Can you believe it?"

"Did you say it back to him?" she questions with a saucy lilt to her voice.

I pause, replaying the moment in my head.

"I didn't," I confess feeling foolish.

"Why not?" she snaps, catching me off guard.

I think for a moment before answering.

"He said it really fast then hung up before I could process what he said," I explain, hoping she will understand.

There is a long pause before Nicole speaks again.

"You're an idiot," she snickers, but I can tell that she is not joking like she normally would.

"Huh?" is the only sound that comes out.

"Did I stutter?" Nicole's tone is harsh and mean.

"That's not fair," I pout, feeling as if I have been verbally slapped.

"The guy of your dreams confesses his feelings for you, and you mess it up," she chastises rather severely. "As usual."

"Wait one minute!" I bark, refusing to be attacked. "What the hell is wrong with you, Wong? You're being a complete witch!"

"Thank you for noticing," Nicole brashly replies then clicks off our call. All I can do is stare at my cell wondering what just happened.

My head is reeling and about to explode. In all of the months that I have known Nicole she has never behaved this coldly. Honestly, it is rare for the teen to even raise her voice. She is normally even keeled and caring to a fault.

"I've never seen her act this way," I confess to my mother and brother during dinner.

"It's definitely out of character," Mom mumbles as she pushes her lasagna remnants around her plate with her fork.

"Combine that with her strange behavior when I spent the night," I add, analyzing everything that has happened and wishing Jenny was back from Ireland so I can pick her brain. After all, Jenny and Nicole have known each other since elementary school. Jenny would be able to figure out what in the world is going on with our best friend.

"Mommy?" Ando speaks up.

"Yes, my baby."

"What were those things that attacked us?" he questions, changing the subject.

"They were vicious," I declare with a growl. "And ridiculously fast too."

"Don't forget strong," Ando pipes up as he reaches for another serving of lasagna which turned out perfectly, if I do say so myself.

Then I smell it.

It is that overwhelming scent of wildflowers. The fragrance permeates the entire kitchen to the point that I feel like I am being suffocated by potpourri.

"Can you smell that?" I wince, pinching my nose and breathing through my mouth.

"Smell what?" Ando counters then takes another forkful of the pasta directly from the baking dish.

"It smells like wildflowers," I add, also taking a second helping of dinner.

Mom sniffs the air.

"I don't smell anything except dinner." She smiles, reaching for the pitcher of cold hibiscus tea sweetened with coconut sugar. "Thank you for making such a terrific meal. I'm so grateful."

"You're welcome." Ando grins, taking the credit, but we all know that it was a shared endeavor.

"Really?" I gasp, practically suffocating. "You can't smell it?"

My brother and mother both shake their heads.

"Maybe I'm imagining it." I pout, taking several bites in a row then following it with a long drink of iced tea. However, my sinuses beg to differ. As I sit facing the glass door that leads outside to the balcony, a shadow darts past. Immediately, my stomach lurches.

"Something is outside!" I shout, standing up and knocking over my chair. "It ran past the door!"

"Are you sure?" Mom asks as she abruptly stands then dashes to the glass door and gives it a strong tug making certain that it is locked. "Ando, run upstairs and make sure all of the windows are locked. I'll do the same down here."

"What should I do?" I ramble, feeling useless and frightened.

"You're already hurt," Mom reminds. "I don't want you—"

She pauses and I already know what she is worried about.

"Just stay here, please," she requests as she bolts toward the living room area.

As I continue standing, waiting for my family to return, two more shadows rush past the glass. One stops and taps, the other disappears around to the far-side of the house. Terrified of them getting indoors, I hobble to the kitchen drawer that contains

Mom's carving knives. These things are deadly and can easily cut through bone and sinew without missing a beat. Scared out of my wits, I grab the largest, sharpest butcher's knife… and pray.

"If you take one step inside this house, I'll carve you up myself," I threaten with a trembling voice.

"Tsk… tsk… tsk," it mocks, still tapping its long talon against the glass pane. "Baby Sirens talk boldly when they are inside, and we are out."

"What do you want?" I shout to my foe, this time, not recognizing if it is male or female.

"We want what you have," it sneers. "We want what you took from us… what you *stole* from us."

"What did we steal?" I ask, genuinely interested. "What do we have that you don't?"

Then my eyes adjust a little more and I can see an outline of the creature. It has pale, almost transparent skin that glows like the moon. Its eyes are black as midnight, and its hair is a startling platinum blonde. It is a vision made of nightmares, and it is currently staring at me.

"Selena!" Mom barks as she runs into the room. "What happened? Why did you sh—"

Abruptly, my mother ends her comment.

The thing outside hisses and howls and before we know it, all three creatures are standing at the glass door glaring menacingly at us; their facial expressions are those of pure unadulterated hatred.

Suddenly, I feel cold. It is the same iciness that I felt when I was at Nicole's house. My bones begin to ache, and goosebumps cover my skin. The creature hesitates for only a second, but it is enough time for my mother to see it. She growls low in her throat and bares her teeth like a she-wolf protecting her cubs. Then Mom does something I have never seen her do, ever: she shows her true Siren form on land.

Without hesitation, my mother shifts from skin to her obsidian battle scales. Her sharpest most menacing teeth and talons emerge from beneath the protective armor-like covering. Her usually lovely silken strands of ebony hair are now thicker with tiny razor-like barbs at the tips of the curly ends, and even her aquamarine irises have shifted and swirled into a deep, terrifying, bloody maroon.

From deep inside her diaphragm, the most chilling, blood-curdling wail escapes shaking the walls and windows alike. The shrill inhuman sound attaches to my spine and travels to my brain, almost shutting down all of my mental capacities. Unexpectedly,

I need to concentrate on staying on my feet and continuing to breathe. All around me the blast echoes, bouncing and bounding across the solid surfaces, shattering the salt and pepper shakers, toppling several canisters and the dish soap dispenser, until it slowly begins to subside. When it finally stops completely, all but one of the creatures have fled.

Still shocked, I stand motionless with my mouth gaping.

"Do not leave this house alone at night," Mom's demeanor is steely. "Do you understand?"

"But—" I begin to speak, but I am rebuked.

"This is not a request, Selena!" my mother growls, eyes swirling from maroon to a gray-hued cobalt.

Without further debate, I nod my understanding.

"Ando!" she bellows, ignoring me. "Come to the kitchen! Now!"

I hear running upstairs and then my brother's voice behind me.

"What is that?" he whispers pointing at the creature who stares at us like we are dinner.

Mom shudders. Her gaze locked onto her enemy. Her hands clench even with her talons drawn.

"Mermaid!"

CHAPTER SEVEN

I do not think that I will ever feel safe again. Even after Mom and Ando scour the grounds, as well as the cove below the house, and assure me that they are gone, visions of Mermaids keep haunting me. Sadly, even though I try focusing on other things, I soon realize that it does not matter if I am awake or asleep; all I can think about are the hideous creatures that have their sights set on us.

"Mom, have you contacted the Aunts?" I question, biting my bottom lip with exasperation.

Mom leans back and takes a deep breath.

"I tried for more than an hour to contact the aunts, but without any success."

"What's the deal with Mermaids and Sirens anyway?" Ando probes. "What do they want?"

"I hope they do not come back," I whisper to the room.

Mom seems to be mulling over her words.

"Those are all great questions, son," our mother sighs, still not answering.

Ando glances at the windows for the tenth time in less than five minutes. I know this because every time he looks, I do the same.

"I've never personally met a Mermaid," she confesses at last. "The Three scattered what was left of their clan eons before I was born."

"Why?" Ando grills as he gathers the items from the pantry that Mom has requested. "What did we do to them?"

Mom frowns.

"Selena?"

"Yes, Mom?" I answer immediately.

"Please get Grandpa Theo's journal," she demands firmly and I obey.

Before attempting to stand, I look down at my swollen pulsating ankle.

"I'll get it for you, Lena," Ando volunteers. "Where is it?"

"It's in a wooden box in my closet under a stack of magazines," I divulge my hiding place to my brother because I have no other choice.

"I thought it was under your bed wrapped in a sheet," he slips then covers his mouth knowing he has been caught.

"How do you know that it was under my bed?" I cross-examine, wanting to pinch his cheek, hard.

Pretending to be clueless, he shrugs.

"Why did you hide it anyway?" he questions with a confused look. "Technically it belongs to me too."

Of course he has to hit me with logic. That boy should be an attorney. I swear! He would never lose a case.

"Ando," Mom interjects, getting him back on track. "Please get the journal. We'll discuss sharing later."

Patiently, we wait as Ando goes upstairs to find my — I mean — *our* journal. It does not take him long to return. Gently, he sets it on the dining table and waits for further instructions.

"Go ahead and take it out, sweetheart," Mom smiles and Ando practically jumps for joy.

Carefully, my brother removes the old leather journal from its box.

"It looks really old, and the pages are all yellowed and stained," he whispers like he is afraid of insulting Mom, me or our family heritage.

I thought the same thing the first time I saw it.

"Hey!" he exclaims with realization. "The cover of the journal is decorated with the same design as Mom's volcanic glass charm."

Mom nods.

"Lena has her own charm now," he says out loud as he touches his bare neck. "I'm the only one who doesn't have one."

I suddenly feel bad for him.

"You will get yours when you turn sixteen," Mom informs, messing-up his hair.

"When I complete *The Calling*?" He beams with anticipation.

"Exactly," Mom replies with a bright smile.

With slightly trembling hands, he touches it, feeling the smoothness of the leather against his fingertips just as I had done so many months ago. It is a feeling that cannot be explained to someone not of the bloodline. Although it is an inanimate object that cannot speak, it communicates with us in other ways, more heartfelt ways. It is like reconnecting with an old friend that you have not seen in years, but when reunited, it feels like no time has passed at all.

"What does this symbol mean?" Ando probes, his gaze still lingering on the journal.

"It is the ancient symbol for Siren," Mom answers with a bright smile.

"This is so cool!" he proclaims enthusiastically, slowly removing his hand from the book.

Mom laughs a full belly laugh at my brother's excitement. I have to agree; it is quite contagious. It almost makes me want to be a Siren again.

Almost!

"I agree," she smirks touching her own necklace. "It is extremely cool."

"Since Lena isn't a Siren anymore, do I get to keep it?" he blurts, and I feel as if I have been stabbed in the back.

Mom looks out of the window disconcertedly; lost in thought as she tries to find an appropriate response.

"Well," she begins. "I haven't really thought about who will look after my stepfather's journal."

"I'll take good care of it," he promises, cocking his head to one side as he runs his fingers gingerly over the raised leather relief once more.

"I'm sure you will," Mom agrees, but sees the hurt in my eyes.

"Why are there carvings of Mermaids on this box?" he queries with a disgusted expression.

"It is so we will always remember our enemies," Mom reveals with a snarl. "According to the aunts, they are our most hated foes."

"Why?" Ando presses, not quite understanding, and to tell the truth neither do I.

"I'm not sure," Mom states emphatically. "Whatever it was almost killed-off both species."

"Tia Ligeia told me that mer-people are snooty and self-righteous," my brother pipes up.

"I don't understand why we hate each other so much," I blurt, thinking over the death sentence on my head.

As Mom and I watch, Ando opens the journal to the first page. Like me, he reads the dedication which says:

> *To Parthenope, Marina, and the sea for*
> *bringing meaning to my life. I will*
> *follow forever your Siren-Song.*
> *—T.T.*

Ando just stares at it.

"The title of the journal is called *The Truth about Sirens by Dr. Theodore Thermopolis*; Grandpa Theodore was a human who loved a Siren," he mutters, talking to himself. "So cool!"

And so, it begins…

Feeling that a second-floor room would be safer, Mom ushers us upstairs. Not wanting me to put any unnecessary weight on my ankle, she scoops me up into her arms and carries me to my bedroom as if I weigh nothing at all. Glad for the assistance, I do not bother to complain; I simply keep my mouth shut and enjoy the kind gesture. My brother follows closely behind, tucked securely under his left arm is Grandpa's journal.

Once settled in my room, we wait. *For what?* None of us know. We just wait.

"Grandpa Theo really wrote this?" Ando asks as he lies on his belly at the foot of my bed, obviously confused.

"Yes," Mom answers with a proud smile. "He did."

"I thought he made buildings?" my brother counters, trying to remember Grandpa Theo's profession.

Our mother grins.

"He was an architect, but he was also an expert on Greek Mythology," Mom educates. "The Siren lore was his specialty. He knew absolutely everything about them."

Ando beams.

"I want to be an arch-ee-tect when I grow up," he states firmly.

Mom grins.

"Your grandfather would be very proud if you followed in his footsteps," she praises, handing the book back to my brother. "It belongs to you *and* your sister."

I take her proclamation under protest, mumbling heavily under my breath. Unexpectedly, Mom stands and begins pacing back and forth like a wild animal trapped in a cage. Ando begins to read:

> *This is the history of the gods; before Adam and Eve… before man walked upright; mighty Zeus and his brethren walked the Earth and made the mountains shake and the oceans churn with their awe-inspiring power. It was in these days that Melpomene the Muse bore to Tethys' son Akheloios three sea nymphs named Parthenope, Leukosia and Ligeia. The ancient world came to know them as the Seirenes.*

He stops reading and closes the journal; on his face is a broad grin.

"I know what Mom told you," He giggles, feeling extremely proud of himself.

Mom stops at the window and peers outside. I guess she is looking for mer-people. Right now, I am trying to forget about them. All I want to do is go back to the days when Sirens were the only creatures that mattered. Now, I have to come to terms with merfolk wanting to kill me along with every Siren currently alive.

Our mother sighs: the sound is painful to hear. She is about to respond, but I recite it for her. Actually, I quote her verbatim:

"'Our entire history—both good and bad—is in these pages, and even though the words may sound unbelievable, you have to look into your heart then you'll know that every word is true.'"

Mom blows me a kiss then turns quietly on her heels and exits the room; never looking back at us.

"Where is she going?" I ask Ando, missing the telepathy we once shared.

"She's going outside to do a perimeter sweep," he answers like a soldier in an old-World War II movie.

"They'll get her!" I snap, grabbing my crutches. "Let's go!"

With one hand, my brother halts my advance from the bed.

"Wait, Lena!" he forcefully urges.

"Can you hear her?" I interrogate, feeling my upper lip beginning to perspire.

"Mom has their scent now," he informs with a devilish grin.

"What does that matter?" I question our mother's common sense.

"She'll be able to track them anywhere," he says matter-of-factly. "They won't be able to sneak-up on us again."

Whew! That's good to know.

Then his eyes swirl green then brown and finally back to aquamarine.

"Ando?" I rest a hand on his small shoulder. "What just happened? Your eyes are doing a freaky-Melody-swirly-thing."

He does not respond, only stands motionless.

On instinct, I take a step back. Why? Because I am human now, that is why!

Jeez!

"The aunts are coming," Ando blurts with a mischievous grin.

"The aunts are coming?" I repeat, hoping that I heard him correctly. "Here?"

"Yup!" he replies, still grinning.

"When will they be here?" I probe, suddenly feeling lighter than air.

Without warning he walks to the locked window and stares up at the cloudy sky. He mumbles something under his breath then hurries back to the bed. Again, his irises start swirling, changing colors, and finally returning to normal.

"Ando?" I exclaim, getting his attention. "When?"

"Before the next full moon," he answers as he thumbs through the journal.

"When's that?" I ask, hopping over to the window to see if I could find Mom.

In the distance, near the cliff, our mother waves to me from the backyard and I wave back. From my aerial view, I can see everything below. My window has the perfect view of both the side of the house and the backyard. Unfortunately, the front yard is out of my sightline.

"Does Mom know that they're on their way?" I query, wishing I could talk to her from up here.

"Yup!" he speaks again. "The aunts told us both."

I suddenly feel a pang of disappointment that I no longer have that ability.

"Don't be sad, Lena," Ando encourages.

My heart leaps for joy.

"Did you hear what I was thinking?" I question with exuberance.

He just looks at me then shakes his head.

"No," he finally answers. "You just looked sad is all."

"Oh," I respond with a loud exhale. "I see."

"Hey!" Ando shouts, making me jump out of my skin.

"What's wrong?"

"I found something in the journal about Mermaids." He smiles like he has found buried treasure.

Hopping back over to where he sits, I peer over his shoulder.

"What does it say?" I grill, tapping my fingers on his back. "Is it something important?"

"Lena?"

"Yes?"

"Stop tapping on me," he chastises. "It bothers me."

"I'm sorry," I apologize. "I'm just anxious."

"It's okay." He smiles warmly.

"What does it say?" I beseech one more time. "Read it out loud."

Ando pauses for a moment.

"What's the matter?" I wait, holding my breath.

"It's Mom," he informs.

"Is she alright?" I hop back to the window.

"The coast is clear," he states with a military phrase like *G.I. Joe.*

I release a held breath.

"She's coming back inside," he informs nodding. "I think she's going to eat some more lasagna."

I giggle.

"Thanks for the update," I tease. "Perhaps you should become a news anchor instead."

My brother crinkles up his forehead.

"Nope, I'm gonna be an arch-ee-tect like Grandpa Theo," he reemphasizes with determination.

"Read the entry for me, please," I beg, making him focus again.

Ando clears his throat before he begins:

> *In the time of Demeter's great ice storms, when the Earth was new and the laws had not yet been set, there came to be two tribes of sea nymphs. The Sirens, daughters of the great Muse, Melpomene and the River God, Akheloios, direct descendants of Zeus himself. The second tribe was the Merpeople who are the offspring of the Assyrian goddess, Atargatis. According to ancient lore, Atargatis*

transformed herself into a Mermaid out of shame for accidentally killing her human lover.

As it was told to me by the Siren, Parthenope, the Merpeople helped the God of the Underworld, Hades, abduct the Princess Persephone from the care of The Sirens. From this act of betrayal arose The Great Nymph War *which waged for decades until most of the Merfolk were destroyed by* The Three *who swore vengeance.*

Zeus, feeling magnanimous one day, bartered with the Sirens that if they ended the fighting, they would be allowed to keep their wings given to them by the goddess, Demeter. However, Poseidon, who had allied with their brother Hades, drugged The Three with a powerful sleeping potion and had the leader of the Merfolk, A'hd, steal their wings while they slept. Although they could not break their pact with Zeus, The Three sworn by a blood-oath that no merpeople would ever leave the fifth quadrant upon penalty of instant death…

He stops reading and closes the journal; on his face is a strange expression.

"Do you remember what the Mermaids said?" I say, turning to my brother.

"About us stealing something from them?" he recalls with a scrunched-up forehead.

"Yeah," I sigh, wondering what it could be. "And what is the fifth quadrant?"

Ando shrugs.

"I don't know," he huffs, returning to the worn pages.

"Does it say anything else about the fifth quadrant or what was stolen?" I question, wishing I could pace.

Ando continues to scan the book but finds no mention of either of these things. *Huh!* Maybe whatever it is, is so horrible that Parthenope could not reveal it to anyone, even her own offspring. Maybe Grandpa Theo was not privacy of it because he was a lowly human being.

"Your ankle looks worse." Ando grimaces as he looks at the disturbing shade of purple that my ankle is turning. "Are you going to see the doctor?"

"Yes," I lament. "Mom made an appointment with Dr. Pak tomorrow morning at ten."

Ando smiles.

"I like Dr. Pak," he admits freely. "She has a treasure box."

"I know," I roll my eyes. "The last time I went to see her, I got a ring pop as my prize. It was red."

"I got an eyepatch," he grins. "You wanna see it?"

"Maybe later," I grin too.

He stops for a minute, and I recognize the look. He and Mom are talking to each other telepathically. I really am starting to miss doing that.

"What did Mom say?" I watch him longingly, wanting to hear Mom's voice in my head too.

"She says we are all going to sleep in your room tonight," he frowns. "I've gotta shower. Here, Lena."

Gingerly, he hands me the journal.

"Please put this back for me."

"No worries," I smile. "See you in a few minutes."

"See ya!"

Carefully, I place the book back inside of the cedar box that it was housed in. Then it goes back into the closet under the same stack of magazines. I debate for a brief moment on changing its hiding place, but that would not be fair to Ando. Mom is right. The journal belongs to both of us.

Before I can close the closet door, Mom enters my room. She smiles as she sets the *Scrabble* box on the end of the bed. Her mannerisms are light, but her eyes are dark with anxiety.

"Are you worried that the Mermaids would break into the house and kill us in our sleep?" I probe in a ramble.

"No," she grins. "The aunts told me a few helpful facts."

"What kind of facts?" Ando asks as he runs into the room wearing his *Superman* pajamas and jumps onto my mattress. His body is still slightly damp from his shower. My brother is notorious for not completely drying off.

Mom settles on my bed too. She, on the other hand, smells of soap and jasmine-scented lotion along with her own unique Sireny scent. I never realized how intoxicating she smells. No wonder humans flock to her like hungry birds to a worm.

"Some really interesting tidbits," Mom giggles like me.

"Tell us, Mommy!" Ando begs.

"Well, did you know that Mermaids can only come out at night?"

Ando and I both shake our heads.

"Why can't they come out during the day?" I grill, leaning back on a pillow to get more comfortable.

"Tia Leukosia said it is because sunlight burns their skin," Mom lowers her voice as if it is a secret.

"That's weird." Ando makes a face.

"Supposedly, they were banished to the fifth quadrant which is in the deepest darkest part of the ocean," she continues, adjusting her position so her back is leaning against the headboard. "There is no light at all there, so they have become very sensitive to sunlight… to the point that it physically burns them."

"Oh, wow!" Ando whistles. "Like vampires."

Mom nods.

"Is that why their skin looks like moon jellyfish?" I add, remembering the moon jellyfish off the coast of Capri.

"Apparently," Mom acknowledges. "Do you want to know another fact about them?"

Ando and I both nod again, riveted by our mother's recon work.

I have to admit that I am impressed.

"According to Tia Ligeia," she continues. "They can only stay on land for short periods of time."

"That's great!" I proclaim. "But how long is that exactly?"

Mom does not know.

"Anything else?" Ando presses for information too.

"Well… I think I can explain Nicole's strange behavior," Mom informs.

"Tell me," I plead, starting to feel nauseous.

"Mermaids can control their human victims while they sleep," she frowns.

"What do you mean?" I respond, more than a little confused.

"Tia Ligeia said that Mermaids are telepathic just like Sirens," Mom explains. "But unlike us they use their enhanced mental powers to make humans do their bidding."

"How do they do that?" Ando's mood darkens.

"They creep into their minds and plant their essence," Mom continues with a frown. "The person doesn't even realize it. They just continue losing periods of time until—"

Our mother suddenly stops her explanation.

"Until what?" Ando and I both ask at once, reminding me of the good old days.

"If the person isn't released before the end of one lunar cycle, they will… " her voice trails off.

"What?" I whisper, already figuring out her next words.

"Nicole's gonna die?" Ando blurts with tears in his eyes.

"I didn't say that!" Mom shouts, trying to avoid eye contact.

"You thought it!" Ando shouts back as tears begin streaming down his face. "We can't let them hurt Nicole! We can't! I'll kill every last Mermaid myself!"

"Don't say that!" Mom's tone is sharp even though she loves Nicole like a daughter. "I won't let them hurt her!"

"I'll stop them!" he sniffles and all I want to do is hug him.

He has been through so much. We all have. I am certain my heart cannot take much more of this, and neither can his.

"Calm down!" Mom yells, trying to finish her comment.

"I won't let them hurt her!" he yells, still freaking out.

"Ando stop!" I snap, feeling his rage.

Unsure of what else to do, Mom grabs him by the shoulders and stops him from flailing.

"She can't die, Mommy," my hysterical brother sobs until I am sobbing too. "Not like Daddy. Not like Daddy. We can't let her die like Daddy did."

"We won't baby," Mom soothes as she holds him close. "We won't."

After a few minutes of Mom rocking him back and forth like when he was little and had colic, Ando calms down. Sometimes it would be so bad that our parents would be up for hours trying to comfort him. Occasionally, when they were exhausted, they would let me help. I would do the *'mom-bounce-rock-shuffle'*; like a mother would do soothing her colicky infant.

"Can we help her?" he mumbles at last.

Mom nods as she smooths his hair away from his sweaty face.

"Tia Ligeia gave me detailed instructions on how to *'dispossess'* her," Mom smiles warmly.

"What do we have to do?" I ask, wiping my face with the back of my hands like my brother does.

Ando sits up ready to listen as our mother begins her explanation.

"Here's what we have to do… "

CHAPTER EIGHT

The next morning is fast paced. By nine-fifty we arrive at Dr. Pak's pediatric office downtown. After x-rays and a thorough examination, it is determined that my ankle is only sprained and not broken.

Great! At last, some good news.

"Selena," Dr. Linda Pak says with great intensity. "You must stay off of your ankle and put an ice pack on it for the next few days, twenty minutes on, twenty minutes off or it will never heal."

Hmm…

Should I tell her that I used to be a powerful Siren, a protector of the seas, a caller of storms, but now I am a vulnerable human, and a group of blood-thirsty Mermaids are after me? Not only that, should I mention that one of my best friends is being controlled by these malicious creatures, and if I do not save her before the next full moon, she will either go crazy or outright die?

I think not.

"I'll make sure she follows your instructions," my mom states with a no-nonsense tone as she glares at me sternly.

"I'll make sure she does too," Ando emphasizes with a determined smirk.

Dr. Pak laughs and pats his head.

"I know you will, Ando," the doctor replies with a grin.

"I promise," I add, raising my right hand as if under oath. "No weight on my foot."

"Come back in a week for me to reevaluate her ankle," the soft-spoken woman says, shaking Mom's hand then mine and, finally Ando's. "If there are any problems before then, please don't hesitate to bring her back."

"I will." Mom beams at the professional, yet genuinely caring physician.

"See you in a week young lady." She winks at me. "Keep out of trouble, young man."

Ando nods.

"Bye!" He waves and smiles at the same time. "See you next week!"

Mom pays our deductible and we head straight to the car. Usually after doctor visits, Mom takes us out for ice cream. It is a ritual that we have always done. I think it makes her feel better, especially if we had to get shots. However, today there is no time to waste on sweets.

As we pile into Mom's Rav4, Ando turns to stare at me. Granted I just threw-on a pair of jeans and t-shirt, but I am positive that Mom would not let me leave the house looking like I have 'no owner' as she likes to say.

Tired of being stared at, I glare back.

"Why are you looking at me?" I snap with annoyance.

"You look terrible," my brother brutally informs on our way to David's workplace.

Tired and irritated, I stick my tongue out at him making him giggle uncontrollably.

The boy is such a goofball!

"So, what do we need from Dad's office?" I ask no one in particular as Mom pulls out of the parking lot, and onto the main street that leads to the far side of the island where we live.

"The aunts said we need to create a tonic for Nicole," Mom states as she merges into the outer lane. "Apparently, it has several unusual ingredients that your dad had access to at Ocean World."

I pause briefly, pondering what my mother is suggesting.

"Are we going to steal stuff from Dad's office?" I question as my temples begin to throb. I am definitely not cut-out for espionage. I would make a terrible Jane Bond.

Then, as luck would have it, an unexpected piercing pain shoots up my leg from the direction of my ankle. Every muscle in my body tenses and locks as I clutch helplessly at the injured area. Maybe being human is not all it is cracked up to be.

"Oww! Oww! Oww! Son of a B—*biscuit!*" I howl emphasizing 'biscuit' which is not the right word to say. Correction, it is not the word I *want* to say, but instead chose the more acceptable term, the one that will not get me grounded.

"What's the matter?" Mom gasps, glancing toward me which makes the vehicle swerve into the other lane and then back. Thank goodness there is no one beside us or we would have caused an accident. "Are you alright?"

Waiting for the pain to subside, I finally speak.

"I'm good," I lie through gritted teeth.

"Lena, you're pale!" my brother informs, his skinny finger pointing directly at my face.

"What do we do with the tonic?" I change the topic while adjusting myself on the backseat to place a cold compress on the puffy spot.

Immediately, Mom's posture straightens like she is contemplating whether or not to tell us the bad news. I know the motion well. She does it when she is biding time.

"We have to get her to drink it," she blurts, looking straight ahead, her hands now gripping the steering wheel even tighter.

"How are we supposed to get her to do that?" I respond meekly. "Isn't she being controlled by the Mermaids?"

Ando looks over his shoulder again in order to talk to me face to face.

"I don't care what we have to do to get Nicole back to normal." Ando's expression is stern and uncompromising. "If she needs to drink, whatever, she'll drink it."

Determination creeps over my features as I nod in agreement.

"Exactly!" I agree with a wink. "Whatever it takes."

Mom looks at us both but remains silent.

"Mom?" I ask, needing her to say the words. "Please repeat."

"Whatever it takes." The centuries-old Siren grins, her eyes twinkling with resolve.

That declaration seems to pacify my brother and his smile reappears.

"Let's put these ugly witches in the ground," Ando states firmly.

The nervous knots in my stomach have transformed into heavy cannonballs.

"Who's getting us through security?" I wonder out loud, staring at the back of my mother's head, her bouncy, shiny onyx curls perfectly in place. No styling products are needed. I, on the other hand, am sporting a frizzy bird's nest quaff that is going in several directions at once.

I did not miss bad-hair days when I was a Siren. Not at all.

Mom points toward the security gate as we pull into the employee parking lot.

"A friend." She smiles.

Just as she speaks, I notice Dr. Dorinda Khan waiting for us at the Ocean World security gate. Mom efficiently parks the SUV, and we all exit; anxious to get the ingredients we need to make Nicole's tonic. Ando being Ando, runs towards Dr. Khan who scoops his small body into her arms.

"I didn't know you were gonna be here," Ando beams, his eyes sparkling.

"I couldn't pass-up the chance to see my favorite family," Dorinda answers proudly. "Hello ladies."

Mom and I quickly give her individual hugs and kisses on her left and right cheek as is her custom.

"You always wear the scent of bread," Mom praises, inhaling deeply. "It's so comforting."

"Yeah," Ando and I sniff the scientist too.

"I do not know if I should take that as a compliment or a slight," Dorinda responds with a chuckle and an amused wink.

"It's a compliment!" Mom, Ando, and I exclaim at once causing that sense of déjà vu that was once extremely commonplace but has now become rarer than a Myanmar ruby.

"Come with me, I will get you in and out in a jiffy!" Dorinda lowers her voice, so the guard does not overhear, as she hurries us past. "I am so sorry that David is not well."

Huh? Not well? That's an understatement.

Mom's face turns pale, and I can tell that her stomach is flip-flopping since she is covering it with her hand.

Why doesn't she just tell everyone the lost at sea story? Now he's sick? The flu doesn't last forever, but death certainly does.

"He came down with the flu," Mom fibs without missing a beat. "He told me to say 'hi' for him.

"Tell him I hope he feels better soon," Dr. Khan requests sympathetically. "Everyone in the department misses him like crazy."

Mom clears her throat nervously as she continues the charade.

"I'll relay the message," the mournful half-Siren replies weakly. "We really need to find his… umm… medical card."

Nice save!

"He thinks it's in his office," Mom continues the subterfuge.

"No worries, Marina," Dorinda smiles warmly. "Make sure he goes to the doctor. You know how men are."

Mom laughs and nods.

Quickening our pace, we all keep up with Dr. Khan's long strides. For a short woman, she moves speedily, her feet barely touching the pavement. *Weird.* She is also one of the rare people that cannot be seduced by a Siren's Song. I am not sure why, but she and her daughter have never mentioned the riot during last year's Winter Concert. Which is surprising since the love-struck mob of human males is hard to forget. Maybe they blocked it all out. It is possible, I suppose. I, however, will never forget it.

As we continue our short journey, a painful stomach cramp hits me, so I lag behind unexpectedly feeling queasy. I am not sure what is causing it. It might be the pungent scent of marine life combined with the buckets of fermenting bait fish used for feeding, are overloading my sense of smell. Taking a piece of hard candy out of my pocket, I pop it into my mouth hoping the sweetness will mask the foul smells around me.

Suddenly, that strange frigidness slams into me again, but this time I cannot tell if it is something supernatural or just the industrial-strength, state-of-the-art air conditioning system. Either way, my body feels like it has been dunked in a bathtub filled with ice cubes.

"Are you still not feeling well?" Mom probes as she feels my forehead.

"I wasn't until a few seconds ago," I answer honestly. "Do you feel cold?"

My mother shakes her head.

"No sick talk," Ando states blankly. "We gotta do this."

Mom and I concede with a nod of agreement.

"Hi Bobby," Dr. Khan greets the first security officer, taking her badge out of her lab coat pocket. "How are you?"

The man grins and blushes.

"It's going well, Dr. Khan," Bobby replies pleasantly.

Similar to celebrities, we enter the private grounds through an unmarked gate. With a huge smile, Bobby the security guard checks Dorinda's identification then has her sign several pieces of paper. When everything is in order, he allows us inside.

"Nice to see you again, Mrs. Marquez, Selena, Ando!" The tall dark-skinned gentleman welcomes kindly.

"You remembered us!" Ando exclaims, giving him a bright smile.

The security officer winks at him then returns to his original 'Don't-mess with-me' attitude.

"Thanks a lot, Bobby!" Dorinda adds. "See you later."

Chatting away, Dr. Khan leads the way down a ramp to a long concrete pathway that circles the administration building. Just as before, we arrive at another entrance where she flashes her ID, and we are waved through by another guard.

"It always amazes me that there is so much security," Mom admits below her breath. "It's like visiting the FBI building at Langley."

"It is a cutthroat business we work in," Dr. Khan explains with animated arm and hand motions. "It does not help that we are also a research facility that specializes in top-of-the-line marine equipment. Believe it or not, we have a great deal of competitors who would give their right arms to take a look at our prototypes."

Her zeal for what she does makes us all smile.

As we continue walking, we arrive at another station where a female guard sits behind a small desk. A few feet away from the officer's desk is a thick steel door with an ID reader. It is the same door we entered with David when we first visited almost a year ago.

"Welcome back, Mrs. Marquez… little Marquezes," the friendly guard says with a welcoming smile.

Dorinda chuckles as she swipes her badge then places her thumb into the scanner and waits.

"Having a good day so far, Margie?" Dorinda grins from ear to ear. "How is the new grandson?"

"He's so adorable." Margie giggles, pulling out her wallet and turning to the picture of a newborn. "This is Steven… Stevie for short."

Ando grins at the photograph of the round-faced baby boy with the ruddy cheeks and the tuft of blonde hair at the top of his head.

Mom's face lights up.

"Oh, my gracious!" she coos, admiring the sleeping infant. "He's precious."

My brother chuckles at our mother's reaction, which causes the new grandmother to turn towards him.

"What's your name, Marquez Junior?" Margie addresses my brother.

"My name is Fernando." He smiles sweetly. "But everyone calls me Ando."

"Aww!" Mom gushes, still enthralled with the photo. "His cheeks are so pinchable!"

Uh oh! No baby-fever please!

"He truly is adorable," Dorinda grins widely. "Bring him in for a visit. I would love to see him in person."

"I have next Wednesday off, I'll bring him in then," the proud grandmother beams. "I'm sure his mother will appreciate some time to herself."

Patiently, Margie waits for Dr. Khan's credentials to be verified by the computer system. After a few seconds, we hear the salutation of a pleasant artificial male voice.

'Clearance verified… Hello, Dr. Khan… Have a great day.'

"I can't wait," Dr. Khan says as she waves goodbye, moving us along once more.

Inside, there is one last card reader.

"Good morning, Dr. Khan… Verification complete… Please enter."

Automatically, the light on the door turns from red to green and Dorinda pushes it open for us. The room is dimly lit, and the air is comfortably conditioned. Around the room's perimeter are transparent tanks with a wide variety of sea life including moray eels, fierce-looking barracudas, bumpy starfish, wiggly sea anemones, graceful stingrays and several baby nurse sharks. There is even an area specifically for moon jellyfish. Several technicians that know us well are observing the marine creatures and logging data into handheld tablets.

Cindy, a college intern who David recruited at the beginning of the summer who we have had over for dinner several times, looks up and smiles when she sees us. Speedily, the college senior walks over. Excitedly, she hugs Mom who smiles at the friendly gesture.

"Hey, Cindy!" Ando greets giving her a high-five. "How's Howard?"

Howard is a sixty-year-old male loggerhead sea turtle that got caught in a fisherman's net and had to have one of his front flippers amputated. The sassy marine reptile has lived at Ocean World for as long as David had worked here. My stepfather was actually the one who saved the turtle's life; caring for Howard twenty-four hours a day for almost a week until the turtle was out of harm's way. He was also the one who figured out that Howard loves head and neck rubs and also has an affinity for peeled red delicious apples.

"How's Dr. Marquez?" the twenty-something-ish woman questions. "Please let him know that Howard is doing much better using his prosthetic front flipper."

Mom looks like she is about to start crying.

"I'm sorry, did I say something wrong?" the young biologist blushes. "I talk way too much or at least that's what people tell me."

Mom shakes her head.

"No, Cindy," Mom reassures, giving her a smile. "I'm just having problems with my allergies. I'll let my husband know about Howard."

Cindy releases a held breath.

"I've got to get my foot under control," Cindy pretends to put her foot in her mouth for real, making us all snicker, especially my brother. "Oh! How's Miss Khan?"

"My daughter is doing well," Dr. Khan smiles. "She went to India this summer to visit a family friend. She loves all of the attention she gets there."

"Will Indra be teaching Chorus this year too?" Mom asks with great interest. "She's a terrific music teacher. Her students love her."

"I know I do," I smile. "High school would be boring without her."

"Don't tell her that," Dr. Khan chuckles. "I don't want her getting a bigger head."

"I won't," I reply humoring her. "Next time you talk to her, could you please tell her that I miss her."

"I will." Dorinda winks, playfully.

Ando suddenly clears his throat.

"Dr. Khan, my dad needs his medical card," he reminds. "Can we get it?"

"Of course!" Dorinda blushes, forgetting why we are here, and turns to Mom. "I am so sorry, Marina. Let's get what you need."

Then the strangest thing happens.

Dr. Khan gently rests her hand on my mother's shoulder and whispers a phrase. What the phrase means? I have no idea. It does not sound like English or Hindi, which is her native language, I believe. During my brief time as a Siren, I could translate many different languages, from Swahili to sea cucumber, but the doctor's words, although rapidly muttered, reminds me of the ancient language of the Greek gods which Melody and the aunts often revert to when being covert.

Mom's body instantly relaxes and her tension fades just a tad, just enough for her lovely eyes to sparkle and her heavenly beauty to return to full strength. Her skin emanates a soft glow as if she has gotten a slight tan to her already naturally olive complexion. Even her hair darkens and appears fluffier than usual. Mom, Ando, and Cindy do not seem to notice, but I definitely do.

After a few seconds, my mother grins and gives her a tight hug which is now habitual for her. For some reason, Mom immediately felt comfortable with Dr. Khan. We used to tease her all the time about her being a social hermit, but now she is like a different person, chatty and personable.

Well, I'll be…

"Follow me," Dorinda instructs, leading the way out of the main area toward the back hallway as Cindy waves goodbye to us and we do the same to her. Once we are out of earshot, Dorinda speaks again.

"I don't know how I would have made it without her this past week," the scientist confesses with a large grin. "It has been a blessing that she applied to do her internship here instead of at our sister park in India."

We nod in agreement. Cindy is a great person, so it seems, and is extremely intelligent. She knows as much as Dad does when it comes to sea animals. I think her mom, who is somehow related to Jacobs, is a marine scientist as well. It is hard to believe that she is even remotely related to Amy and her father, Stuart Jacobs.

"I like having someone to boss around," Dorinda jokes.

Again, we start to chuckle. David's friend and colleague is always kidding and playing practical jokes. She and my stepfather are constantly trying to outdo each other with innocent pranks.

"Thanks again for doing this, Dorinda," Mom smiles. "You don't know how much this means to us."

"Do not thank me anymore, Marina." Dr. Khan blushes and smiles at once, her Indian accent sounding stronger. "You are making me all blushy."

Wasting no more time, our friend escorts us to a spiral staircase leading into the main observatories, but instead of going up the stairs to the common area, we go down the stairs to the offices and conference room. Staying together, we make our way through the corridor between the glass encased rooms. The outer walls are shatterproof plexiglass that look out into the vastness of the Caribbean Sea. As a pessimist, I have often imagined the sea will push against the glass panes, hoping that one day it will find a weak spot to crack, and kill us all. Well, not Mom or Ando, that is.

Dr. Khan clears her throat to get our attention.

"Mr. Jacobs wants to expand this facility next year," Dorinda informs, proudly. "This particular underwater observatory tower is approximately two-hundred feet offshore and descends almost forty feet beneath the water's surface. He wants to double that."

"Is that safe?" Mom immediately chimes.

"If done correctly… absolutely," she educates with all honesty, and I believe her.

"Will the fish still be able to come and go as they please?" Ando questions as he runs his fingertips across the glass, his expression seemingly deep in thought.

"Definitely," Dorinda smiles. "That is something we would never change. Your father and I would never allow them to be trapped here."

Almost at a whisper, Ando click-clack-whistles to a passing stingray. The male… *Wait!*...female, stops long enough to answer his question and then quickly disappears around the corner of the observatory.

"They are happy that there are no barriers keeping them here," my brother continues emphatically. "They come and go freely, which is what they want. To be free."

"I've always loved that about Ocean World," our mother beams. "I have to give props to Mr. Jacobs for that."

"We have a pod of dolphins that regularly visits," Dr. Khan informs with exuberance. "There are at least a dozen of them."

"That's Whistler's pod," Ando blurts and then pretends that he did not say anything even though we all heard him.

Dorinda only studies him with a confused expression before she speaks again.

"Early yesterday morning, I saw a couple of white-tipped sharks and today an enormous hammerhead shark came looking for food." The Indian scientist pauses to gather her thoughts. "It ate a few bait fish that the divers were handing out then left."

"Did he have a propeller scar over his left eye and a wildlife tag in its dorsal fin?" Mom exclaims.

Dorinda nods in surprise.

"That's JJ. He'll be back," my mother mumbles so only we can hear. "He's always hungry."

"We keep getting sidetracked." Our friend laughs. "Let us continue."

"Yes, lets," Mom agrees, and begins to quicken her pace.

"I am sure that you remember that David's office is at the end of this corridor," Dr. Khan reminds. "I do not know if he has mentioned it, but his office was redecorated at the beginning of the summer."

"No, he didn't mention that." Mom frowns slightly.

"It is quite lovely," the kind-hearted female praises with enthusiasm.

"I'm sure it is," Mom replies, but her tone is anxious.

"David's office has been locked all summer, but he gave me a spare key because he kept losing his," Dr. Khan continues with a smile as she reaches into her lab coat pocket and comes up empty. "What the—"

"What's wrong?" I ask, wondering why she suddenly looks so flustered.

"I cannot find the key." Dorinda stares blankly as she starts to rummage through her trouser pockets.

"When was the last time you saw it?" Mom questions without heat.

"I had it this morning," she informs with a scowl.

"Could you have left it in your office?" I add, feeling sorry for her.

"It is a possibility," she sighs.

"We'll wait right here until you get back." Mom smiles.

"I will be back shortly," Dorinda mumbles as she goes to the adjacent door which leads to her office. When she returns, she is even more frazzled. "I might have left it in the cafeteria. I stopped this morning to get a coffee. Be back soon."

"Take your time." Mom grins again.

As soon as the other woman turns the corner, Mom gives me my mission orders.

"Selena," she starts. "Go to Dad's office and get these ingredients from his laboratory fridge. Everything we need is written on the list. Hurry!"

"What about the key?" I grill.

Mom opens her hand and places the missing key in my palm. *Wow!*

Not only is she a skilled Siren, an amazing photographer, and a dedicated parent, but apparently, she is also a talented pick-pocketer.

"Mom!" I gasp. "You stole the key from Dr. Khan?"

Mom sighs and turns me toward Dad's office door.

"Hurry up before she comes back!" Mom adds, not making me nervous at all.

Before I can say anything else, she disappears into Dr. Khan's office. How she managed to open it is a mystery to me. I guess we will leave it as magic. It is better than the alternative idea that my mother used to be a thief. Well, she did steal back her portrait from the Vatican vault.

"Ando, you're the lookout," Mom designates as she pokes her head through the doorway. "Use your enhanced hearing to let me know when she's on her way back."

"Okay, Mommy," Ando acknowledges, giving her a salute.

Inside David's office is freezing and his refrigerated walk-in cooler is even more so. Quickly, I enter the four-digit code that my stepfather had me memorize that opens the secondary door. Glancing at the list, I peruse the bottles of items for a few specific ingredients: billings root, coral snake venom, seaweed extract, distilled water, and moon jellyfish flesh.

Jellyfish flesh! Disgusting! What are we? The freaking Witches of Eastwick?

With shaking hands, I wrap the small containers in a hand towel and shove them in my large purse. I usually never carry a purse, but today Mom insisted. Now, I know why. Little did I know, we were going to reenact *Ocean's Eleven* or *The Italian Job*!

"Lena!" Ando pokes his head inside. "She's coming back! Get out! *Right now!*"

Immediately, my hands begin to shake even more, but I still manage to zip up my purse completely. Dad's saltwater tank filter bubbles catch my attention along with a curious blue, yellow, and black angelfish that swims up to the glass. Missing my ability to communicate with sea animals, I try to mimic my family's unique Siren-language and to my amusement the fish turns toward me and blows a tiny stream of bubbles.

What the heck? Maybe my powers are coming back!

Ando's squeal brings me back to the moment. Bored with my weird noises, the fish swims away. At least I know my powers are still absent.

"Dr. Khan is at the front entrance!" he whisper-shouts from the doorway.

My brother is now jumping in place and waving his hands reminding me of one of those toy monkeys that play the cymbals.

"We're gonna get caught!" he proclaims as he paces. "We're gonna go to jail! Do they have prisons for six-year-olds?"

"Stop saying that!" I snap, locking Dad's office door behind me. "Where's Mom?"

"Right here." Mom startles us. "Got the stuff?"

"Yes!" I reply, patting my purse. "I got everything on the list you gave me."

"Great!" Mom winks then locks back Dorinda's door and throws David's key up the hallway in Dorinda's potential path.

Waiting nervously for Dad's coworker to return, Ando begins clicking and clacking his tongue and before we realize it, there are several types of fish gathered near the glass where we are standing. They all seem to be excitedly chatting with Mom and my brother. Sadly, they just ignore me.

"I cannot find that key," Dorinda huffs as she rounds the corner, her expression bleak as she looks down at her feet. "Wait a second! Here it is!"

Guilt ridden, we all blush.

"I looked everywhere for this bloody thing!" she half-laughs, half-growls as she holds the shiny object above her head.

"You found it!" my brother shouts, keeping up the charade.

"I thought I was losing my mind." The woman laughs at herself. "Here you go."

Gently, she places it in our mother's hand.

"Thank you," Mom tells calmly. "I won't be long."

Then she quickly unlocks David's office and returns in less than a minute holding his insurance card.

"I got it!" She whistles. "It was on his desk like he said."

"I am glad I could help," Dr. Khan exhales loudly, wiping the sweat from her brow.

"How about we treat you to lunch, Dorinda?" Mom invites, wanting to make-up for our deception.

"I would love that." The elated lady beams. "Today is veggie-loaf day in the cafeteria. It is my favorite."

"Mom, we have that *thing* that needs taking care of," I remind anxiously, trying to get us away from the crime scene. "Don't you remember?"

"Yeah, Mommy." Ando joins the ruse. "That *thing* we need to do."

Mom grimaces and gives us both a pensive stare.

"It will be alright," she mumbles below her breath. "We can't do it during the day."

"Oh!" Ando and I both say at once.

Slowly, all four of us turn to leave when Dorinda stops.

"Hold on." She is staring under her office door.

"What's wrong?" I gulp.

We've been caught!

Speedily, Dr. Khan unlocks the door and reaches inside.

"I must have forgotten to turn off the light." She smiles as she switches it off. "I do not like to waste energy, even if I am not paying for it."

Out of my peripheral vision, I notice that Dr. Khan is staring at the three of us with a puzzled countenance. Filled with nervous knots, I hold my breath. If I do not breathe soon, I will probably pass out, but that might be a good thing. Me fainting would definitely be a distraction.

"Are you ready to have some lunch, Dorinda?" My mother distracts, temporarily forgetting the heist we just pulled off.

"Yes, of course." Dr. Khan glances at her watch. "The cafeteria should still be empty."

"That way we won't have to deal with long lines," Mom continues making small talk.

Our friend gives us a huge smile, completely unaware of our ruse.

"Can we please go to the deep reef tank before we get lunch?" my brother suggests, returning Dr. Khan's smile.

Mom nods.

"I don't see why not," our parent replies, using her fingers to push his hair away from his eyes.

"Yay!" Ando cheers. "Let's go!"

He then begins to pull me along and I temporarily refocus on our awaiting lunches. The last time I was here, Dad treated me to fish tacos and fries. This time I think I will substitute the fish for a double bacon cheeseburger. The cafeteria has surprisingly delicious food. It is like eating in a fancy restaurant instead of at a place of business.

As we pass the deep-water shark tanks, a sense of déjà vu comes over me. After the accident with the young girl, David made much needed improvements with the barriers as well as security—both hidden and overt—so that both the sharks and humans could enjoy each other without fear of another catastrophe happening.

In the mood to shop, Mom convinces us to stop at the gift store and pick out a few souvenirs. However, after a couple minutes of browsing, Dorinda and I decide to go without. So instead, we wait outside on a bench under the shade of a gigantic flamboyant tree.

"How are you, Selena?" The curious scientist investigates as she fills her lungs with the salt-perfumed air.

"Great!" I lie, trying desperately not to think about David, Nicole, or The Mermaids, instead closing my eyes to enjoy the warmth of the sun against my cold face. "Fantastic, as a matter of fact!"

As if already knowing my pain, Dorinda studies me then glances upward at the scarlet blossoms of the massive flamboyant tree towering above us. As I watch, she mutters the same mysterious language she spoke before. In that moment, a blossom falls from an overhead branch and lands in her open palm, but that is not what intrigues me. Immediately, another flower follows, then another, and so forth until at least a dozen are in her open hand.

It is then I realize that the delicate buds are not actually resting there but hovering an inch above!

"Are you sure?" she queries with a mischievous grin.

"Yup!" I respond with a huge lump in my throat, adding another false grin to sell it.

Holy crap! What is she?!

The intelligent *'woman'* merely smiles at me, and for whatever reason I am not afraid, I simply accept what is happening. My human heart and brain both agree that the wily scientist would never harm me or my family… *Ever.*

"You can tell me anything, you know that, right?" Dr. Khan adds sincerely, making me wish that I could tell her absolutely everything, but I do not.

Siren business is meant for only Sirens.

Suddenly, I feel the need to change the subject.

"How has it been since my stepfather has been away?" I question Dr. Khan as I glance at Mom and Ando at the cash register paying for their items.

Dorinda frowns before answering.

"Selena," she begins. "I can honestly say that this place is not the same without Dr. Marquez."

Then, as if the invisible strings holding the flowers above her palm are cut, they land rather haphazardly, some unable to fit are left to land on the concrete below our feet. Unable to remove my gaze from them, I continue staring, mouth slightly ajar, eyes wide with bewilderment.

Without warning, what she is saying about David truly sinks in. Like an anvil, I feel the first pang of guilt slam into my chest, accompanied by a rush of unwelcomed memories of the *'incident'*, and then the punch of loss, despair, and disbelief as all three jab my broken soul like the world's sharpest blade.

To my relief, only one tear escapes and I quickly brush it away before my companion notices.

"He is the heart of Ocean World," his associate continues as her kind eyes become misty. "Unlike Mr. Jacobs, the wellbeing of the animals is always his first priority."

Her heartfelt comment almost makes me start to bawl, almost.

"Your father does not care about the bottom-line or the end of the quarter projections," Dr. Khan informs with all seriousness, her dark eyes bright with admiration toward my stepfather. So much so that I feel even prouder to be his daughter. "I hope you and your family realize what a special person he is."

"We do," I reply, biting my nails which I never do. "David was… I mean, *is* an amazing man."

With that, the tears begin to fall, hard and fast as if the dam that has been holding them back has been broken and nothing can stop the flood that is released. To my surprise, Dorinda gently lays her hand on top of mine, whispers something unrecognizable and a slow-moving wave of serenity rolls over me.

This comforting feeling manifests itself as warmth, is the only way to describe it. The sensation spreads throughout my body into every part of my being and fuses to everything that weighs me down, both physically and spiritually, freeing me. This warmth was stolen from me when David died, but somehow it has been returned. If only for a brief moment by the enigmatic Dr. Dorinda Khan.

"What's happening to me?" I ask with a breathy exhale.

"Shh," she implores, placing a finger to her lips. "How do you feel?"

"Better," I acknowledge the gift she has bestowed onto me with a brilliant smile.

Instantly, she returns my lighthearted expression.

"I'm glad we talked," I gush, giving her hand a gentle squeeze. "Thank you!"

Then, returning to her true Dorinda style, she adds, "If I was younger, I would give Marina some competition for that man of hers."

The sassy minx winks and blushes at the same time which causes me to blush too. Unable to contain it, I laugh a little too loudly and an elderly couple passing by hand-in-hand turn to stare at me. I suppose they are of that mentality that children—and teens—should be seen, not heard. Not caring what they may think of my boisterous outburst, I continue chatting with Dr. Khan while we wait.

"Lena!" Ando beams as he comes running out of the store holding his newest Ocean World poster. "I got the last poster of Howard!"

Our mother chuckles.

"The poor salesclerk had to rummage through the stockroom to find it," Our mother answers quickly, and then takes a sip of the bottled water she also purchased.

"What did you get, Marina?" Dorinda grins at her friend's new and improved attitude.

"I got a refrigerator magnet in the shape of a conch shell." Mom chuckles.

As my mother, Dorinda, and Ando make small talk, I bask in my euphoric state, finally able to expel, at least for the time being, my guilt and self-hatred. It is the first time since being back on Isla Flora that the overwhelming fear that I will fall apart in front of the entire world vacates me.

"I'm starving, Mom," I relay, moving the conversation along, suddenly very hungry. "Shouldn't we be heading to the cafeteria before the lunch rush? We still have lots to do today."

"Yeah," Ando agrees, and his mind quickly switches to food. "Can I have sushi?"

Mom's brows arch.

"I don't think they have sushi, son," our mother smirks.

"They make a Ceviche that is amazing," Dorinda speaks up.

"What's that?" my brother asks, making a face.

"Ceviche is a seafood dish made from fresh raw fish cured in either lemon or lime juice, and spiced with ají, chili peppers along with other seasonings," Dr. Khan patiently explains. "It has some onions and cilantro too. Believe me, it's delicious!"

"I like those things." He grins and pats his belly.

Dr. Khan gives Mom a wink and leads the way.

"Next stop, the cafeteria," the intriguing lady announces as we walk to the building that houses the staff facilities along with the gym, indoor pool, and locker rooms.

"What are you hungry for, Marina?" Dorinda queries as we walk among the tourists. "They have grilled chicken and shrimp, all sorts of sandwiches, salads—"

"I think I might get the same as Ando," Mom replies.

"What are you getting, Dr. Khan?" I question, curious to know what she is in the mood for.

"I'm craving their eggplant parmesan," she grins.

"No meat?" Mom asks.

"I am a vegetarian," Dorinda tells proudly. "So is my daughter."

"That's good to know," Mom smiles back. "I'm planning to have the two of you over for a meal soon."

Just as we enter the building, a short man moving at the speed of light almost barrels into us. It is Stuart Jacobs, co-owner and general manager of Ocean World, not to mention Amy, my rival's, father.

"Pardon me," he begins then recognizes us. "I'm so sorry, Mrs. Marquez… children."

"That's quite alright," Mom counters, letting him off of the hook.

Flustered, Mr. Jacobs shakes Mom's hand, then Ando's and finally mine.

"It's been a crazy day. So much to do… I'm late for a conference call and wasn't paying attention," he rambles, obviously discombobulated and stressed. "Please accept my sincerest apologies."

Mr. Jacobs is a short man about 5'2", with large plump features, a noticeable bald-spot that he tries to hide with a comb-over, and small dark eyes that appear to have no distinguishable irises. The only thing that is pleasing about him is his extremely expensive dark pinstriped Armani suit and designer shades.

Why is he wearing sunglasses inside?

"No harm, no foul, Mr. Jacobs," Dorinda genuinely comforts.

"Nice to see you, Dr. Khan." The man frowns as he readjusts his black-framed Versace sunglasses. "By the way, I have the updated specs on the newest submersible in my office. I'll bring those over to you sometime before the end of the workday. You'll need to stay late tonight to review them."

Wow! Is he serious?! Way to give her notice.

His employee simply nods her understanding.

Next, he turns to my mother.

"Mrs. Marquez, when is that husband of yours coming back to work—" Mr. Jacobs begins.

"Umm… hopefully very soon," Mom quickly retorts, her cheeks turning red.

When is she going to tell them that Dad is never coming back?

"Please let him know that we've got a lot of balls up in the air and we need him back in the line of fire A-S-A-P."

As he says this, his sunglasses slip down again, just enough for me to notice the plum-sized purplish-blue bruise over his right eye.

How did that happen?!

Quickly, he pushes his eyewear back into place and begins to fidget nervously.

"This facility has financial obligations, Mrs. Marquez, and your husband's inventions bring in much needed revenue," Mr. Jacobs' voice lowers to a threatening tone. "It also means job security for him."

Didn't he say almost the same thing when our parents saved that little girl from the sharks?

As Amy's dad blathers on, Ando's hands clench into fists, alerting everyone in the room to take cover. He, like his father, is known for a lot of things, but holding his tongue is not one of them. Mom, noticing my brother's ire, quickly speaks up.

"I'd be happy to relay your message and stress how much he is needed at work." Mom presents her most mesmerizing smile. "Don't worry about a thing, Mr. Jacobs. I'm on it."

"Thank you," The man breathes a sigh of relief and gives a nod. "I appreciate it. He's a real asset to the company."

Then without any further niceties, we watch as Mr. Jacobs scurries away.

Rubbing her hands together, Dr. Khan breaks the silence.

"I can smell the eggplant from here." Dorinda sniffs the air. "Let us eat."

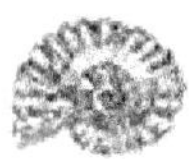

After lunch, we say goodbye to Dorinda and head home with our *'borrowed'* ingredients to make Nicole's tonic. During the short ride home, I continue scrutinizing the bottles, wondering how this is going to help my possessed friend. If it works, she will be extremely upset that Mermaids used her to get to me, but at least she will be alive, even though it might cost us our friendship. If it does not work, she will be dead.

There is not a clear win as far as I can see.

"When do we make the tonic?" I grill, putting the substances in the fridge to keep them cold.

"Tonight," Mom mumbles below her breath.

"Why not now?" I question, wanting to free my friend.

"We need moonlight," Mom educates without any further explanation.

"What are we going to do now?" I utter, losing patience.

"We're going to spend some quality time together," she informs with a wink. "Go change into your bathing suits. Meet me at the shoreline in fifteen minutes."

Not wanting her to get upset, I do as I am told.

These days, the only thing that keeps my mind off of David is reading, but Mom and Ando insist that I cannot stay home alone, even though it is daytime. They have both informed me that until the Mermaid threat is neutralized, I am always to be with one of them. That means, unfortunately, I have to accompany them on their swim. I still do not understand how I will be able to keep up with them.

"Here you go," Mom smiles.

I look at her like she has two heads.

"What's this?" I sneer, scrutinizing the seafaring object before me.

"It's a speedboat silly." She places her hands on her hips and gives a patented Marina Marquez *don't mock me* glare.

"Isn't it cool?" Ando grins as he sits inside of the sleek, almost-new vessel.

"What am I supposed to do with this?" I whine, climbing aboard with Ando's help.

He firmly holds my hand since the water beneath our house is so choppy. As a human who has experienced drowning once before, I do not want to try it again.

"I don't know how to drive one of these things," I remind, suddenly feeling worse than I did before.

"I know how to do it," Ando reassures. "Daddy and I rented one on our guy's day out."

Mom smirks.

"We've got everything covered, Selena," she reassures encouragingly, waiting for me to be seated.

"Where are we going?" I ask, putting on my life jacket, just in case.

"Your favorite place." Ando grins and starts the boat. "Where the sea meets the shore… where the creatures raise their young… where the—"

"Stop speaking in riddles," I warn, cutting him off in mid-rant.

"I'll meet you over there," Mom states with an amused chuckle, then dives into the water disappearing from view.

Twenty minutes later, we arrive at our destination. Ando turns off the engine and dives in, leaving me alone. When he reappears, Mom is in tow. She wears a large toothy smile.

"Come in," she urges with newfound exuberance. "The water is lovely."

"I'm not a Siren anymore, remember?" I pout, leaning over the side to splash them both with water.

"You don't have to be," my mother scoffs. "I won't let anything happen to you."

"I don't know," I whimper, contemplating my options. "Before I was a Siren, I wasn't a strong swimmer. Now, I'm like a rock."

"All you need to do is hold your breath, Lena," Ando encourages.

"Okay," I hesitantly agree as I remove my t-shirt and shorts to reveal the plain black one-piece swimsuit beneath, but before they can protest, I slip back into the life vest. "Don't let anything bad happen to me."

"I won't," he swears, and I believe him. "But you have to take that *thing* off."

Hesitantly, I take off my life vest and swing my legs over one side of the boat. To fortify my nerves, I take several soothing breaths. I have to do this otherwise I never will.

"Here I come," I announce as I enter the barely moving water. Immediately, Ando takes my hand as I hold my breath and dive under the brackish water.

Beneath the waves, my thoughts are erratic… my heart is pounding… I have no purpose, and in this moment; all that matters is getting back in the damn boat. Panic-filled, I wrench my hand away from my brother and make a beeline to the surface; gasping and sputtering as I exit my watery tormentor.

"What's wrong?" Ando questions, appearing beside me.

"I can't do this!" I spit and swipe the liquid from my eyes. "I can't!"

"Calm down," he speaks gently as he tries to pacify me.

"I'm going back in the boat," I gasp, doggy-paddling to the ladder, not stopping until I am back in the safety of the speedboat.

"At least we're all together," he sighs happily after pondering our strange situation of a former Siren afraid of being in the sea.

"When can we go home?" I beg, pulling a towel around my shivering shoulders.

"Soon," Mom answers, popping up beside my brother with three spiny lobsters still squirming in her hands. "But first we feast."

Unable to stop myself, I grimace.

"I can't eat it raw," I complain, hearing my stomach gurgle. "It'll make me sick."

"I'll cook yours," Mom reveals as she asks Ando to retrieve the stockpot with the steamer basket insert, and a plastic gallon Ziploc bag with smaller individual baggies of various seasonings she had stowed onboard earlier. I was wondering what those were for.

Obediently, my brother followers her orders, catapults out of the water and lands gracefully on his feet then disappears into the bowels of the ship. Several seconds later, we hear clanking and clinking before he returns carrying the items. Mom takes them and swims back to the small clearing among the mangrove trees. There, she builds a fire, and when the flames are vigorously crackling, she partially fills the stockpot with seawater, places it on the heat and allows it to boil. Next, she puts mine and Ando's lobsters in and covers it with the lid. In ten minutes, we have two perfectly steamed lobsters.

Happily, we devour the tender, succulent shellfish. It is fresh, sweet, and naturally salted. All that is needed is a ramekin of drawn butter. Other than that, it is perfect.

Not surprising, our mother eats hers raw. Unapologetically, she breaks open the shell with her talons and begins to nom; not stopping until the shells are picked clean. It is a sight to behold.

"I have to admit, that was incredible," I compliment, licking lobster juices off of my fingers.

"It was really tasty, Mommy," Ando agrees, rubbing his tummy and smacking his lips.

"Thank you!" Mom grins as she throws water onto the fire and listens to it hiss, making sure that every last ember has been extinguished. "I think we are ready to head home."

In a better mood, I stand to start the boat but stop when I hear the strange croaking sounds. Ando must hear it too because he stops as well, straining to decipher what is making the noise. Mom looks just as puzzled as we do.

"What's that sound?" Ando quizzes with a confused grimace.

"It sounds like… crocodiles," our mother professes with a blank expression.

"Crocodiles don't live in the Caribbean," I educate, recalling my *National Geographic* magazine reading.

"I'm aware of that," Mom says in a hushed tone.

Before I can make another comment, my mother motions for me to remain quiet. Speedily, she closes her eyes and then suddenly opens them. She looks terrified.

"Selena, start the boat… *now!*" she whispers. "Ando, no matter what happens, stay in the boat."

Ando nods his understanding.

Immediately, I start the boat without a problem, but just as I am about to pull out of the peaceful inlet, I feel something hit the underbelly of the craft, hard.

"Jeez!" I gasp. "What the hell was that?"

"Head home!" Mom shouts. *"Now!"*

Completely confused, I turn to answer, but instead of seeing just Mom, I see two pale-faced Mermaids clawing and pulling her under into the caliginous shadows that lurk beneath the undergrowth of the mangroves. It never occurred to any of us that Mermaids could be sneaky or smart enough to use the small patches of darkness to avoid detection. I guess they are not as stupid or inept as I pictured them to be.

"Momma!" I yell, wanting to jump in and help, but knowing that would be disastrous.

"Keep going!" Mom commands just as she gets pulled under.

"Go Lena!" Ando yells at me. "Step on it!"

"Okay!" I shout back, heart beating out of my chest; sweat beading on my forehead, wet palms gripping the steering wheel. "What about Mom?"

Ando shakes his head.

"She's fine!" he informs. "Just go!"

With those words, I throttle-up and race out of the inlet, but halfway out of the cove another hard crash hits the boat, this time sending Ando and me out of the vessel and somersaulting several times over the surface like a stone skipping across the surface until we get sucked into the water. Before I know what is happening, something grabs my legs and tugs me below.

Refusing to die this way, I grab the creature's platinum hair and pull with all of my might. I know that it is such a cliché chick-way to fight, but at the moment I do not care. The Mermaid lets out a high screech then temporarily releases me. Taking the opportunity, I rush to the surface and barely have enough time to take in a couple of full breaths before being yanked under again.

What the hell is up with these bit—

This time we are face to face… nose to nose… aquamarine eyes to onyx eyes.

"Lena!" I hear Ando's muffled voice above me, calling frantically. "Lena! Where are you?"

With burning eyes and barely any oxygen left in my lungs, I kick and flail enough to be freed. A few feet away, I see Ando fighting like a superhero, kicking butt and taking no prisoners. He may be small, but he packs quite a wallop.

A few more kicks and I breach the surface and quickly scan the area for the craft. Thankfully, I spot it about twenty feet away. Fueled by terror, I manage to freestyle swim to the vessel and pull myself halfway inside of the boat before I am pulled back. Everything is moving in slow motion. Suddenly, I feel something sharp rip open the flesh on my inner arm and then my outer thigh.

All around me is red. Then I feel the smooth skin of something rubbing against my legs.

About to lose my mind, I scream as I resurface once more. Beside me is the rounded dorsal fin of Whistler or one of his pod members. I grab his fin and hold on for dear life as he leads me out of the cove. He is flying through the water just like the speedboat would and surrounding us are his family, protecting me from those bloodthirsty merfolk.

Thankfully, they do not stop until we are at the rocky coastline below my house. Quickly, Whistler deposits me near the rocks and waits as I heave myself up onto dry land.

"Ando!" I scream at the top of my lungs. "Mom!"

Dear God! Please let them be alright!

"Anybody!" I wail out of control and desperate.

Ignoring my wild behavior, the pod remains guarding me, but I can tell they want to rejoin the fight. I cannot communicate with them anymore, but I am afraid of being alone. Suppose the Mermaids come after me.

What would I do then?

Thirty minutes pass before I see the speedboat in the distance. Squinting, I see Ando at the wheel and Mom sitting beside him. Even from this distance, I can tell that she is pretty badly beat-up.

To my surprise, Ando expertly parks the boat and carefully Mom climbs out. My brother throws me the rope, and I secure it to the hitching rod that Mom drilled into the rocks. Impatiently, we wait as Ando disembarks and helps me carry our mother up the steep steps.

"How many were there?" I pant under Mom's slumped weight.

"Three," Ando answers without any labored breathing. "I can carry her faster on my own."

Without argument, I stop and let him take her full weight.

"Go open the door, Lena," he commands and like a good soldier, I run ahead to unlock the front door and switch off the security system that Mom had installed.

"May I help?" I request watching as my younger brother helps our parent.

"No." he gives a small smile. "I've got it."

"Alright," I mumble, wishing I could be helpful.

"Lock the door, please," he reminds then takes Mom to her room.

I do as I am told like a good little human. Looking around at the empty room, all I can do is wish that I had not misused my powers. If I had listened to Gaia, I would never have lost my natural abilities, David would be alive, Mom would not be hurt, and I would be able to heal her right now.

Leaving the lights on, I leisurely climb the flight of stairs to my room. Despite how the day ended, I cannot help but reminisce that it was my first full day out of the house since spending the night at Nicole's. It was enjoyable visiting Ocean World and spending time with Dorinda. Even our premeditated 'heist' allowed me to shed the shroud of unhappiness that I had wrapped myself in for a brief time, and as always, the cove where the aunts trained me to be a Siren, still feels like a second home. I guess it always will be.

The secluded area in the dense mangrove forest located on the uninhabitable side of the island, affectionately nicknamed by David 'Siren-Central' used to be my home away from home. It was my sanctuary, like the Blue Grotto was for my mom. It was in the secluded cove where Leukosia, Ligeia, and Mom taught me everything they knew about being Sirens.

The mangrove cove was also where I was introduced to Shu'a-ma, one of the greatest wonders of our supernatural world. Who or better yet, *what* is Shu'a-ma? Simply translated; she is *The Mother Tree*. There, in that hidden alcove, deep inside the dense mangroves, guarded by heavy thickets of spiny thorn bushes lives the great Mother Tree. This ancient banyan, with a trunk the width of ten sumo wrestlers and branches as thick as several elephant legs put together, is the guardian of the enigmatic alcove. On its many limbs, hundreds of songbirds of every color and species, build nests and raise families. Sometimes, if you are lucky, they will grace you with angelic songs as their individual voices combine to create a magical choir.

However, birds are not the only inhabitants. In hidden nooks and crevices along the massive trunk live small mammals such as squirrels, chipmunks, and mice; along with reptiles like lizards, iguanas, and insects of all kinds... even snakes! Despite their species, they are all living harmoniously in one incredibly special tree.

Shu'a-ma provides for them all.

At her base and up her trunk grows the most impressive collection of mushrooms: morel, button, shitake, portabella, and enoki, to name a few. Growing beside them are patches of edible flowers with tender stalks and sweet grasses intermingling with generous amounts of mealworms, grubs, ants, and beetles for the carnivores of the bunch. For the herbivores, there is an endless supply of seeds, nuts, and berries that inexplicably replenish several times a day like clockwork.

Needless to say, the sheer sight of this magnificent tree both humbles and overwhelms the watcher; but unlike other trees that pull nourishment from the earth, this Mother Tree *feeds* the grove. Magically, it injects the land with mystical nutrients, released through roots as thick and impressive as its branches. In turn, the soil becomes a deep pitch which keeps the area lush and verdant.

How does it do this? Not even the aunts know.

Legend has it when the tree was just a struggling sapling. Gaia, determined to see it survive, touched the sickly sprout, blessing it with good health and long life, aiding it to become what it is today.

But I digress…

Sadly, that has all changed. The Mother Tree, grieving for the loss of The Sirens and saddened by the invasion of the Mermaids, has lost its potency and will to live. Shu'a-ma's leaves once bright and robust have lost their luster and hang limp, almost completely lifeless from her unused branches. The earth of the mangrove forest, no longer dark and fertile, is now dusty-gray and barren with only dead twigs and weeds as covering.

No longer do the birds call the banyan home. Fearful of the merfolk, they have abandoned the inlet and the branches of their mother. As for the reptiles and mammals, they have found new places to hide, knowing they are the prey. Now, instead of the lovely tune of songbirds, there is only the hollow echo of what resembles crocodile croaking, accompanied by the stifling scent of decay and hopelessness.

This does not surprise me.

The Mermaids have taken over our sanctuary and now it belongs to them.

CHAPTER NINE

The rest of the night, Ando stays with Mom in her room while I campout in the living room armed with my brother's water gun, a string of garlic and a bottle of holy water just in case Mermaids really are similar to vampires.

Hey! Do not judge me. I do not know anything about these freaks except sunlight hurts them. Just like vampires!

Near dawn, I hear Mom stirring and I peek in on her. Even in the dimly lit room, I notice the scratches and bruises on her limbs and face. She looks like she has gone twelve rounds with Muhammad Ali and Joe Frazier at the same time. Painfully, she stands and heads to her bathroom returning a few minutes later.

"I'm going to be okay," Mom whispers as she climbs back into bed. "Stop fretting."

"I wish I could give you a scale or two," I confess, feeling pathetic.

"Me too," she winces then stops herself.

"Can I get you anything?" I ask, stepping inside of the doorway.

"Just some water," she whimpers, pulling the covers under her chin.

"I'll be right back." I cringe, seeing her in this condition. "Don't go anywhere."

She attempts to laugh but grips her side instead.

"Stop making me laugh," she groans softly.

Playfully, I give her a thumbs up before going to the kitchen and fixing her a glass of ice water. When I return, she is already asleep, so I rest the tumbler on the bedside table and go back to the living room. Getting tired, I settle on the couch and close my eyes. Before I know it, I wake.

"Hello, Selena," Melody greets, staring lovingly down at me.

"Melody!" I exclaim, bolting to my feet and hugging her tightly around the waist. "I'm so glad that you're here!"

She laughs and the sound of Champagne bubbles dance around my ears. For some reason, the sound always comforts me, always makes me smile; even now when the world around me is brimming with murderous beings waiting to kill us.

"It has been a long time, my beautiful great-granddaughter," the ancient Muse compliments, hugging me back.

"Where have you been?" I question, pulling her down to sit on the couch beside me.

"I have been busy," she replies, but does not elaborate, which is completely like her.

"That sounds cryptic," I tease, hugging her again.

"I see things are not going well here on Isla Flora," she frowns, gently touching the swollen scrapes on my neck and arms.

"Ha! That's an understatement." I chuckle, suddenly feeling uplifted.

"How is Marina faring?" the original Muse questions, nodding toward Mom's bedroom.

"Not well," I confess with a sad expression. "Not well at all."

"Tomorrow when she wakes, have the bathtub filled with seawater and throw some seaweed into it," she instructs as I listen intently.

"Why?" I query, thinking it is a strange request.

"Trust me." She grins, and I do.

"I've missed you," I express filled with joy.

"I have missed you as well," Melody reveals with a brilliant smile.

"How long will you be here?"

"Not long," she says, touching the charm around my neck.

"I'm glad you're here regardless." I giggle, resting my head on her shoulder and closing my eyes. She smells intoxicating, fresh and woodsy like the dense cypress trees surrounding her cottage on Capri. The fragrance comforts me on so many different levels.

"Get some rest, my lovely," Melody suggests, stroking my curls away from my face. "There is a lot to do when you wake."

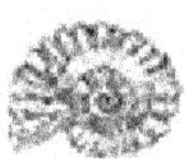

The house is quiet. Too quiet, but the rays of sunshine filtering through the sheer drapes inform us that it is morning and for now, the Mermaids are restricted to the dark places.

Sitting up, I stretch my arms above my head towards the ceiling and enjoy as my limbs unfold. I have not felt this invigorated in weeks. With renewed purpose, I tiptoe to Mom's doorway. Inside, fast asleep, are Mom and Ando, both lightly snoring.

On a mission, I go to the first-floor storage closet and get two plastic buckets. I disarm the alarm that secures the back entrance, completely forgetting to put on my sneakers and jog across the side yard and down the steps. Speedily, I fill the buckets with seawater and laboriously trek back to the house where I then climb the stairs and empty the buckets into the bathtub. Several times, I do this until the bathtub is three-quarters of the way full.

As I descend the staircase, Mom is already in the kitchen fixing herself a cup of tea. She is moving slowly and limping, favoring her left leg. That is not good.

"Morning, Mom," I whisper, hoping not to startle her.

She turns, giving a weak smile.

"Hey, baby!" she hails sweetly then returns to stirring a teaspoon of sugar into the hot caramel-colored liquid. "Have you been up long?"

"Not really," I smile. "But I have a surprise for you. You have to come upstairs though."

"Ugg!" Mom groans. "Then I'll have to *climb* the stairs."

"I'll help you," I volunteer, and she takes my hand.

It takes ten minutes for her to climb fifteen stairs. With every step, Mom whimpers and squeezes my arm. It takes all of my self-control not to take the speedboat, along with the crossbow and the quiver of arrows I brought back from Paradiso and kill every last Mermaid at the inlet.

At last, we enter the bathroom. Mom looks into the bathtub and smiles.

"What's all this?" She grins, slowly removing her clothes.

"Melody said that this would help." I grin back, helping her disrobe.

"Melody?" She repeats, observing me. "Your great-grandmother, Melody?"

"Uh huh." I beam. "The one and only."

Mom's features brighten as if a light is switched on beneath her bruised skin.

"She's here?" Mom halts her movement and turns to leave the bathroom.

"Uh huh." I chuckle, stepping in front of her so she does not attempt to go looking for our beloved visitor.

"Where is she?" Mom demands as she tries to get redressed.

"Umm," I pause. "I don't know. I woke to an empty house."

Mom rubs her temples.

"Now, I'm confused." The Siren chuckles as she leans against the nearest wall.

"Me too." I laugh and slowly scratch my head. "At least I thought she was here."

Huh!

"I guess it could have been just a wonderful dream."

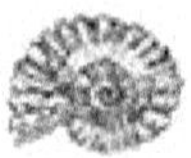

Mom soaks in the seawater-filled tub using the clump of seaweed as a makeshift pillow while I prepare breakfast. I do not understand the affect Melody has on me, but I am thankful for whatever it is. I even find myself humming as I prep the ingredients for the omelet and count out eight pieces of bread to toast—

"Shucks!" I correct myself, putting two slices back into the plastic bag.

"Need some help?" I hear my mother's voice behind me.

I smile, but do not turn around.

"How are you feeling?" I inquire, crossing my fingers.

"I feel incredible!" she confirms as she does an arabesque and a spin. "Dream-Melody was right on the mark. I wonder how she knew what to do."

I chuckle.

"She is the original Siren-Momma," I remind with a smirk.

Mom thinks about it.

"She certainly is." My mother snorts which she has not done in forever.

"What's going on?" Ando yawns as he enters the kitchen, his hair all askew.

"Mom and I were talking about Melody," I tell, cracking the first of six eggs.

Instantly, my brother perks up.

"Did she contact us?" he interrogates with wide wild eyes.

"Sort of," Mom speaks up, coming around the counter to help pour three glasses of pink grapefruit juice.

"Huh?" he hums glaring at us.

"She came to me in a dream." I giggle. "Can you believe it?"

Ando thinks for a moment.

"Lena?"

"Yeah?"

"Have you had any other dreams?" he questions. "Ones that come true?"

"Nope," I answer without hesitation.

"Oh," he replies and sits on his favorite dining chair, waiting for breakfast to be finished.

"Why do you ask?" I wonder out loud, adding some milk to my egg mixture along with a sprinkling of salt and pepper. Knowing that Mom loves cheese, I sprinkle some cheddar into it as well.

Ando pauses before explaining.

"That's how Melody talks to me," he confesses with an adorable smirk. "She visits me in dreams."

"Really?" Mom and I state together.

"I think she can sense when I need inspiration or comfort and then when I fall asleep—"

"She appears," I finish his sentence. "But it doesn't feel like a dream, does it?"

Ando shakes his head.

"It felt like she was right next to me," I state to myself. "I could even smell her perfume mixed with cypress wood."

"Sometimes she smells like chocolate-chip cookies." Ando snickers.

This has never happened to me before. Melody has only appeared to my brother while he sleeps. I wonder why she chose me this time. Whatever the reason, I am just thankful that I got to see her even if it was for only a moment.

"Mom?" I announce, getting her attention. "When are we making this tonic for Nicole?"

"Tonight," she says without hesitation. "Before the moon is at its pinnacle."

"Sounds good to me." I shudder, returning to making our food.

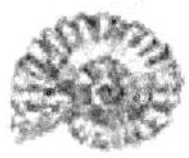

At eleven-forty-six p.m., when the moon is at its apex, Mom, Ando, and I gather up all of the ingredients and head to the back deck overlooking the Caribbean Sea. I am not sure why we do not have weapons, but Ando is carrying a paring knife in his back jeans pocket just in case Mermaids decide to crash whatever it is we are doing. All I know or care about is that this 'tonic' will save Nicole from being a Mermaid slave.

"What do we do first?" I grill Ando and Mom, suddenly feeling like I am being watched.

Our mother is already using one of David's Bunsen-Burners from the garage to heat the distilled water. When it begins to boil, she adds a one-inch chunk of billings root, which is another name for ginger. I learned that from the aunts.

"This is so weird," Ando grumbles as he wiggles the moon jellyfish flesh between his thumb and forefinger. "It feels like your webbing, Lena."

I grimace at the thought.

"Wanna touch it?" he asks, holding it out to me.

"No, thank you." I frown, waiting for Mom's instructions. "I'll take your word for it."

"Hand me that vial over there," she points to a thin cylinder that contains a thick, green-tinted goo.

"What is it?" My eyes widen.

"That, my dearest Selena, is seaweed extract." Mom grins wickedly.

"Why is it so thick?" I swirl the substance around in the vial before handing it to my mother.

"It's thick because it has been boiled down and reduced," she informs like a tonic-making pro.

"Like demi-glace!" I exclaim, recalling the last *Chopped* episode I saw before we left for the Mediterranean.

"Excellent reference," Mom praises. "Just like that."

Before I can ask another question, Mom and Ando grasp hands. Closing their eyes, they begin to silently chant. I am not sure what they are saying, since I no longer understand Siren, but whatever it is, the sea becomes still. Still like glass. Next, dark rain clouds roll in blackening the horizon, and overhead thunder begins to boom as streaks of lightning illuminate the sky. When they stop, it instantly goes back to normal.

"Now, we wait for it to boil again," Ando states since he also knows the procedure.

As we wait for the first part of the cure to come to temperature, Mom takes a walk around the grounds searching for any signs of our new *'friends'*, but as luck would have it, we are all alone. I hope.

"Do you think this will work?" I suddenly blurt, studying the bubbling concoction.

Ando smiles and nods.

"Tia Leukosia said they've used it before," he educates with a smile.

Before long, Mom turns down the temperature to a low simmer. The liquid begins to turn into a deep sage.

"What do we do now?" I probe, feeling lost, wishing I could help.

"We have to add a two-inch piece of the jellyfish flesh," my brother answers as he carefully places the portion he was playing with in the container.

As the ingredients intermingle, multihued sparks begin to escape from the open vessel. One lands on my arm, but it does not burn, in fact, it is ice cold.

"You are really good at this," I praise, feeling extremely jealous.

"Thanks," he blushes.

While we observe, the drink turns into a lovely shade of emerald.

Before our eyes, our mother calls her scales along with one extra-sharp talon which she uses to slice off one small scale over her heart. Quickly, she throws it in. As if adding water to a pot of hot oil, the mixture starts to violently bubble, and squeak then returns to a steady simmer. The tonic is now a vibrant tangerine-orange.

"We've got to put two drops of coral snake venom into it now," Ando informs.

"Alright." I grab the dropper and carefully count out exactly two drops of the clear poison. The brew spits and hisses as it shoots out more colorful sparks. "Now what?"

"Now," I hear Mom's voice behind us. "We wait."

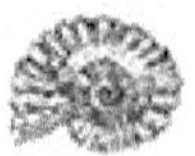

It takes approximately two hours for the medicine to cool and turn clear. Mom and Ando take a sniff then hand it to me. I sniff too, but the scent only confuses me.

"It smells like peppermint," I apprise, shocked.

"Great!" Mom exclaims and smiles. "It's ready!"

"How long is it good for?" I ask, transferring it to a small plastic *Tupperware* container. We do not want this to spill.

Next, Mom sets the alarm on her watch.

"We've got twenty-four hours to use it," Mom advises flatly. "After that, we'll need to make another batch."

Ando and I both nod our understanding.

"Did you call Nicole like I asked?" My mother folds her arms across her chest.

"Of course," I divulge with anxiety. "I asked if she wanted to spend the night tomorrow."

"Well?" Mom frowns. "What did she say?"

"She said… *yes*," I reveal dramatically.

"Perfect," Mom says, doing a quick moonwalk embarrassing both Ando and me.

Carefully, she then grabs the *Tupperware* and heads back into the house.

"We'll need to get ready for our houseguest." The excited Siren grins mischievously. "We've got a lot of work to do."

CHAPTER TEN

The wait is killing us. Ando has looked out of the front window more than five times in ten minutes. Mom is keeping busy in the kitchen making snacks. While I am busy biting my already jagged nails and trying not to hyperventilate.

"When is Nicole coming over?" Ando stares nervously out at the driveway.

Reluctantly, I look at the wall clock. My stomach lurches and I say a silent prayer that it will behave. This is the moment that I have been dreading, confronting Nicole. Well, not really Nicole, but the Mermaid that is currently controlling her.

"She'll be here in a few minutes," I inform, wanting to continue biting my fingernails, but deciding against it. "She texted me when she and her mom left their house."

"Do you remember what you have to do?" Mom questions as she enters the living room carrying a tray of tortilla chips, salsa, guacamole, and bottled water.

Wearily, I nod.

"You put it in the water." I stare at the three bottles. "Which one?"

"All of them," she admits, craftily, admiring her work.

I examine the bottles too, proud to not be able to tell where my half-Siren mother injected the healing medicine for my unsuspecting friend.

"I just have to make sure she drinks it," I repeat for the umpteenth time. "How much?"

"Doesn't matter." Mom grins. "A few gulps will work."

"Good to know," I exhale, loudly.

"The aunts said that there would be a *'reaction'*, but they didn't say what kind." The woman scowls. "So be prepared for anything."

Be prepared for anything? Anything? Like what?

All of these horrible images flash through my mind. Is her head going to spin around and will she vomit pea soup? Will she start speaking in tongues and floating above the ground like an evil phantasm? Or will she start sprouting hair and turn into *The Wolf-man*?

"That sounds ominous," I respond, glancing out of the front window, in time to see Nicole's mom's minivan pulling into the driveway. Things feel tense as I catch a glimpse of them sitting in the van not speaking or making eye contact. Usually, Nicole and her mother have a terrific relationship. Right now, it looks as though they are strangers.

That can't be good.

"She's here," I blurt, starting to get more nervous.

"Don't worry," Mom replies taking one of my sweaty hands in hers. "We're all in this together."

Ando nods and takes my other hand.

Without even knocking, Nicole comes bursting in wearing a tight denim miniskirt and a red halter top. A four-inch pair of red heels completes her outfit. Her eyes are wild, and her pupils are dilated as if she has just gone to the ophthalmologist's office. Unfortunately, she is nothing like her former self. It is a good thing that we made the tonic.

"Hey!" Nicole chuckles. "I'm here."

"Yes, you are." Mom forces a smile.

"I'm so sorry," Mrs. Wong apologizes as she runs in behind her daughter. "I don't know what's wrong with her."

Defiantly, Nicole turns and glares at her mother. Her face is blank and there is not even a glimpse left of her humanity. Every aspect of her personality seems artificial.

"It's fine." Mom gives Mrs. Wong a brief hug.

"Hi, Mrs. Wong," Ando and I say at the same time, reminding me of old times.

"Hello everyone," Nicole's mother answers with a small tense smile. "Thank you for having Nicole over."

"Oh, mother," Nicole speaks at last. "Could you please stop being so *sweet*?"

We all glance over at Nicole then at her mom and finally at each other. The *'thing'* inside of her is not even trying to appear human anymore. Looking more closely at my friend, I notice that there is a slight translucence to her normally mocha complexion. Even her irises appear darker and rounder instead of their usual soft amber.

Mrs. Wong, on the other hand, looks completely and utterly frazzled. Her hair is slightly rumpled, and her eyes are red-rimmed from lack of sleep. There is a nervous quality to her behavior, and her hands have not stopped shaking since she arrived.

Poor Mrs. Wong.

"Are you sure you want her here?" The lovely West Indian woman accidentally blurts.

We all look at her.

"Don't you worry about a thing," Mom reassures, walking the obviously unhinged woman to the front door with an arm around her shoulder. "I'll bring her home tomorrow afternoon. Good as new."

"I really appreciate it, Marina," Mrs. Wong gushes as she gives our mother another hug.

"Get some rest, okay?" Mom gently urges.

"I'll try," she replies with a barely-there smile. "Thanks again, Marina."

"*Grrr!*" Nicole growls. "Enough already. Why don't you just leave?"

Mrs. Wong's eyes well with tears, but she still holds it together long enough to get back to her vehicle. Seeing her like that makes me want to slap the smugness right off of Nicole's haggard face. That would teach her a lesson, or it might throw her into an uncontrollable frenzy. Who knows? Either way, the thought gives me a little satisfaction.

"Why don't you two go upstairs and watch a movie?" Mom encourages with a glint in her eyes. "Please take the snacks up with you, Selena."

"Sounds good," Nicole agrees patting her stomach. "I'm famished."

"Do you want a drink?" Ando asks with a sweet grin.

"I'll take juice," the teenager answers flippantly. "Any kind, I love the taste of juice."

Weird!

"We have apple juice," Ando informs, glancing at the bottles of unopened spring water. "Is that okay?"

"Yup!" she responds only half paying attention. "C'mon, Selena. Let's go upstairs."

"You know where my room is," I jibe. "I'll be right up."

"Take your time," Nicole purrs, sauntering up the stairs like she is a model on a catwalk. "I'll just make myself at home."

"You do that," I mumble below my breath, waiting for her to be out of earshot.

"Oh! Darn it!" Mom suddenly shouts. "The apple juice is finished. Of all the luck."

Nicole pauses on the stairs.

"Don't worry about it," she replies with a flip of her long dark hair. "I guess water will do."

Thank goodness!

"I'll be right up with the snacks." I wink, grabbing the tray and as carefully as possible, I begin to climb the stairs to the second floor, my brother at my side.

"Be careful, Lena," my brother reminds. "She's not really Nicole."

"I know," I sigh, shaking my head, knowing this is all of my fault. "I know."

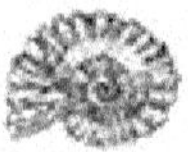

Steadying my nerves, I make my way up the stairs to the second floor. As I climb, I have to remind myself to act like I normally would, otherwise Nicole will become suspicious. Determined to do this, I take the steps two at a time. When I get to the landing, the young woman is nowhere to be seen. Speedily, I walk to my room, but she is not there either.

"Nicole?" I call, going back into the hallway. "Nicole! Where are you?"

With great haste, I speedwalk to Ando's adjacent room.

"Have you seen Nicole?" I pant, glancing around the space for my guest.

He frowns and sits straighter, ignoring the superhero comic book he is pretending to read.

"You lost her?" he gasps, standing up.

"I didn't *lose* her," I growl, my anxiety growing by leaps and bounds. "She was supposed to go to my room, but she's not there."

"What are you guys doing?" Nicole queries from the hallway, causing both my brother and me to jump out of our skins. "I thought we were going to hang-out?"

"Where were you?" I ask, feeling queasy, wondering what mischief she was up to.

"In your room," she replies suspiciously, twirling her hair around her left index finger.

"No, you weren't," I counter, narrowing my eyes. "I checked my room, and you weren't there."

"What's that in your hand?" Ando gasps, walking toward Nicole, pointing to the item she is carrying.

Oh no!

It's our grandfather's journal!

"Where did you get that?" I feel the blood draining out of my face.

She smiles innocently as she gives it to Ando who snatches it away.

"In your closet," Nicole purrs then sits at the foot of my brother's bed.

"What were you doing in there?" I interrogate, wanting to shake her until her head falls off.

"I was snooping." She chuckles. "What else?"

Ando growls low in his throat, baring his teeth at her. If he thought he could get away with it, I am certain that he would bite her… *Hard!*

"Why don't we go back to my room, Nicole?" I suggest; maneuvering her by the elbow out of Ando's room before things escalate. Her skin is cold to the touch. "Here Ando, take care of this please."

"You got it!" he exclaims, glancing at the journal.

"Thanks," I wink.

"Are you coming or not?" Nicole calls me from my room.

"What movie would you like to watch?" I ask, going over to the stack of Blu-rays. "Something with action or—"

"Let's talk," she interrupts, patting the mattress where she perches like a feline. "Like we used to."

Hmm.

"What do you want to talk about?" I sit at my desk, not wanting to be too close.

"Andrew," she boldly discloses, staring at me hard.

"Andrew?" I huff, not wanting to engage in that subject with someone who is currently being controlled by other worldly creatures. "What about Andrew?"

Nicole stands, her eyes flash onyx then back to amber. Slowly, she saunters over to the window and stares out at the sea. As if something heavy weighs on her mind, she sighs heavily.

"The sea… it's so beautiful," she whispers, enthralled at the rhythmic motion of the waves. "Isn't it?"

Without warning, she turns to face me, her face slightly paler than moments before, and wearing the most vicious expression. Suddenly, my knees begin to knock.

"I guess so," I answer, staring at her staring at me. "What about Andrew?"

I change the subject away from the sea hoping to not feel so awkward.

"I like him." Nicole suddenly pouts.

"Huh?"

I must be dreaming again.

"You heard me!" she snaps.

"When did this happen?" I gasp, feeling bile in my esophagus. "You and Andrew are best friends. You've always been in love with Mike."

Quickly, she walks toward me, and by instinct, I move and relocate to the bed. Mockingly, she laughs, and slithers toward me again, sitting beside me, our thighs touching. It takes all of my determination to stay seated. Sensing my apprehension, she moves a few inches away and just glares at me.

"Pfft!" she sounds, admiring her own manicured nails. "Mike is cute, but he is nothing compared to Andrew."

"Mike worships the ground you walk on, stupid," I ramble without thought, losing my temper. "Where is this coming from?"

"I have feelings for Andrew, and he has feelings for me," she continues ignoring my pale appearance. "You're simply a distraction."

"A distraction?" I huff, rage igniting. All I want to do is grab her by the scruff of the neck and toss her headfirst out of the window. I have not felt this violent since… *Amy!*

"Listen to me, Selena." The imposter stands again, peering down at me like an eagle sizing-up a field mouse, and finding it wanting. As she continues to stare, I notice that her eyes are turning… *blue?*

Nicole has amber eyes, **not** *blue.*

Ignoring that for the moment, I stand to face her, refusing to be intimidated.

"You're behaving like Amy," I insult, observing as her expression changes for a second.

"Intelligent, self-confident… amazing?" She grins.

"No. Prissy, ignorant, bossy." I grin back, knowing that I have struck a nerve.

"Selena!" Nicole pleads, but it is not her current voice. The voice she speaks with now is higher, a little squeakier, and smooth as silk. This other voice is weak and scared. *"Help me!"*

"What was that?" I interrogate, taking a closer look at her eyes, wondering if it was just my overly active imagination or a trick of the light, but it is not. I am positive; it was real, as real as the teenager standing before me.

When she notices what is happening, Nicole closes her eyes and when she reopens them, she is back to her previous haughty, annoying self.

In my heart, I know that it was the real Nicole able to break free from the Mermaid's control for a brief second. Sadly, she disappears just as quickly as she had appeared. I just want her back.

"Here are some more snacks." My mother surprises us. "I hope you're hungry because I made a lot of caramel corn."

"I am." Nicole pushes past me as if I were invisible; the scent of wildflowers seeping out of her pores is stronger than ever. "What about you, Selena? Are you hungry?"

"Uh huh." I smile through the anger.

"Is everything alright?" Mom asks curiously, studying us. "Why is it so cold in here? It feels like the Arctic."

"Uh huh," I respond, keeping my cool.

"I feel quite comfortable actually," my *'friend'* smirks.

Mom's eyes widen, but she says nothing.

"Are you okay?" she directly questions me, her 'worry' face glued on.

"Everything is glorious," Nicole answers instead.

"Yeah, Mom," I pretend, and force a smile. "Everything is fan-tab-u-lous."

I'll tell her all about it later.

"Alrighty-then." The second-generation sea nymph sighs. "If you all need anything, just give me a holler."

"We will, Marina," Nicole sneers. "I mean… Mrs. Marquez."

Without a retort, my mother exits the room but leaves the door open.

"C'mon," the body snatcher encourages. "Let's watch that movie."

Slowly, I nod my agreement but continue to mentally dissect my companion's strange behavior. I remind myself that this will all be over soon, and Nicole will be free of the control of the Mermaids. She will be back to normal, and we will be best friends again. Hopefully, we can put this whole nasty incident behind us.

A few minutes later, the movie is queuing up, and we are settled comfortably, me on the floor and Nicole on the bed. Am I afraid of her? *Hell yes!* I am not a Siren anymore. I do not have enhanced senses, super-human strength, or the ability to fight like *Wonder Woman*. All I have now is my innate ability to be cautious and my instinctual desire not to be dead.

Silently, I study Nicole and am completely shocked when the teenager begins to eat like I have never seen her eat before. Nicole is a healthy eater and has been raised with manners. This thing obviously has not been raised with either. Not even testing the temperature of the food, Nicole grabs a pizza roll and shoves it into her mouth like she has not eaten in days. Next, she takes a homemade cheese puff and does the same. Her eyes roll back in her head like a shark's right before they attack.

"Mmm," she moans in delight. "Your mom is a great cook, Selena."

Terrified, I manage to smile.

"Thanks, Nicole." I blush and reach for my first cheese puff.

"But it's lacking something," my guest implies, making a face of disgust.

"What does it need?" Mom asks as she reappears in the doorway, her right foot tapping with agitation.

"I few splashes of vinegar," Nicole grins. "I love that flavor, don't you?"

"Sometimes," Mom mumbles. "Depending on the meal."

"I'm surprised someone like you could make such a delicious meal," my friend sneers, still shoveling food into her mouth.

"What do you mean by *someone like me*?" Mom crosses her arms across her chest, indignantly.

Nicole suddenly stops scarfing, and her eyes transform from amber to black as she stands.

"You know," she smirks. "A dimwitted, slow-moving, moronic, piece of trash, Siren."

With those caustic words, Nicole lunges at my mother who deftly throws the teenager off balance. The young woman tumbles backward and lands on top of the mattress. Thankfully, she is startled but not hurt.

"Grab her arms!" Mom orders, reaching for the nearest bottled water.

Of course, I do as I am told and manage to keep the wildly thrashing Nicole in place.

"My goodness!" Mom huffs and puffs as she restrains Nicole with her left hand while desperately trying to unscrew the bottle cap with her right. "She is strong!"

All the while, Nicole is howling and screeching like a banshee on fire.

"Let go of me, you freak!" she screams at the top of her lungs. "I'll kill you! *I'll kill you all!*"

With a flail of her leg, she kicks the still closed bottle from Mom's hand, and it quickly ricochets off the wall and rolls under the bed.

"Damn it!" my mother yells, as the much-needed object disappears from our sight.

Ando hearing the ruckus comes rushing into the room.

"Did you do it? Did you give it to her?" he shouts over the din of Mom and I wrestling Nicole, who has managed to wriggle off the bed and onto the floor.

"Ando!" I yell, noticing that my grip is loosening on the struggling young woman. "Get the bottle… under the bed! It's under the bed! *Hurry!*"

With lightning speed, my brother dives under the bed, and soon reappears holding the miracle beverage.

"I got it!" he squeals. "I got it! What do I do?"

"Give it to her!" I roar, getting kicked in the chin.

Ando pauses, his eyes wide with horror.

"Me?!" he exclaims, loudly. "Shouldn't one of you do it?"

"No!" I snap, securing her wrist.

"You're going to have to force her to drink it!" Mom yells, and I feel a sharp blow to the chin from Nicole's elbow.

"Ouch!" I bellow. "Ando! Hurry up!"

Finally, following my directions, my brother twists open the top while Mom and I attempt to open Nicole's mouth, but she refuses to be compliant, instead she doubles her effort to keep it tightly closed. It takes both of us to hold her in place so that Ando can straddle her chest.

"Stay still, Nicole!" Ando snaps, prying open her mouth with one hand and tipping the bottle into it, but only a mouthful runs out before his *crush* knocks the bottle out of his hand and back onto the floor. I feel the water splash on my leg right as Nicole hits me in the face with her head and wriggles away from Mom's grip.

As we try grabbing her again, the amped-up teen leaps out of the window, jumps off of the roof, and races around the side toward the rocky steps. She moves swiftly, but not as fast as a true Mermaid. Determined to catch her, Mom jumps out of the window and so does Ando. I, on the other hand, grab the water bottle which still has more than half of the tonic still available and race with it through the house like a mortal.

With my ankle still a tad bit swollen, I do my best to run as fast as possible. Down the steps I go, avoiding the slippery patches. When I reach the bottom, I glance around. No one is there.

"Mom!" I shout, feeling afraid. "Ando! Nicole! Where are you?"

"Over here," I hear Nicole sputtering; her body is soaking wet and smells of the sea.

"Nicole!"

Filled with relief, I sprint to her, getting on my hands and knees in order to sit, and then resting her head on my lap. She is frightened and tired, and I make the mistake of feeling sorry for her. Before I can correct my error, she punches me in the nose.

Immediately, my vision blurs and I see stars as I gently coddle the throbbing area.

"Damn it!" I screech at the top of my lungs. "That's it!"

Without hesitation, I ball my right hand into a tight fist and get ready to beat her to a pulp, but before I can land my first punch, she speaks.

"Help me," she groans, spitting out excess water, and sounding like the real Nicole. "I don't know how long I can keep this *'thing'* suppressed."

"Try not to wig out," I tell, realizing that Nicole is truly back in control for the moment, laying her on her back. "I've got to give you this."

I hold up the bottle of clear liquid.

"What is it?" Nicole asks, looking at me strangely.

"Medicine," is the only word I say.

"What kind of medicine?" My friend's eyebrows hitch.

"You're possessed and without this you'll either go braindead or die," I blurt then wait for her reaction.

Speechless, she lies still for a moment watching the clouds passing by. It is a beautiful late afternoon, clear and cool. It would be perfect if Nicole was not in this predicament.

Nicole braces herself.

"Give it to me," she whimpers. "Do it now!"

"Okay," I pant, trying not to have a panic attack.

"Selena?" Nicole gazes at me innocently.

"What is it?" I ask, getting ready to unscrew the cap.

"You're so freaking stupid!" She snarls, eyes black like the blackest hole.

Thrown off guard, I grab her hands before she can hit me again. She struggles almost rolling into the water. It only takes a split second for her to wrench free and before I can grab her hands, she punches me in the nose; *again!*

"*Crap!*" I scream, holding my nose while my eyes continue to water. Losing my temper, I punch her in the same manner and place that she punched me.

"*Oww!*" she yells, the sound reverberating against the stony cliff side. "You're so dead!"

Thankfully, it hurts her just enough to make her grab at her face, and not at me. Taking the opportunity, I uncap the bottle, drain the remaining tonic into her mouth and pinch her nose shut. Unable to breath, she inhales through her open mouth and the liquid rushes down her throat.

"That's it," I calm in a soothing tone. "Drink it… good girl."

Once more, she starts to thrash, but I straddle her like Ando did and then cover her swollen nose with my hands. Unable to breathe, she gulps down the remaining liquid that fills her throat.

When the last bit of medicine enters her system, she begins violently coughing and wheezing uncontrollably: arms and legs thrashing. Her face turns from ghostly white to her normal mocha complexion then to an intense shade of maroon. For several minutes, she lies gasping and sputtering. Several times, she even convulses to the point that she slams the back of her head onto the unyielding stone surface. That blow knocks her out cold.

A few minutes later, Mom and Ando emerge from the water, frantic and badly scratched and bruised. Seeing Nicole unconscious, they smile. I just shrug.

"Where have you two been?!" I bark with an annoyed tone. "I could have used the help."

"There were at least a dozen or so of them," my mother huffs as she pulls herself and her son up onto land.

"One of them got me really good," my brother informs proudly as he shows us the deep cut on his neck which is already starting to heal.

Then they both turn their attention to Nicole.

"Did you do that?" Mom questions with a shocked expression.

"Do what?" I exhale loudly, pulling Nicole's limp body back onto my damp lap.

"Did you kung-fu chop her and knock her out?" Ando grins, pretending to spar.

All I can do is blush, smile, and nod.

"Did she drink the tonic?" Mom questions more seriously, her jet-black curls sopping, but still perfect.

I nod and grin again.

"You never cease to amaze me," she mumbles, but I still hear her. "Even without your powers."

"Thanks," I blush, feeling my cheeks heat.

I chuckle, wiping the stray hairs out of my eyes. Mom comes over and sits beside me. Her smile warms me from the inside out. I can tell she is proud and that makes me blush even more.

"How will we know that it has worked?" I feel Nicole's damp forehead. "She's got a fever."

Mom touches her head to confirm.

"Let's get her inside," she orders looking up at the sinking sun. "Before they come for her."

"*What?!*" Ando squeals.

"Why would they come back for her?" I yelp, helping Mom get the unconscious girl over her shoulder in a fireman's hold.

"According to Tia Ligeia, Mermaids are very possessive," she states flatly. "What belongs to them… will always belong to them. Even in death."

"Great!" I proclaim, following her up the steps. "Hurry! The sun is almost completely below the horizon!"

Ando sprints ahead of us, making it to the house in record time and grabs a blanket to wrap Nicole's limp body. We are all nearly in a panic and at first; Mom takes her to my room but then remembers the broken window and totes her back downstairs to her room. There, she lays her down on the bed.

"Ando, can you get me a wet washcloth?" she commands.

"Yes, Mommy," he replies, rushing to complete his task.

"Selena?"

"Yes, Mom?" I respond, looking down at Nicole's purple lips.

"There are a few sheets of plywood in the garage near Dad's tool bench," she starts. "There are nails and a hammer in the second drawer of the tool bench."

"You need me to secure the window?"

She nods as Ando returns to the room holding a bowl of ice water and a clean washcloth.

"I'll take care of it," I inform, staring as my mother calls her scales along with one talon which she uses to slice off a large shimmering lilac one located near her heart. "You concentrate on Nicole."

Wanting to get it done as soon as possible, I rush to the garage and locate the things I will need: hammer, nails and plywood. Everything is where Mom said they would be, in Dad's red metal, industrial toolbox. Then back upstairs I go. Before I can get the first nail hammered in, I hear the similar sound of croaking alligators from down below in the backyard.

Please don't let it be—!

It is what I feared, followed by the sultry, seductive tune that completely surrounds me and threatens to take over my common sense.

Crap!

"Baby Siren looking all discombobulated," the larger of the two Mermaids heckles me from several feet below the window, eyes black as midnight, hair pale as the moon, skin like translucent Scotch-tape, and teeth pointy and razor-sharp.

Double-crap!

"Baby Siren!" the other joins in. "You look tasty! I bet you taste like mackerel."

They both laugh until they are gasping for breath.

That gives me just enough time to hammer the second and third nails into the wood. As I start to pound in the final nail, I feel a powerful blow against the board that blasts it into splinters. The fist in front of my face loosens and grabs me around the neck. Sadly, the grip is strong enough to render me silent, unable to call for help.

"I am starving, Dahlia," the smaller one informs, licking her lips. "This is a tender piece of meat. She will be tasty and moist."

The other creature shakes her head.

"We are not here to eat, Wisteria," the wiser of the two reminds. "Get the human!"

Wisteria studies me.

"What about *this* human?" she pokes me with a sharp talon.

"Smell her," Dahlia orders and I suddenly feel paranoid that I forgot to wear deodorant or something similar.

Loudly, she sniffs at me. Moving closer, she does it again. Finally, she puts her nose right up against my skin and does it a third time.

"She smells like human, but *different*," the inbred Cretan says it like it is an insult.

They croak at each other, but nothing they say is comprehendible to my ears.

"She will not do." Dahlia smirks. "She is tainted."

Tainted? What the hell does that mean?

"Get off of my sister!" Ando suddenly yells as he bashes Dad's shovel over Wisteria's coconut-shaped head.

The scream she discharges almost bursts my eardrums, but the blow is painful enough that she releases me and dives out of the window. Dahlia hisses and lunges at Ando with talons at the ready, but before she can seize him, I grab her ankle and redirect her in midair; the momentum slams her body onto the dresser. Shattering sounds fill the air as her figure slams into the mirror; sending razor-sharp shards of bloody glass splattering everywhere like shrapnel.

"Get out of our house!" Ando yells, picking her up by the upper arm and throwing her outside physically. "Don't come back! Tell the rest of your slimy friends!"

"Thanks, little bro," I say, giving him a relieved grin.

"No worries, sis!" He grins back. "Mom needs us. Nicole is waking up!"

Anxiously, we run downstairs and into Mom's room. There, still laying on the bed, is Nicole, but this time she is wide awake and smiling slightly. The pale quality of her skin is completely gone and is replaced by healthy, rosy-colored cheeks. She definitely looks like her old self.

"What happened?" the confused teenager asks, rubbing the back of her head where she hit on the rocks. "I feel like I've been slammed by a semi."

Relieved, I smile as I sit beside her.

"You hit your head pretty hard," I inform, looking at her eyes… her lovely *amber* eyes. "Mom thinks you may have a concussion, but she gave you the venom from one of her scales, so you should be as good as new by tomorrow."

"Thank you, Mrs. Marquez," she groans and tries to sit up, but falls back against the pillows. "How did I get here?"

My mother examines the large, swollen bump on the back of her head.

"You don't remember?" Mom grills as she gently touches the wounded area, making my friend wince.

With difficulty, Nicole sits up and this time manages to stay upright.

"May I have some water?" she asks with a hoarse throat.

"With vinegar?" Ando queries back, eyes narrowed, little fists clenched.

"Yuck!" The teen snaps making us giggle. "Just regular water will be just fine."

Ando chuckles at her facial expression.

"I'll get it!" he tells as he speedwalks to get Nicole's beverage.

"Thank you, Ando," she grins, and we know it has to be her. "Now, what's been going on?"

It takes all of ten minutes to explain everything that has happened, that we know of, to Nicole. Amazingly, the only thing that she has real issue with is that some skanky Mermaid has put her in a slutty outfit and has made her be mean to her family. With determination, she stands, holds on to the nightstand, and steadies herself.

"I think I'm going to be sick," Nicole announces, holding her head and stomach at the same time.

"I'm so sorry, Nicole," I apologize, feeling awful.

"Mermaids, huh?" she smirks as Ando returns and hands her another bottle of water from the fridge.

"Yeah," I say with reddened cheeks. "Mermaids."

"And why were they using me as an avatar?" She rubs her throbbing temples.

"To get to me... to *us*." I wave my hands around at my surrounding family members.

"I see," she responds, opening the cap with a great deal of effort, but finally getting it done.

She takes a cleansing breath before continuing.

"What kind of person wants to look like a hooker?" Nicole utters as she stares at her reflection in Mom's full-length mirror. "I look like Julia Roberts' roommate in Pretty Woman."

I giggle.

"Actually," Nicole adds. "I look like Amy."

We both laugh at that image.

"Should we tell your folks?" I nervously bite my bottom lip. "I mean about what we are and what happened to you."

Nicole's eyes widen, and she frowns.

"What do you want us to do?" I question, wanting her to know we will do anything she wishes.

Her eyebrows hitch to her hairline as she contemplates the question.

"I'm not sure." She sits back down. "I don't want to put you in jeopardy. After all, I'm sure you don't want everyone knowing your secret."

"Your family is different." Mom smiles sincerely.

Nicole blushes as she rests her hand on her queasy stomach.

"I'll get you some crackers, Nicole?" Ando turns to return to the kitchen.

"No thanks, Ando." Nicole grins and hands me the plastic bottle, so she can lie back down.

Ando stops in midstride.

"Maybe later," she grins, closing her red-rimmed eyes. "More water please."

Without hesitation, I hand it to her again and we are all grateful when she begins to take small sips until she manages to drink the entire thing. "That really hits the spot."

Mom smiles.

"Mrs. Marquez?" my best friend whispers.

"Yes, Nicole?" Mom takes a step towards her then stops.

"Can the Mermaids get back inside of my head and control me again?" the anxious teenager asks, tapping her bottom lip with her finger nervously, eyes still closed.

"Tia Leukosia said that once you have the tonic in your system, it will protect you always." Mom gives a reassuring smile. "From now on, you will have an immunity to all forms of supernatural mind control."

Nicole beams.

"That's good to know," Nicole quiets and her breathing softens as she begins to drift to sleep. "Ando, thank you again for the water."

"Do you need anything else?" he questions, his aquamarine eyes filled with relief and unshed tears.

Nicole pats her belly.

"No, thanks," she says. "I just need… some… rest…"

CHAPTER ELEVEN

The next day, Nicole feels one-hundred percent better and we spend time getting caught up on our lives over the summer. Unbeknownst to me, Nicole had not been herself since the day before my family and I returned to Isla Flora. We both feel like idiots.

"How did this happen?" I interrogate, trying to wrap my mind around Nicole's traumatic event.

My friend reflects for a moment before answering.

"I think it started when Andrew and I went to Amy's birthday party," she confesses, looking bleak.

"Amy invited you to her party?" I ask, confused. "Amy? Amy Jacobs?"

Nicole chuckles.

"Well… not really," the baffled teen informs. "She asked Andrew to go, but he didn't want to go by himself, so he asked me to go with him. I didn't have anything better to do, so I agreed."

Enthralled by the newly shared information, I lean back against the headboard listening to her account. Quickly, she describes the venue where the event was held. Turns out, it was at the same swanky resort that homecoming was. With bated breath, she explains the lavish decorations and exotic food, even the rich attendees like the governor's family, local businessmen, and a butt load of local celebrities. Mr. Jacobs even hired a world-famous DJ to emcee the fancy festivities.

"That sounds spectacular." I whistle, imagining it in my head, not seeing anything peculiar about the evening so far.

"It really was!" Nicole exclaims, reaching for a strawberry jelly and cheddar cheese sandwich on the plate beside her.

"What happened next?" I encourage, reaching for one of the salty-sweet concoctions as well, enjoying the contrasting taste experience.

"I remember having to use the ladies' room," she recalls, holding the almost finished sandwich a few inches away from her mouth. "Amy came in after… we were just talking…"

"Then… " I urge her to continue.

"Then… *nothing*," she frowns. "Everything is kinda foggy after that."

"That's weird." I sigh, trying to add one and one together, but coming up with three.

"Tell me about it. At first, I was just losing small chunks of time," Nicole admits. "Ten minutes here… fifteen minutes there. Soon after, days would be missing."

"Is there anything else you remember?" I probe, completely engulfed in her recollection.

"Just darkness and the sound of rushing water." Nicole gulps uneasily. "Selena?"

"Yeah?" I swallow hard.

"I think I may have *kissed* Andrew," she reveals, bracing for retaliation, but for some reason I do not feel upset with her. "I'm not sure why I did it. I don't even like him in that way. I like Mike."

I frown, and nod at the same time. Mike Taylor: sweet, funny, smart, athletic, one of the kindest people I have ever known has been Nicole's secret crush since I have known her. Never, not even once, has she ever mentioned having feelings for Andrew. They are like brother and sister.

"It's alright." I smile, taking a bite of jelly and cheese on whole wheat. "You weren't yourself."

"Andrew was the perfect gentleman though." The high school senior giggles then turns a deep burgundy. "He thought I had been temporarily replaced by a pod-person. He told me that he loves me like a friend, but he is *in love* with you."

"Aww," I blurt, blushing too. "I think I'll keep him."

"Do you forgive me for everything?" Nicole's expression saddens.

"Absolutely!" I grin, taking her hand in mine.

She looks relieved, but there is no need for her to feel guilty. The only reason Nicole was targeted was because of our close relationship. Whoever is doing this knows they can access me by using her. I should be the only one feeling culpable of anything.

"I'm the one who should be sorry, Nicole." I give her a quick hug.

"Why are you sorry?" She stares at me.

"This is my fault," I mumble. "All of this is my fault: David dying, you getting possessed, me losing my powers—"

"What?" Nicole shouts, almond-eyes widening. "Lost your powers? What do you mean you've lost your powers?"

In a few minutes, I explain that when I was in Capri, I stole energy from the Earth, which, of course, was unacceptable and was a punishable offense. Filled with embarrassment, I also had to reveal that I was warned several times by Gaia the Goddess of the Earth about stopping, but instead of listening I ignored her warnings. Feeling relieved to admit to someone who is not a member of my immediate family, I also confess to kissing Ares, the God of War.

Nicole's eyes widen to the size of dinner plates.

"Ares!" she yelps. "*The* Ares? Mythological bad-ass, Ares?"

I nod, hanging my head in shame.

"Yeah," I reply with my head still bowed low.

"Holy crap woman!" Nicole proclaims rather boisterously. "You made-out with Ares, the God of War!"

"Not so loud!" I beg, turning red.

"I haven't made out with anyone," Nicole reveals with a sad expression. "You're so lucky!"

"Shh!" I chastise, smacking her hard on the arm. "Not so loud!"

"Sorry," Nicole lowers her voice to a whisper. "How was it?"

She wiggles her eyebrows provocatively making me want to crawl under a rock and stay there. How can I tell her that I enjoyed kissing the God of War? Too much, as a matter of fact. For some reason, he appealed to my wild side, my Siren side. He was dangerous and captivating with self-confidence oozing out of his pores, the ultimate bad-boy.

"I'd rather not talk about it anymore," I grumble, wishing it had never happened. "I wasn't myself."

"I know, I know," she whispers. "But was it good? Is he a good kisser?"

I nod and blush at the same time.

"Eeee!" she squeals, playing on my culpability then her face drops as she realizes the inevitable. "Have you told Andrew yet?"

Guiltily, I shake my head.

"Are you going to tell him?" she questions, eyes still wide.

"Should I?" I ask, not knowing what to do. "You know him better than I do."

Nicole thinks for a brief moment then answers.

"I'm not sure," she sighs.

"Me either," I reply, staring at my boarded-up window.

After dinner, my mother drives us to Nicole's house and agrees to come back for me in a couple of hours. At our place, Nicole felt okay, but sadly now, her nausea has returned. Mom advises that she only eat soup and maybe some crackers. Apparently, one of the aftereffects of the tonic is gassiness and bloating. Nicole does not mind though; she is just happy to be free. I, on the other hand, still feel like a heel.

"Are you sure that you're feeling better?" I walk my friend to the door.

"I'm tired, but fine," she smiles like her old self. "How am I going to face my family? Who knows what other evil things I did."

"Don't worry," I reply, walking up the stairs beside her, carrying her overnight bag. "I sort of killed my stepfather and I got forgiven."

Nicole grimaces.

Just as we reach the landing, the door flies open and the twins come racing out, keys in hand, startled looks in their exotic hazel eyes. Without even a hello, they get into their *Jeep* and turn the ignition, but nothing happens. Justin or Jordan swears, but I cannot tell from this far away which one is the culprit.

"What's wrong?" Nicole shouts in their direction.

They both blankly stare at her.

"This is all your fault!" they shout back.

"What are you talking about?" their sister asks, taking her bag from me and resting it on the front porch.

"It's Mom!" they yell, turning the key again, but still the vehicle remains dormant.

"What's going on with Mom?" The teen shouts at her brothers.

They pause and glance at each other doing their silent-wonder-twins-communication thingy they often do.

"Spill it!" Nicole yells, perching her hands on her hips. "What's the matter with Mom?!"

"She's acting just like you!" they shout back.

Nicole and I glance at each other, our hands immediately finding each other as we stand speechlessly staring at them. *Jeez!* Why is this happening? Why do Mermaids keep attacking the Wong women? First Nicole and now her mother. Is this some sort of colossal joke, a prank? Well, it is definitely *not* funny!

Finally, the *Jeep* starts.

"Where is she?" Nicole interrogates as we sprint to the Jeep, hand in hand, pile into the backseat and secure our seat belts.

"Down there!" one of the twins points to the sea below their house.

"H-how… why… w-why would she be down there at this time of the night?" Nicole stammers, her hand trembling in mine.

Not knowing what else to do, I temporarily release Nicole, grab my cellphone from my back pocket, and speed dial my mom's number. Thankfully, she picks up on the second ring.

"Everything alright?" Mom demands with a worried tone to her voice.

"No, ma'am!" I sulk, squeezing Nicole's hand once again. "Please tell me that we have some more of the tonic?"

"We don't," Mom hesitantly informs. "Why?"

"Mrs. Wong is possessed," I whisper, but the twins hear me anyway.

"Huh?" They both sound at once.

"Are there enough ingredients to make some more?" I quiz, pinching the bridge of my nose.

There is rustling then my mother answers.

"Ando and I will make another batch right now, but it won't be ready until it cools and changes color," she reminds.

"Please make it," I beg. "We will bring her to the house."

"Be careful," she replies, flatly.

"Always," I respond then hang-up. "They're going to make some more, but we have to get your mother to my house."

"More of what? What are you saying?" one twin interrogates as we turn onto the main road that goes to Coconut Palm Beach.

"Where is Dad?" Nicole jumps in.

"He went after her," the other twin responds, then adds. "But at least he took his car."

Nicole and I both stare at each other in confusion.

"What exactly happened, Justin?" Nicole probes, needing better answers.

"Mom was fine up until a few hours ago," Justin explains as calmly as he can. "They had just come home from a sunset swim at Coconut Palm Beach."

"Mom looked kind of out of it," Jordan blurts, voice wavering. "Said she had gotten bitten by something when she was swimming and wanted to take a shower to clean the wound, then went upstairs. Next thing we know, she's yelling and screaming and arguing with Dad. She actually pushed him down the stairs because he wouldn't let her go back to the beach alone!"

The young man pauses as the memory replays in his still stunned brain.

"Then she ran out of the house toward the cliff and jumped—"

"*Jumped?!*" Nicole interrupts. "What do you mean she '*jumped*'?"

"Our mother ran to the backyard and jumped off of the cliff into the sea," Justin rambles, his eyes glistening.

With that disturbing visual, my pulse starts pounding in my ears.

"Why was she so worked up?" I grill, pretending to be as surprised as the rest of them.

"I'm not sure!" Justin barks, throwing his arms above his head in frustration, causing us to jump.

"She was yelling about Nicole and something about a cure… then about your family… nonsense about Sirens and Mermaids… I don't know!" Justin shouts, running a frustrated hand through his wavy hair which causes the vehicle to swerve into the other lane then back again. "It's all gibberish!"

"Is Dad alright?" Nicole questions with a green-sickly look about her.

Suddenly realizing his speed, Justin lightly steps onto the brake, slowing to a more manageable rate, all the while taking slow deep breaths.

"He twisted his ankle when he fell, but insisted on following her down there," Jordan states flatly. "What's going on, Nicole?"

"How should I know?!" his sister snaps, turning from mocha to red.

"Selena?" Jordan steps in. "What do you know?"

Tongue-tied, I pause.

"Spill it!" Jordan orders. "This is our mother and father! Anything happens to them and it's on your head!"

Do they need to know? Yes! They need to know what they are dealing with.

"Your mom is possessed by a Mermaid!" I shout at them.

There I said it!

"Nicole was also possessed by a Mermaid!" I exclaim rather loudly, suddenly feeling unburdened.

"Huh?" they respond together.

"Which one… well… we don't exactly know," I ramble, hoping they do not make a U-turn toward the psychiatric hospital. "But we made a cure with jellyfish flesh and other stuff and now… she's cured!"

Woot! This feels great!

"I used to be a Siren!" I spew in a rush of words. "I'm not anymore. My mother and brother are and so are my aunts… they are the original three… they're not here right now… my stepfather isn't lost at sea, he got killed because all of my family members including my great-grandmother, who is a powerful Muse, joined their essences so that David could save me from becoming a blood-thirsty, bitchy, intolerable Siren… the kind that kills humans!"

Dear Father! This feels really *great!*

The twins are gawking at me with wide eyes and wider mouths. The one driving stares at me from the rearview mirror. The other riding shotgun glares at me from over his shoulder. Needless to say, they both look pale and confused. Nicole, on the other hand, just shakes her head like I have lost my mind, but I do not care. They need; no, they *deserve* to know the truth.

I trust the Wong's, all of them, and hopefully they trust me.

"That's enough," Jordan and Justin reply at once. "Are you nuts?"

Nicole sighs, head in her hands.

"She's not crazy," she informs, finally. "Everything she has said is true. I can testify to that in a court of law… under oath."

"You can't be serious," Justin comments; now staring at his sister.

Suddenly, Nicole straightens, staring right back at him.

"Remember the stories Grandpa would tell us about beautiful women sunning themselves on rocks and singing the most beautiful songs?" Nicole adds, her voice steady.

"Yeah," they both answer.

"Do you remember when I got pulled into the sea by a gigantic fish?" she continues, without humor.

"Yeah," they say again.

"Remember when Grandpa and I tried to convince the family that I got saved by a woman with golden hair and aquamarine eyes?" Nicole questions while folding her arms across her chest and narrowing her eyes to appear fiercer.

"Yeah," Jordan is the only one that answers this time.

"Turns out it was Selena's Siren-aunt, Leukosia, who saved me," Nicole jabs.

There is a long pause.

"You are nuts!" Justin laughs.

"Look at Selena's eyes!" his younger sister commands, holding my face with her hands. "What color are they?"

The weirded-out twin gulps.

"Aquamarine," he answers, afraid of what his sister will do if he does not.

"Have you ever seen eyes like hers before?" she continues.

Justin can only shake his head.

"*She's* not crazy!" their sister insists more forcefully. "*I'm* not crazy! There are supernatural beings that walk the Earth. Some are kind, others are not! *Mermaids* are here! And they are coming for us! *They are coming for all of us!*"

Less than five minutes later, we are pulling into the parking area of Coconut Palm Beach. Several yards away, the water is calm and inviting. Tall palm trees are gently swaying to the rhythmic island breezes. In the treetops, tiny creatures are fast asleep in their hiding places.

"I don't see them," Nicole announces aloud. "Do you?"

"I don't see them either," I respond, looking around the desolate beach.

"Dad!" one of the twins shouts out.

"Mom!" the other twin follows.

"*Daddy?!*" Nicole exclaims as she spots her father lying in the sand. "Oh no!"

Speedily, we sprint to where he is with sand kicking up in our wake like horses running the Kentucky Derby. As we reach him, he groans clutching his ribs. His face is badly bruised and scratched, but he is holding on.

"Dad, can you get up?" Nicole helps him sit-up.

"Where's Natasha?" he mumbles, almost too low to understand. "Where's your mother?"

We all stare at him.

"They took her," he groans in agony, gripping his side.

"Who took her?" Nicole gently wipes the drying blood from his nose and mouth with the edge of her t-shirt.

"The women with the white hair," the injured man mumbles, and then loses consciousness.

Gently, Nicole rests his body onto the sand. Immediately, her eyes fill with tears, but her face is full of unbridled rage. I have never seen her look so vicious. It is a new side to my normally reserved friend, and it is terrifying.

"We'll find her," Nicole whispers, gently wiping the sand away from her father's closed eyes. "You just sleep, Daddy. When you wake everything will be back to normal. I promise."

From out in the surf, I see something bobbing with the motion of the waves. It is the right size and shape to be Mrs. Wong. She is facedown and not moving. Quickly, I mumble a silent prayer hoping that it is just a piece of driftwood and *not* the feisty Trinidadian mother of three.

Jordan spots her next.

"Is that—"

"Mom?" Justin completes the question.

"Let's go!" Nicole announces, stripping down to her sports bra and booty-shorts that she wears to dance class.

With that said, the young woman runs toward the sea with both of her brothers running after her. Without hesitation, all three dive-in and within a minute they are almost to whatever it is floating in the water.

"Is it her?" I shout out to them. "Is it your mom?"

They seem confused.

"It's only debris!" Jordan hollers.

As he says this, he gets pulled under.

"Jordan!" Justin yells and then disappears beneath the waves as well.

Nicole screams then gets tugged underneath too.

I really need to learn how to swim again!

As I watch through tear-filled lenses, I see Nicole breach the surface followed by Jordan and then Justin. They are all gasping and coughing. Then I see them, Mom and Ando. Mom is towing the twins while my brother assists Nicole. Her arms are around his neck as he gives her a piggyback ride back to shore.

"Thank goodness!" I yell, running to meet them by the shore. "Are you alright?"

"Thanks to your mom and brother," Jordan gasps for breath.

"What were those things?" Justin barks, spitting water.

"They had freaking tails!" his brother declares, brushing the sand particles out of his hair.

Nicole plops down on the soft sand and squeezes the excess seawater out of her hair. Slowly, she leans back on her elbows and takes several deep breaths, all-the-while staring up at the cloudless sky.

"Those, my dear brothers, were *Mermaids*," Nicole informs without looking at them.

"Freakin' hell!" Jordan exclaims loudly. "Mermaids?! They really freakin' exist?!"

"This can't be real, Nicki!" Justin stares at the dark mysterious sea, shaking his head. "No way this is real."

Nicole stares at them.

"What else could they be?" she questions, turning their way.

"Not Mermaids is all," Jordan states blankly as he sits beside her.

"Maybe it was a shark," Justin adds, sitting on the other side of his sister.

"With the head of a woman?" I blurt, snickering to myself. "I don't think so."

Mom rests on the sand too. Her face is flushed, and she is breathing heavily, but she is unharmed and pissed-off. I would not want to be a Mermaid tonight.

"Where did they go?" I probe, looking out at the black depths. "Are they still out there?"

"Your Mom took care of them," Justin sputters.

"What do you mean by *'took care of them'*?" I ask, curiously.

The twins do a cutting motion across their throats.

"Ugg!" I groan understanding what they mean. "I assume that means that they're dead?"

"Got that right!" Justin proclaims holding his side. That is when I realize he is bleeding.

"You're cut!" Nicole exclaims, unwinding her arms from around her own body, trying to get warm.

"Don't worry about me," Justin gushes. "Did you find Mom, Mrs. Marquez?"

"I couldn't find her," Mom tells our group.

"I saw her," Ando says, breathing heavy. "They have her."

"Who has her?" we all ask.

He pauses, turning back to the sea.

"Mermaids."

CHAPTER TWELVE

Jordan and Justin are on their way to the hospital with their father while we are back at our house coming up with a plan to save Mrs. Wong. Unable to focus her nervous energy, Nicole is pacing and chewing on her fingernails. Ando, always thinking ahead, is bottling more of the cure just in case we need extra. Mom, our very own resident *Athena*, is contemplating battle strategies before we retrieve Nicole's mother from the clan of Mermaids. I, being mortal now, load up some equipment in a waterproof bag in case of an emergency.

"What are you putting in there?" Nicole grills as I pack my surprise.

"A few essentials." I grin, mischievously.

"What sort of *essentials*?" she asks, reaching for the bag.

"Take a peek." I smile, opening the duffle and allowing her to look inside.

Seeing my secret stash of weapons, she immediately perks up.

"Ooh-la la!" Nicole chuckles, wickedly. "Nice! Very nice!"

"I thought these might come in handy." I wink, confidently.

Feeling left out, Ando comes running over. He has always been nosey. Even when he was a baby he would cry if I did not let him open all of my presents before he opened his.

"May I see?" Ando implores as he peers in. "May I use that?"

"No," I respond, zipping the bag closed. "You've never used one of these before. I have."

"Please, Lena," he begs with a whiny voice.

"No way," I huff, picturing him hurting himself and me getting grounded for life because of it.

"Dad taught you how to use it?" he queries with a pouty lip. "Why didn't he teach me?"

"That's right." I grin. "He taught me on one of our water testing trips. He thought I was ready and responsible."

"I'm ready." He beams. "And responsible."

"But you're a Siren, and Nicole and I are not," I remind, pretending to pinch his chubby cheeks.

Not amused, he continues to pout.

"It would still be cool to use one of those," he says with sparkling eyes.

"Maybe another time," I reply more seriously.

"Show me how to use it," Nicole states with trembling lips.

My mind instantly runs through every unfortunate scenario that could possibly occur, all ending with Nicole's inevitable death. I do not want to have to explain that to the Wong family members and I certainly do not want that on my conscience. Sadly, I have to deal with enough blame as it is.

"You don't have to go with us," I remind, sympathetically.

"She's my mother," Nicole jabs.

"But you've got no powers," I fire back.

"Neither do you," she pokes me verbally.

"Girls!" Mom interrupts our banter. "Stop arguing. I can barely hear myself think."

Suddenly, Nicole and I both go silent. I know that I do not have any powers and I could die trying to save Mrs. Wong, but something deep inside of me needs to help with this mission. I love Mrs. Wong, all of the Wong's actually. They have stood by us and welcomed us into their family with open arms. We have gathered together for Thanksgiving, Christmas, New Year's Eve, Easter and every birthday and anniversary celebration imaginable. They are a part of our family.

For good or bad.

"I'll show *both of you* how to use one of these." I grin. "But no playing around. You don't want to take someone's eye out. Even Sirens need to be careful."

Ando gives me a thumbs up.

"I got it, Lena." He salutes. "No being silly."

"Exactly!" I grin, sounding like my mother.

"Nicole," I press. "Do you understand?"

"Yes, sir, ma'am-sir," she teases, saluting also.

Amused, I chuckle at both of them.

"We'll be out back, Mom," I convey as we head outside.

No need to break anything inside the house. Mom would kill us before the Mermaids have a chance to. Mischievously, I smile to myself knowing that we are about to become our own little army of four.

Watch out Mermaids! Here we come!

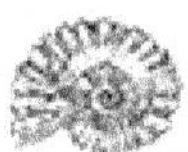

About an hour later, Nicole and I board the speedboat, but before I start it, we say a quick prayer. I have never been so nervous in my entire life. Neither has Nicole, who is still gnawing on her fingernails like a piranha chomping on a finger.

"Would you please stop that?" I request, untying the boat from the makeshift dock cleats. "You're making me more nervous than I already am."

Nicole frowns.

"I'm sorry," she apologizes, refraining from her bad habit. "But you chewing on ice all evening was just as unnerving."

"I chew ice when I'm nervous or upset," I admit. "It makes me feel better."

"Well… biting my nails makes me feel better," she grunts.

"I'll make you a deal." I start the engine. "You don't bite your nails for the rest of the night, and I promise not to chew on ice when we get back. Deal?"

Nicole thinks about it for a second or two.

"Deal!" She smiles.

"Are you ready?" Mom calls from the entrance to our little cove, only her head above the waves.

"We're as ready as we'll ever be!" I shout, waving my hand.

Nicole groans.

"Do you think this is actually going to work?" The teen raises her hand to her mouth but quickly returns it to her side.

"My mom is amazing when it comes to battle strategies," I reply, proudly. "Her father was a captain in the Roman Navy. He taught her everything he knew about winning skirmishes."

"That's amazing," Nicole whistles in awe. "It's hard to believe that your mother is hundreds of years old."

"Tell me about it," I snort.

"When was she born?"

"In one-hundred-seventeen A-D," I confess, recalling the conversation.

Nicole does a quick mental calculation.

"That means she's almost two-thousand years old," my best friend gasps.

"I'll be exactly one-thousand-nine-hundred and one years old in a few months," Mom answers from thirty feet away.

"Wow!" Nicole gleams. "So freaking cool!"

"Don't give her a big head," I joke, knowing Mom can hear that too.

I am not surprised when my mother sticks her tongue out at me.

"Enough chit-chat," Mom states frankly. "We can't stall any longer ladies."

With shaking hands, I grab the wheel and slowly ease out of the cove. The sea is unusually calm tonight which makes me less nervous. No need to worry about falling out of the boat and drowning.

Off we go, cruising across the surface at top speed, the salty spray misting our faces. Mom and Ando are somewhere under the waves, but of course we cannot see them. Nicole sits perfectly still reminding me of a statue. I can tell that she is terrified. I would know since I am about to wet my pants.

"Are you frightened?" I ask, wanting to keep my mind off of what we are about to do.

"Aren't you?" she questions back.

I nod.

With that said, we remain silent for the rest of the short trip.

Less than twenty minutes later, we arrive at the outer reef that protects the inlet where the mangrove cove is located. Privy to what we are about to do, my heartbeat increases, and I hope that I do not have a heart attack. Even without my Siren hearing, I can hear Nicole's pounding heart as well.

To our left, Mom and Ando surface without so much as a single bubble. They are in stealth mode; Mom covered in her hardest scales and talons at full length. Ando is armed with a sharp knife in his back pocket. The night is so quiet that our accelerated heartbeats can be heard. I am sure that Ando must hear it too because he stops as well, straining to decipher what is making the deafening rhythmic noise. Mom looks at us too.

"Sorry," I mouth, embarrassed and turning red.

"Can you hear it, Mom?" Ando whispers.

Mom nods but does not reply. I am guessing that they have now switched to telepathy since they are nodding without speaking aloud. I really wish I could still do that.

"Can you hear it?" I whisper to Nicole.

"It sounds like frogs croaking," my friend tells flatly.

"That's how Mermaids communicate," I educate, swallowing the remaining saliva still left in my mouth.

"That's creepy," Nicole mumbles in a hushed tone.

Just as I am about to make another informative comment, my mother motions for me to remain silent. As is her custom, she closes her eyes and then suddenly opens them. She wears a deadly expression on her beautiful face.

"Selena, get ready," Mom murmurs. "Ando, you've got my six."

Ando nods his understanding.

"Don't forget the plan," Mom mouths, and we notice that she has switched on her Siren-vision.

Nicole and I nod and cross our fingers.

Just as was discussed back at the house, I turn on Dad's fish-finder. The electronic sonar system lets Nicole and I see everything that is happening under the boat, so we can be ready for our part of the plan. Nicole looks like she is about to puke. I feel the same way.

"Are you ready for this?" I inquire at barely a whisper.

"Not even a little," she squeaks. "Do you really think we can pull this off?"

Wanting to reassure her, I open my mouth to answer, but a large blip on the fish-finder catches my attention. As we watch, the one hefty blip turns into two blips then three and finally four. I show Mom and Ando four fingers, and they quickly disappear under the waves.

Good grief! All of this drama is going to give me an ulcer.

"We're up," I relay to Nicole as I restart the engine and gun into the inlet.

Nicole keeps an eye on the sonar screen as I drive, watching for protruding roots, wily clumps of seaweed, and of course, murderous Mermaids.

"There's nothing following us," my friend updates with a smile. "Your Mom and Ando are keeping them busy, I guess."

Expertly, I steer the boat into the shallows and tie it to a thick mangrove root so it will not float out to sea. In mission mode, Nicole grabs the bag and we both exit the vessel to begin our search of the completely dark mangrove forest. It is so dark that I feel as if I have vertigo even though I am on firm ground.

"Did you grab the stars?" I whisper to Nicole as she trails a few feet behind me.

Immediately, she holds up the plastic bag of neon-green glowing, plastic stars and starts dropping them behind us like *Hansel and Gretel* dropping breadcrumbs behind them to find their way out of the forest. In our case, substitute mangroves for woods and Mermaids for witches.

Basically, it is the same ice cream, only a different flavor.

"Pass me the flashlight," I mumble to Nicole who speedily opens the bag and gets the LED flashlight.

"Why are we using such a bright light?" my sidekick queries as she switches it on. "Do we want the Mermaids to know we are here?"

"They already know we're here," I illuminate, breaking her bubble. "Mermaids are sensitive to bright light. I'm hoping if they come after us, we can use this flashlight as a weapon."

"Great idea!" She smiles, liking my logic.

I giggle at the fact that we both are not hiding in the hull of the speedboat.

"I have my moments," I playfully jest, easing our nervousness just a bit.

Determined to be helpful, Nicole quickens her pace and I match hers. I am sure she is eager to locate her mother. I am too.

"Hand me one of the bottles of tonic," I request, traveling deeper into the densely packed trees.

"It smells like mildew in here," Nicole announces, pinching her nose closed and breathing through her mouth.

"Don't think about it," I ease, finding it difficult to ignore the pungent scent of something utterly stinky.

Quite efficiently, she retrieves a bottle of the cure and places it in my hand. Her palm is sweaty, but so is mine. For some reason, we grin at our lack of fortification. As we turn the corner, the light hits something causing it to pull back into the shadows.

"Nicole," I gulp, my hands perspiring even more.

"What is it?" Nicole grabs my elbow as she comes to a complete standstill.

"Over there." I shine the light at a large clump of trees.

Nicole gasps and steps back, but I grab her hand to keep her close.

Several feet ahead of us, we see two pale-faced Mermaids using their hands to shield their eyes from the bright artificial light.

"Turn it on high," I insist, and immediately the light doubles in brightness.

Instantly, we hear several deafening screeches as the creatures race further back into the shadows.

"Do you see her?" Nicole begs, tugging at my arm. "Do you see my mom?"

"Wait," I respond, noticing a mound lying on the damp, muddy ground. "I see something."

Immediately, we start running toward it and almost trip over it.

"Mom!" Nicole bellows, kneeling to examine her mother who appears to be knocked out. "Mom, wake up!"

Using the opportunity to our advantage, I uncap the water bottle and pry open Mrs. Wong's mouth. Without hesitation, I pour some in and pinch her nose closed. To my surprise, she coughs and sputters but manages to drink all of it. I do it again until the entire bottle is empty.

On the brink of tears, Nicole gently taps her on the face, hoping she will open her eyes. Finally, she does.

"Mom, can you walk?" Nicole queries, almost hysterical.

Weakly, her mother nods and allows her daughter to help her to her feet.

"Get her to the boat before the convulsions start," I warn, recalling when Nicole drank the tonic.

Slowly, they turn to leave when Nicole turns back.

"What about you?" she asks with a furrowed forehead. "I'm not leaving you here."

"I'll be right behind you," I fib, crossing my fingers behind my back for good measure.

"Don't be too long or I'm coming back for you," my best friend counters with sass.

"Copy that!" I salute with a grin.

"I'm serious," she frowns, and I know she is.

"Go now," I order and as I turn to retrieve the duffle, I am grabbed by several pale hands clawing and pulling me into the lightless, impenetrable void that lurks beneath the thick canopy of the mangroves.

"Selena!" Nicole screams, turning back to help me, almost dropping her mother's weak form.

"Leave!" I command just as I get pulled down to the ground and several freezing bodies pile on top of me, pinning me to the ground.

"Damn it!" Nicole shouts. *"Selena!"*

"Go!" I yell at the top of my lungs. "Don't look back!"

"Okay!" she shrieks over her shoulder, as she retreats as fast as she can with her groggy mother in tow.

With all my might, I kick and punch at the creatures. In the darkness, I manage to strike one in the chest, another in the groin and still another in the face… possibly. Thank heaven their skin actually gives off a soft glow and by chance I spot the flashlight laying a few feet away. Using all of my strength, I start head butting and wind up bashing a few body parts. When their grip loosens, I crawl on my belly toward the device and grab it. Wasting no time, I click it on to the brightest setting.

"Take that you beast—"

Eardrum shattering squeals and screams echo against the trees, and I know I have only a small window of time to flee. Bolting to my feet, I grab the bow and arrows that I packed from inside of the bag and load one of the spears, tucking the rest under my arm. The duffel bag itself, I sling across my body. It is heavy and uncomfortable, but still manageable.

Then I snatch two more things. The solar flares that turn night into day, according to my stepfather who used them many times and who just so happened to keep them always on hand. Thank goodness for David, always saving the day even though he is not here.

"Selena!" Nicole screams from ahead. "Help me!"

Hearing those words, I ignite the flares and throw them behind me as I run toward Nicole's cries. I manage to glance over my shoulder, shocked that no one is following me.

"Nicole!" I shout back. "I'm coming!"

When I exit the mangroves, I see why Nicole is screaming. In the boat there are two more Mermaids waiting for her… waiting for *us*. Without hesitation, I bring up my bow, aim and fire. Like a bullet, it whizzes through the night towards its target. Everything else goes quiet. It is a direct hit! Right in the short one's heart! The impact of the bolt knocks the dead Mermaid into the water, but the other one lunges at me and knocks the weapon out of my hands.

"Get in the boat, Nicole!" I yell. "Start it! Don't forget to untie it!"

Like a good sailor, the petite brunette follows my instructions and idles as I struggle to get the beast off me. Not caring if I have been reduced to chick-fighting, I grab the creature's platinum hair and pull with everything I have. After several yanks that rip bunches of hair out of its scalp, it lets out a high screech then releases me. Tired of being stalked, I grab one of the spears and ram it straight into its translucent chest, splitting bone and squirting blood without much effort.

Woot! Finally, some payback!

With Mrs. Wong safely in the vessel and with no signs of Mermaids, I search the waves for Mom and Ando.

"Ando!" I yell, but there is no reply. "Where the hell are you?"

"I'm here Lena!" I hear Ando's voice as he hoists himself into the boat. "Mom is right behind me."

Mom bursts out of the water holding the decapitated head of a Mermaid in her left hand, and I almost lose my lunch. Carelessly, she tosses it aside like a hollowed-out coconut husk then leisurely, she swims to the boat and pulls her body inside.

"Let's go home," she gasps, out of breath.

With sweat dripping in my eyes and hardly any oxygen left in my lungs, I throttle the boat and aim in the direction of our house. Behind us, it is clear of Mermaids.

"How did it go?" I ask, finally relaxing after our ordeal.

"Better than expected." Mom smiles as she hugs Ando to her side.

"Ando?" I glance at him. "What about you?"

He chuckles.

"I got to karate-chop some Mermaids!" he proclaims animatedly.

Mom musses his hair.

"I was a good helper," he brags with a broad grin.

"Yes, you were." Mom laughs. "Yes, you were."

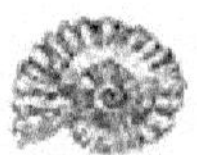

Mrs. Wong sleeps for over an hour before the symptoms of taking the tonic reveal themselves. Unlike Nicole, she does not have a fever but develops a migraine that completely incapacitates her. It is so debilitating that we must keep her in a dark room with the air conditioner set to a continuously cold temperature. When she does finally wake, she is a bit stiff and queasy, but besides that she is back to her regular spirited self.

"Mermaids, huh," Mrs. Wong whistles with bewilderment as she sips a hot cup of herbal tea.

"What do you remember, Mom?" Nicole rests a small saucer of dry toast on the table in front of her. In her weakened state, her mother takes a couple of bites before she pushes her plate away.

"Not much," Mrs. Wong shares with us. "Your father and I were taking a walk along the beach, enjoying the sunset when we heard a female voice calling for help from the surf near the reef."

Natasha, Nicole's mother, takes another drink of her cooling tea.

"Of course, since your father is a fantastic swimmer, he jumps in first." The female smiles proudly. "I bring up the rear, but when we get to the spot where the woman was… she's gone."

Natasha stops talking and just stares out of the window at the rising sun. We all can guess what she is thinking.

How can this be happening? How can any of this be real? Who could blame her?

Not me.

"Keep going, Mom," Nicole encourages, sitting beside her at the dining table.

"We searched the water for several minutes, when something grabbed my leg." Mrs. Wong's voice lowers, and she begins to nervously play with the cross pendant on her necklace.

"That must have been terrifying," Nicole soothes as she holds her mother's trembling hands.

"It was," Natasha gulps then returns to her tea for comfort.

"Please, go on," my mother presses, wanting to hear the entire story.

"It pulls me under, but Donald struggles with it and it lets me go for a second," she whispers as a tear rolls down her flushed cheek. "Your father got scratched up pretty good, but it wasn't anything life-threatening."

There is no noise in the kitchen, not even that of us breathing. Nicole's mother just sits silently, holding her tea in between her palms and staring outside. My heart breaks for her.

"Is there anything else, Natasha?" Mom pipes up.

"When it pulled me under, it dug its claws into my leg, then it bit a chunk of its own flesh off and held it against the wound on my leg," Mrs. Wong explains with confusion.

"There's a lump at the base of your neck," I add, hoping she will remember.

Mrs. Wong sits straighter in her seat, her hands tightening on the cup.

"That happened when I returned to the beach," Natasha explains as she closes her eyes.

We all are intently listening. I can actually see the events playing out in my mind's eye. I can even smell the scent of the sea mixing with the hibiscus bushes that line the path that leads to the beach from the parking lot.

There is a pregnant pause before she continues.

"I felt a blow to the back of my neck and when I woke up, I was... *here*." She scans around the room.

"Do you remember anything else?" Nicole questions.

"I vaguely recall getting back to the house, but I wasn't myself," she admits, rubbing the back of her neck.

"The boys said you and Dad got into a fight," Nicole inserts the thought, wanting to jog her memory.

"Your father was cleaning my wound... I d-don't know what—" her explanation stops abruptly.

Nicole shrugs, not knowing what to do or say next. How can you comfort someone who now has intimate knowledge that true unadulterated evil actually exists? There are no pamphlets for this sort of trauma.

"Donald mentioned something about my eyes being black and then… " her words trail off as she returns to looking out of the window at the slowly rising ball of fire.

"I have flashes of memory," Nicole confirms in a sheepish tone. "It's like I'm watching television, but I can't rewind or fast-forward or change what's happening."

"You never told me this," I say, feeling even worse.

"I didn't want you to feel guiltier than you already do," the young woman replies with a compassionate glimmer in her eyes. "You've been through enough, Selena."

"The aunts said that this would happen," Mom reveals. "When a Mermaid possesses its victim, the person's personality is suppressed and theirs takes over. They are the puppet master, and you are the puppet."

"That really sucks," Nicole groans.

"I bet it does." I pout, sitting beside her.

"How are we supposed to live with this?" Natasha questions, her temper rising. "How do we feel less violated?"

"I don't know—" I start.

"Ando and I can wipe your minds," Mom offers with red cheeks.

"Like brainwashing?" Natasha probes, uncomfortably.

"No, not at all," Mom explains. "We can take everything that's associated with the supernatural and wipe the slate clean."

"We wouldn't know about any of this?" Natasha asks with bright eyes.

"That's right." Mom smiles.

"Wait!" Nicole looks at each of us individually. "Will you also take the memories of what you are too?"

My mother nods.

"We would be just regular, normal, run-of-the-mill friends." Mom chuckles. "Not *supernatural* friends… neighbors who enjoy each other's company."

"Does it have to be done now?" Nicole's eyes well with tears.

"I'm just putting it out on the table," Mom states sweetly.

"Will you eat our brains if we don't comply?" Natasha queries with saucer-sized eyes and a gaping mouth.

Everyone else in the room laughs.

"Absolutely, not!" Mom blushes and smirks.

"Are you Mermaids too?" Mrs. Wong confronts, glancing at the exit.

"Nope!" Ando joins the conversation at last. "We're *Sirens*. We don't have tails."

"Sirens?" Nicole's mom repeats with a chuckle. "From Greek mythology? *Those* kinds of Sirens?"

"Yes and no," our mother educates with a grin.

As if she has rehearsed this particular speech umpteen times, Mom explains our origins using a more simplistic and easily understandable format. I can tell that she has done this many times before and will probably do this many more times in the future. When all is said and done, Mrs. Wong whistles, shakes her head and after moments of silence finally speaks.

"I could use a drink," she replies on a loud exhale.

"More tea, Mrs. Wong?" I ask, standing at the ready.

Natasha shakes her head.

"I was thinking more in the line of *wine*," Nicole's mother sighs as she returns to staring out of the window at a brand-new day.

CHAPTER THIRTEEN

The house seems so quiet since Mrs. Wong and Nicole have returned home. The twins and Mr. Wong were anxiously waiting for them. According to Jordan, his father only has a swollen ankle and all that is needed is a few cold compresses. The scrapes will heal on their own with just a little bit of *Neosporin* or something similar.

"Have you spoken to Nicole since this morning?" Mom checks the temperature of the charcoal grill.

"I thought that she might want a little space," I admit, searching the utensil drawer for a sharp knife. If I cannot find one, I know where my brother has them stashed in his room. He told me they are there in case we get attacked again. He refuses to be caught off guard and who could blame him. I have been sleeping with the flashlight and my bow and arrows near my bed.

"How are we going to take care of this Mermaid situation?" I ask, seasoning my ribeye with salt, pepper, granulated garlic, and onion powder as Mom lightly sears a whole salmon on the grill for her and Ando.

The Siren does not answer, only makes herself busy tending to the charcoals.

I have to admit that the aroma of the fish does not entice me in the least. Since I have become human, I have been craving things like pork chops with mashed potatoes, pizza with extra pepperoni and less seafood. It is strange that only a few short weeks ago, I was eating raw seafood right out of the ocean. Scales and all.

"My steak is ready for the grill," I say with anticipation of tearing into the succulent piece of meat.

"You're more than welcome to have some of our salmon." Mom smiles and winks playfully.

I make a gagging face.

"No, thank you." I giggle, chopping the vegetables for our shared salad.

Everything is neatly laid out on the countertop: lettuce, tomatoes, carrots, beets, mushrooms, red and yellow sweet bell peppers, and croutons. Every salad, in my opinion, needs croutons. Croutons are the best part of the entire thing. Without them there would be no need to consume leafy greens.

Mom disagrees with me of course and so does Ando, who once ate an entire bag of mixed greens in one sitting. If he were not a Siren, he would be a rabbit or some sort of herbivore. I, needless to say, have always been a true-blue carnivore. The meatier it is, the better it is as far as I am concerned.

"There's enough space on the grill," Mom lets me know. "Go ahead and put it on so we can all eat at the same time."

"Sounds like a plan," I grin, gently placing the steak on the area of grates above the hottest glowing coals. It sizzles beautifully and immediately begins to cook. The aroma of salmon intermixed with the tender ribeye is a thing of beauty.

"How do you want your steak done?" Mom queries as she checks on its progress. "Rare or medium-rare?"

I make a disgusted face.

"Medium-well, please." I smirk, licking my lips.

"That's surprising." She grins. "Before you liked your steaks cooked rare or barely medium-rare."

I smile.

"Now I prefer them medium-well," I state without hesitation.

Obviously starving, Ando sniffs the salmon.

"I think it's ready." The boy beams, his eyes fixed on the large fish. "It smells ready."

Mom grins.

"I think you are correct," our parent responds with enthusiasm as she removes the fish and places it gingerly on an extra-large serving platter.

"Is the salad done, Lena?" Ando asks, running to the fridge to get the bottles of salad dressing.

"It's ready." I smile at my colorful and healthy creation. "How much longer on my steak, Mom?"

Just like a professionally trained chef would do, my mother pokes the piece of beef with her finger like Dad taught her. When it is at the perfect firmness, she removes it from the heat and places it on a plate to rest. It looks and smells amazing. My stomach growls in agreement.

"Food's ready!" Ando announces before anyone else can.

Thinking ahead, my brother has already set the dining table and gotten us glasses of water. He has even placed a paper napkin near each plate. The table looks wonderful. All it needs is us.

"Lena, please pass the blue cheese dressing." My brother points to the bottled salad dressing near my dish.

"You got it!" I smile.

Carefully, I hand it to Mom who hands it to him. He wastes no time squirting a hefty dollop of the thick, rich, creamy mixture. As is his custom, Ando uses his fingers to break off chunks of the semi-raw fish, dip it into the dressing, and then pops it into his awaiting mouth. Next, he uses his fork to eat his salad. He goes between his fingers and fork until all of his food is finished.

"Jenny comes home tomorrow," I proclaim to everyone at the table.

"She's been gone all summer," Mom replies as she uses her utensils to cut her fish into bite-sized pieces. "I'm sure her grandparents have missed her."

"*I've* missed her." I smile. "She's the crazy glue that holds our group together."

"Yeah," Ando agrees. "She promised to bring me back an Ireland t-shirt."

"That was thoughtful of her." Mom grins as she loads her fork with salad.

"Nicole and I can't wait to see her," I confess with zeal. "We've got so much to tell her."

"Are you gonna tell her about the Mermaids?" my brother asks, still chewing a mouthful of salmon.

"Of course we will," I answer then cut a piece of steak. It melts all over my tongue.

"Do you want to taste my fish?" Ando asks, eyeing my meat.

"No, I do not," I say then stick my tongue out at him.

With a salivating tongue he continues to stare at my dinner.

"Would you like a piece of my steak?" I playfully roll my eyes.

"Yes, please." He grins and opens his mouth like a baby bird waiting for its momma to feed it a juicy worm.

"What time is she landing?" Mom asks then takes a drink of water.

"Around noon," I reply, taking another bite. "Jenny promised to call us when she arrived home."

"Are you going to see her?" Ando questions as he finishes his supper and looks over at Mom's. "Can I have that?"

He points to the last bit of salmon near the tail end of the fish. I cannot believe that my brother can eat more than my mother. It will be impossible to feed him when he is a teenager. Mom will need three jobs just to keep him supplied with cereal.

"Do you and Nicole need a ride?" Mom inquires, helping Ando get the remaining fish onto his plate.

"One of the twins is meant to give us a ride," I inform, pouring myself another glass of water. Sadly, I look down at my plate and realize that my steak is almost finished.

"When can I take my driver's test?" I ask, out of the blue.

"Are you ready to take it?" my mother probes, taking another bite of salad.

"I've been studying," I admit, reaching for more salad. "And Dad said I was a terrific driver. He described me as 'extremely conscientious and safe'."

"I do remember him saying that." The beautiful Siren smirks, and this time the memory does not make her cry.

"If you let me drive with you a few times, I should be fine," I beg with hands clenched in prayer.

"We can start again tomorrow," Mom replies with a nervous glimmer.

"Great!" I proclaim, eagerly, imagining the wind blowing my hair as it rushes in the open driver's side window. "I'll get the crash helmets from the garage."

Mom's eyes widen and she almost chokes on her water.

"I'm just joking around." I laugh, figuratively patting myself on the back. "When can I take the actual test?"

"Whenever you can get an appointment at the DMV." Mom grins.

"Are you serious?" I rest my fork on my plate, knowing that the local DMV has been backlogged from the beginning of forever.

"Extremely serious." Mom smirks, handing my brother his napkin so he can wipe a smudge of dressing off of his chin.

Still overjoyed, I jump up and give her a tight hug and a kiss on the cheek.

"Why all the urgency to get your license?" Mom grills with narrowed eyes.

"Nicole is going to take her test next week and Jenny, Mike, and Andrew already have theirs," I say with disappointment. "I don't want to be the only one without one."

"Makes sense to me." She motions for Ando to go and wash his face and hands. I think that boy misses his mouth half of the time. If we had a dog or cat, it would never go hungry because there are always scraps under Ando's chair.

"Mom," he states in a low tone.

"Yes, my baby," Mom answers, turning to him.

"I'm still hungry." He pretends to pout.

"Would you like a sandwich?" she offers, shaking her head.

"Do we have any more tuna salad?" my brother questions as he gets up from the table and makes a beeline to the refrigerator.

"There's a bowl of it on the second shelf inside of a blue-lidded container," Mom informs as she looks over her shoulder at him. "Please don't make a mess."

Ando smiles as he takes out the container of tuna fish along with the bread. After he constructs the sandwich, he goes to the pantry to get something to accompany it. A second later, we hear him rustling around and Mom and I both look at the pantry door then at each other.

"What are you looking for?" Mom grills from her seat.

"Do we have any more pretzels?"

"No, you finished those last week, remember?" our mother chuckles then takes her last bite of fish.

"What about those pita thingies?" he adds.

"They're finished too." Mom smirks and rolls her eyes.

"I saw a bag of granola in here this morning." His voice is muffled.

"Mrs. Wong and I snacked on those," Mom tells her still starving son.

"Mommy, are we out of Crackleberry Crisps too?" he huffs.

"That one is on me," I confess, guiltily. "I ate the rest of it a couple days ago."

"Did you put it on the grocery list?" The unseen six-year-old sulks from inside the enclosed space.

I simply give her a puppy-dog face hoping to look cute enough to be reprieved of a lecture.

"What can I eat with my sandwich?" The desperate male complains from the pantry making Mom and I giggle.

My brother, the bottomless pit. Hopefully, he does not eat us out of house and home. Mom and I will turn into skeletons at this rate. I feel sorry for whoever marries him.

Jenny's flight lands right on time, and the reason I know this is that Nicole and I have been tracking it by app as it flies across the Atlantic toward Isla Flora. Unfortunately, Isla Flora's airport cannot handle huge continental jets, so Jenny will have to land at a neighboring island with a bigger airport then take a smaller shuttle plane to our tiny island. When the app shows that she has made her connecting flight and is now landing, Nicole and I ask the twins to drive us to Jenny's grandparents' house.

Jenny's grandparents live on the opposite side of the island and have an amazing view of the lush Isla Flora valley. It is a small home, big enough for three people comfortably. In my opinion, it is quaint, cozy, and filled with love. Jenny says she never wants to leave. In contrast, her grandparents both hope she will change her mind. They love their granddaughter, but they want the opportunity to miss her.

"Do you think she will be surprised?" Nicole asks, holding up her *'Welcome Home Jenny'* sign.

I laugh at her.

"I think she will be ecstatic," I snicker, looking at the artfully decorated banner that we painted in pastels at Nicole's house.

"How's your mom and Dad?" I query as we drive through town. "I didn't see them."

"They had to go to work today." Nicole frowns. "My brothers are going to close the store tonight so they can get some rest."

"If they need any help, I don't mind taking a couple of shifts," I say as we pass the waterfront. There are a group of islanders standing in line to buy freshly caught fish, but the area is not crowded like it usually is.

"May I ask you a question?" Nicole's brother glances over at me, since I am sitting beside him in the passenger seat.

"What's your question?" I counter, looking out the window.

"You've made it clear that you're not a Mermaid," he states, firmly.

"That's right." I chuckle. "I'm… I mean I *was* a Siren."

"Sirens lured sailors to their death with their singing," he answers using a monotonous tone.

"That's not exactly right," I reply, still not making eye contact.

"But you are a killer," he sneers, and I can feel his stare burning into my face. "I mean your entire line are killers."

"Justin!" Nicole snaps. "Be quiet!"

"But it's true," he continues. "I read it on the internet."

Nicole laughs.

"Don't believe everything you read on the internet," his younger sister smirks. "You should know that."

With his aggravation growing, Justin growls.

"Several websites claim that *'to follow a Siren is to follow death'*," Nicole's brother quotes. "Is that true, Selena?"

"Yes," I manage to say, hating where this one-sided conversation is heading.

"Why aren't you a Siren anymore?" Justin questions with fervor.

"I was doing things that I shouldn't have, and lost my powers because of it," I confess, wiping the tear that is rolling down the side of my face.

"So, the *'Greek gods'* are punishing you," he interjects, boldly.

"The *Earth* is punishing me," I whisper, wanting to jump out of the moving vehicle, but I cannot since humans do not heal like Sirens do.

Nicole snarls louder and hits the back of his seat with her hand.

"Justin, leave her alone before I kick the crap out of you!" she threatens calmly.

"It's okay, Nicole." I sniffle, feeling like I deserve to be verbally bashed. "I deserve it."

"It's because of you that our parents were attacked." Justin ignores his sister's threats.

"I'm sorry," I mutter, feeling more hot tears streaming down my face.

"You're sorry?" the twin glares at me then turns to face forward once more. "Sorry doesn't help."

The next thing I know, Nicole smacks her brother on the back of the head.

"Ouch!" he shouts, rubbing where she struck. "Cut it out! I'm driving! Do you want us to end up in a ditch?"

"Be quiet, you jerk!" his sister chastises, and I see her right hand ball into a tight fist.

"You need to choose your friends more carefully," Justin states matter-of-factly. "She's bad news, Nicole. Her whole family is trouble."

Nicole rolls her eyes in protest.

"I should have asked Jordan to drive us," Nicole exclaims, loudly.

"That wouldn't have happened." Justin smirks.

"Why?" Nicole whines at the edge of her extremely short rope.

"Because Jordan is terrified of her… of *them*," the twin reveals his brother's secret without shame.

Thank heavens, just then we pull in front of Jenny's house. It is a welcomed sight after such a grueling trip. Justin won't look at me, Nicole is furious with her brother, and I am just wishing that a meteorite will land on my head and squish me into pudding.

"I'll get my mom to pick me up from Jenny's," I say as I get out of the Jeep.

"Good idea," Justin replies, not making eye contact.

With great haste, Nicole exits the backseat, her lips pursed together tightly.

"I'll pick you up in a few hours," Justin apprises his sister.

"Don't bother," Nicole responds, slamming the door. "I'll catch a ride with Mrs. Marquez."

"Fine," Justin snarls. "Good luck not getting your face ripped off."

"You are a complete moron." Nicole smacks him again as she walks past his open window.

"Maybe this isn't such a good idea," I express, wanting the day to reset. Actually, I wish the entire last few months could be reset.

"Don't let my annoying brother ruin our visit with Jenny," Nicole pleads, nudging my arm with her boney elbow.

"I don't want anyone else to get hurt," I proclaim out of nowhere.

"No one is going to get hurt." Nicole smiles, warmly.

As we stand discussing Justin's newfound hatred for me and 'my kind', Jenny comes flying out of the house. She looks wonderful. Her face has filled-out, her hair has darkened a few shades into a deep auburn, and she is wearing contact lenses.

"Oh, my gravy!" I squeal like a happy piglet. "You look fabulous!"

Jenny hugs me first then Nicole.

"Wow!" Nicole gasps. "You look like a supermodel!"

"Well, I did do a couple of photoshoots over the summer," Jenny blushes.

"You never told me that," Nicole gushes and grins.

"How did that happen?" I pull Jenny onto the front porch as we all settle on the porch swing. "C'mon! Spill it!"

"My cousin, Rory, is a fashion photographer," Jenny enlightens with a braces-free smile that lights up the room. "He took me to work with him one day, and one of his models called in sick. So, he asked me to take her place."

"Wow!" Nicole repeats, touching our friend's softly flowing auburn tresses. "I'm so jealous."

"Don't be." Jenny snickers. "I hated every minute of it."

"Why?" Nicole and I both ask at once.

"I had to starve myself for the rest of the summer," the sassy redhead blusters. "Thank goodness I got a head start on piling on the pounds when I first got there."

"Was the food good?" Nicole questions with a grin.

Jenny's eyes light up.

"It was fantastic!" She beams, blue eyes glazing over. "My aunt, Fiona, is an amazing cook. She's just like your mom, Nicole!"

"Is that why you've gained a few pounds?" I tease, poking her on the side with my finger.

"Ha! Ha! Ha!" she mocks sarcastically. "You're so funny!"

Unable to help ourselves, we embrace each other again.

"Aunt Fiona taught me how to cook," Jenny reveals with a grimace.

"Really?" Nicole and I say in unison.

"What can you make?" I interrogate, settling onto the comfortable cushion.

"Simple things like cottage pie, Irish soda bread, colcannon —
"

"Colcannon?" Nicole and I both repeat. "What is colcannon?"

Jenny smiles.

"It's mashed potatoes with cabbage," she explains, rubbing her belly. "My aunt puts bacon and lots of butter in it. It's basically a heart attack in a bowl, but it's amazing!"

We both look at her and give a cheesy grin.

"We've missed you," Nicole gushes. "A lot."

Jenny's brow furrows.

"What happened while I was gone?" the intuitive redhead demands. "Tell me everything."

"What makes you think that something happened?" I question, avoiding eye contact.

"Yeah." Nicole tries to play it off too but is terrible at it. "Suppose it was completely uneventful."

"Spill it," Jenny insists, propping her lower back with a cushion. "And don't leave anything out."

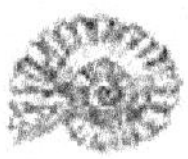

After twenty minutes of Nicole and I tag-teaming our spiel about David dying, me making-out with the God of War, turning into a full-fledged Siren, and losing my powers. Followed by Nicole's Mermaid possession, the abduction of Mrs. Wong, and a series of strange and unfortunate events that have led to this moment, Jenny lets out a long, high-pitched whistle.

"Repeat everything you just said," our best friend orders, taking a long breath. "This time, slowly."

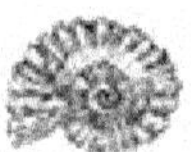

After approximately forty-five minutes, Jenny rubs her head and squints, her narrowed eyes making Nicole and I extremely nervous. Neither one of us can tell if she is stunned into silence, or if she is figuring out how to respond to our tale. All I know is that this is the longest period of time that the high school senior has ever been quiet.

"Can you please say something?" I beseech, nudging her left side.

"Anything?" Nicole hopes, nudging her on her right side.

Another moment passes as she remains immobile.

"I'm not exactly sure what to say," the usually outspoken young woman replies at last, scratching her head in total confusion.

"It's a lot of information at once, we know," I continue, wanting the Jenny of old to give us a tongue lashing, or start slapping us silly. Unfortunately, this new and improved Jenny sits with her legs crossed just thinking.

"You're going to have to give me a few days to process all of this," Jenny advises as she stands. "After all of that, we deserve some snacks."

Ahh! There's the old Jenny that I love!

"C'mon inside, ladies." The former tomboy ushers us inside of the neatly kept house. "We've got a great deal to figure out."

CHAPTER FOURTEEN

After Mom and I drop Nicole home and begin the short drive back to our house, my mother attempts to make conversation. I am not certain why she thinks I need cheering up, but she does. My brother is also studying me like I have sprouted another eye in the middle of my forehead.

"Please stop looking at me like that." I frown, hiding from my mother's reflection in the rearview mirror with my hands.

"Sorry," Mom mumbles and continues to drive. "Is there something you'd like to talk about?"

"No," I ponder the question and come up with nothing. "Why?"

"I have some bad news," Mom informs as she turns onto our street.

"What's the bad news?" I ask, bracing for the worst. "Tell me quickly."

"Mr. and Mrs. Wong don't want you and Nicole hanging out together anymore," Mom speaks speedily as if saying it fast will somehow hurt less.

"But why?" I blather; already my vision is becoming blurry.

"Why do you think?" Mom responds with a bit of sarcasm.

"It's not my fault that Mermaids attacked them," I sputter, indignantly.

Pfft! Of course it's my fault. Everything is my fault.

"Does Nicole know about this?" I interrogate as my blood pressure begins to rise.

Mom just glances at me using the glass.

"That's a stupid question," I grumble. "I know that it is not up to Nicole."

"I tried to reason with her parents, but they were unmovable." The disappointed Siren sighs.

"Wouldn't you be?" I retort, feeling my temples beginning to throb.

"What about you?" I grill Mom, who considers Mr. and Mrs. Wong her closest friends.

She shrugs her shoulders as if none of this matters, but it does.

"I'm sure Mr. and Mrs. Wong aren't going to be your friends either," I ramble, waiting for a response, but receiving none.

I cannot believe this is happening. *Wait!* I can believe this is happening. Not only do we still have a group of Mermaids after us, but now I am down a best friend. Things could not possibly get any worse. *Wait!* Of course it can.

"We should have seen this coming," I huff as my mother turns into the driveway.

"How could we have seen any of this coming?" Mom questions as she puts the vehicle in park and unlocks the doors.

"It's okay, Lena," Ando comforts, patting my shoulder. "I'm still your friend."

With tears threatening to fall, I still smile.

"You will always be my *bestest* friend in the whole wide world," I reassure using nonsensical words to make him laugh and blush.

"Thanks, Lena." Ando grins as he opens the back car door for me.

"Am I your best friend?" I probe, hoping his answer is yes.

"Nope," he surprises me.

"But I'm your sister," I gasp, appalled.

"Sisters can't be best friends with brothers," he tells without heat.

"Why not?" I demand as he opens our mother's door as well.

He shrugs his little shoulders.

"Because it's a rule," he pouts.

"I've never heard of that rule," I poke him as we wait for Mom to unlock the front door and turn off the security system.

"I was wondering when you were getting home." Melody grins as we march into the living room.

Stunned, we all stand staring at her. All except Ando who races toward her to hug her, but his entire body goes through her as though she is not really there. Mom steps in front of us, guarding us with her own body.

"Who are you?" Mom snarls, showing her teeth. "What are you doing in my house?"

"I thought Mermaids couldn't shapeshift," I say to Mom, so only she can hear.

"They cannot," the specter speaks, all the while it walks around the living area nodding in approval at our choice of furnishings. "Marina, this is quite lovely, by the way."

"Who are you?!" Ando snaps as he walks over to it and tries to kick it with his foot, but of course there is nothing there to kick.

"For goodness sakes, it really is me," the thing claiming to be Melody turns and goes into the kitchen.

"Prove it," I insist, keeping my distance.

"How?" the Melody look-alike questions from the other room, but before she can say anything we hear a tapping at the front window.

Turning around we see—

"Belen!" Ando shouts as he lets the horned owl inside. "Mom! Lena! It's Belen!"

"How can you tell that that is the *real* Belen?" Mom questions as she studies the bird's mannerisms. "It might be that witch's crow. Remember when she tricked us into thinking that it was Belen, but it turned out to be an imposter?"

Hearing that comment, Belen begins to chirp and hoot, and just as before, Ando understands him, but for some reason, so can I. Only Mom does not.

Weird!

"What's he saying?" our mother probes, inquisitively.

"He's describing Melody's cottage and the surrounding woods," I translate before my brother can. "He told us about the first time we saw him in the back garden when the rabbit stole a carrot, and it magically grew back."

Satisfied that he is who he says he is, I reach out to touch the magnificent bird, but as usual he puffs up his feathers and tries to bite me. Thankfully, my reflexes are better now that I am human, so I am able to pull my hand away before he can snap off one of my fingers with his beak.

As Ando and Mom stroke Belen's feathers, Melody returns from the kitchen. She looks just the same, like a beautiful robust grandmotherly type with pitch-black hair highlighted with tiny streaks of red, gold and bluish-purple. At this moment, her eyes are as aquamarine as ours are.

"Marina, your garden needs tending." Melody frowns, but like all of the women in my family it does not mar her beauty. "It is overgrown with weeds. They will suffocate the plants."

Mom folds her arms across her chest defiantly.

"You still need to prove your identity," our mother reminds harshly, turning away from the charming, yet temperamental owl.

Melody gives a saucy wink.

"As you wish," the transparent form states, cordially. "Please remember that I have not spoken Siren in thousands of years, so I may be slightly rusty. Here goes nothing."

First, she clears her throat and when she is ready, she begins.

Surprising us all, the woman claiming to be Melody speaks to us in perfect Siren. However, when she speaks it, it sounds lyrical and more like a love song instead of clicks, clacks, and whistles. Her version of Siren has us all in awe.

Too bad I can't speak or understand Siren anymore!

"Wow!" Mom, Ando, and I state with wide eyes and even wider mouths.

"How can you speak Siren so well?" Ando asks the question that we all want to know the answer to.

"I am the mother of *The Three*." Melody laughs and it reminds me of gently blowing wind chimes. "Who do you think helped invent the language?"

Touché!

"How can you *be* here, and *not* be here?" I query, moving my hands through her clear form.

"*Astral projection…* it is one of my gifts as a Muse." Melody smiles and turns to the sea. "You will have company tonight."

Ando's brows furrow.

"What does ass-tral-pro-jection mean?" he repeats, totally dumbfounded.

Mom speaks next.

"In simple terms it is when a person's soul or consciousness separates from their physical body and is able to travel throughout the universe on its own."

Melody presents Mom with a regal bow making her smile for only a moment.

"What kind of company?" Ando's eyes shine and his question brings us back to the problem at hand.

Melody's posture, which is impeccable, straightens even more. Her eyes automatically switch to an almost blood-red. Everything about her is more intensified and more intimidating. History and Literature always describe Muses as these dainty creatures that play the harp and sit half-naked on pianos, but that is not my great-grandmother. She is the original *Terminator*.

"The kind of company that cannot come out during the day," Melody warns, making the hairs on my arms stand on end.

Mom sits, then stands, then does the ritual all over again until she decides to remain on her feet.

"Why tonight?" Mom gulps, starting to pace.

"Tonight, will be a full moon," the Muse explains. "Just like Sirens their powers will be at their greatest strength tonight."

"Terrific!" Mom shouts, flailing her arms. "Just freaking terrific!"

Ando and I watch in silence.

"Can't we ever just get a break?" Mom is now shouting. "Just once!"

"I am sorry, young one," Melody apologizes with concern in her now gray eyes.

"We just culled almost a dozen of those things!" Mom still continues to rant; her demeanor is hardening and that scares the crap out of me and Ando.

Melody's face hardens too.

"More are on their way," she says simply, and to the point.

"How many?" Mom interrogates with an expressionless face.

"Too many to count," the Muse reveals with lowered eyes.

"When will they be here?" our mother presses for more information.

"When the moon is at its apex, they will come for you," Melody states flatly. "And the children."

Dear Father!

"There is no time for self-pity if you are going to survive the night, young one," Melody does not mince words. "The time has come for all good Sirens to put away their human façade and pick up their battle axes."

Battle axes? Is that symbolic? Or did we actually have battle axes at one point in time?

Hearing this, Mom clenches her hands into fists and stops pacing. She is wearing a look that I have never seen before and hopefully will never see again. On a mission, she goes to the garage and retrieves the same shovel that Ando attacked the

Mermaids with and marches into the backyard. Utterly enthralled, we watch as the Siren counts out ten paces from the blooming flamboyant tree that shades that part of our property.

When she reaches her mark, our mother begins to dig, first with the shovel then with bare hands and talons. Almost three feet under the ground, she removes something wrapped in burlap. Carefully, she unwraps it and brushes the dirt off. For a long moment, she stands and inspects her bounty and when she finally turns around, we see them.

"These are Agamemnon the Steadfast, Heracles the Glorious, and Athena the Wise," she introduces them as if they are alive, then like a warrior of ancient times she holds all three up to the sky.

It is obvious to see that Agamemnon, Heracles, and Athena are impressive armaments made from an unbreakable black material, probably obsidian, with intricately carved handles, handles that depict a mighty battle between two factions of sea nymphs: Sirens and Mermaids.

"We really do have battle axes!" I gape, looking astonished, but not caring if I do.

"Yes, we really do." Mom smiles.

"What are they made of?" Ando asks, touching one.

"Black volcanic glass." Our mother grins, her eyes gleaming. "And the metal of the gods."

"Like you and Lena's pendants?" Ando seems impressed.

"Exactly like our pendants." Mom laughs and unexpectedly looks exactly like me.

Our mother beams, and so does Melody who has followed us out into the yard. Her form is still transparent, but after a while you get used to it. Plus, we know who she is and just having her near makes me feel better, stronger, and wiser.

"These were designed by Hephaestus himself," Mom continues. "They were forged in the fires of Mt. Olympus and were created to do only one thing."

"Hephaestus forges all the weapons used by the gods," Ando educates in a hushed tone, but I already know all of that due to my studies at school and with the aunts. They take great pride in teaching us about our heritage.

Nervously, I swallow the remaining saliva in my mouth, hard, before I ask my question.

"What were they made to do?" I inquire, feeling foolish for asking, but needing to know.

Mom smiles roguishly as she grips the handle of the largest axe.

"To slay Mermaids… "

CHAPTER FIFTEEN

I t is strange to be drawn to something that does not belong to you. In my case, at this moment, I am drawn to these unfathomable weapons that are currently laid out before me. Mesmerized by their shiny metal surfaces sparkling under the waning sunlight, it is all I can do not to take one for myself. I cannot explain it, but their strength calls to me even in my human state. I hear them *speaking* to me on a primal level. One axe in particular calls to me.

"Mom?"

"Yes, baby," she replies as she sits cross-legged holding the largest axe on her lap like she is meditating.

"Which one is this?" I ask, pointing to the second axe lying on the grass.

Mom smiles.

"That's *Athena the Wise*," she educates patiently.

"How can you tell them apart?" I question with a stupefied expression.

Mom shrugs her shoulders.

"I don't know," she admits, blushing. "I just can."

"Which one do you have in your lap?" Ando joins the discussion.

Mom beams.

"This," she answers holding the axe toward us. "Is *Agamemnon the Steadfast.*"

"Do you know how to use them?" I grill my mother, who returns Agamemnon to the grassy area and picks up another. She does this with all of them and keeps examining the three weapons until she decides on one.

"It should be self-explanatory," she jests, eyes glistening in the fading light.

Enjoying our playful banter, I choose the perfect comeback when out of nowhere, my body feels like it is *literally* being pulled in different directions. As if I have been doused with gasoline, my limbs begin to burn and there is a loud, high-pitched squealing in my ears. At the same time, my stomach starts to twist and churn, and everything becomes blurry.

Like when I was drowning; my mind is racing in multiple directions at once. One moment it is on tonight's battle, but then it flashes back to ancient days where I see *The Three* fighting hordes of terrifying Mermaids. All around them, bodies are being slashed and things are on fire. The echo of metal striking metal, bone and flesh being ripped apart, and the shrieking, my goodness… *The shrieking!*...death surrounds me and there is chaos everywhere.

A few seconds feels like an eternity when finally, my body starts to experience that pulling sensation again. As if bound to a medieval torture device, my limbs and muscles stretch to their limit and whatever is left in my stomach comes spewing out. I am unaware of how long it lasts, but when I open my eyes, I am back in the yard with Mom and Ando. They have queasy looks on their faces and Ando looks like he will lose his stomach contents too.

"Woah!" I shout, returning to the present on legs that are barely holding me upright.

"What's wrong?" Mom interrogates, glaring at me strangely as she stands to steady me. "What just happened?"

Ando frowns.

"You looked like you were going to faint," he says in a hushed tone as he holds my hand.

"I think I had a… *flashback*," I whisper as I swipe my left arm with my right hand, and somehow, I feel blood on my skin.

"A flashback?" Mom questions, quizzically. "It happened right now, while you were standing here?"

Unable to hold my own weight anymore, my legs buckle, and I am thankful that Mom and Ando are there to catch me. Gently, they rest me on the lawn. The blades of grass are soft against my bare legs, and sitting is the greatest gift anyone could give me at the moment.

"Lena." Ando touches my forehead. "You're burning up."

"Tell me about your flashback," Mom pushes for clarification.

I squint as my vision returns to normal.

"One moment we were talking, the next I was witnessing a war," I admit, feeling dizzy. "I could hear loud explosions, and people dying, and everything around me was on fire: buildings, and ships that were docked in the harbor. There were dead bodies floating in the water and laying on the battlefield. It was horrible."

Obviously out of her element, my mother rubs my back like she did when I was little and kisses my forehead.

"Hopefully it doesn't happen again," she replies with an almost impossible to decipher expression.

On shaky legs, I stand, still in a daze as my stomach complains and my temples throb. My mother simply watches and is unable to offer any advice or suggestions. Lost in what is happening, I clear the 'hallucination' out of my mind, chocking it up to stress.

"Are you positive that you're alright?" Mom checks my temperature again, still worried.

Needing her to focus on our Mermaid problem, I nod, not wanting her mind on me, but rather on her strategy for tonight. Both she and Ando need to concentrate on their plan of action. I will try to be as supportive as I can.

It is then that I see my opportunity, and before I can chicken out, I make my move.

"May I hold one?" I ask, holding my hand out, but she shakes her head. "Why not?"

"It is too heavy for you," she mentions casually, only upsetting me further.

Ando steps forward and asks the same thing.

"May *I* hold one, Mommy?" he requests with an innocent face, and an even more innocent tone.

"Sure." Mom hands one of the axes to him without a second thought.

Curiously, he examines it too.

"Is it meant to be so *light*?" he queries with a long face. "Are you sure this is made of metal? It's as light as one of Belen's feathers."

"Please, let me hold one," I beg, feeling left out and useless.

Mom nods to Ando who hands it to me, but as soon as the axe touches my palm, I feel the full weight of it. Immediately, it drops to the ground. Unsure of what is happening, I bend and grab it with both hands, bending at the knees, I try to lift it off of the ground, but nothing happens. Stubbornly, it does not budge.

"What in the world?" I mumble to myself as I try again. "This thing weighs a ton."

"It is meant for a Siren," Mom informs, coolly. "You are no longer one."

"Thanks for rubbing it in, Mom," I grumble and pout. "Love you too."

"I'm sorry for being so blunt, but during this fight, you are confined to your room," Mom orders, sternly.

"But Mom—"

"But nothing, Selena!" Mom snaps back with fervor.

"I can't just sit around and—"

"You *can* and *will* just sit around," our mother commands. "Do you understand?"

"I understand," I answer, but all the while I am protesting internally.

Disheartened and disappointed, I retreat into the house and back to my room. From my window, I can observe Mom and Ando in the backyard discussing something that I cannot hear since I am no longer a Siren. How unfair is that?

At the same time, from my peripheral vision I see movement.

"How is my favorite great-granddaughter?" Melody's astral form appears in the doorway.

"Fan-freaking-tastic," I sulk, still staring at my family members down below.

"May I come in?" she beseeches respectfully in her gentle manner.

"I guess." I smile, her close proximity starting to make me feel happier.

"Why are you upset with your mother?" the wise old Muse questions as she materializes beside me.

"I'm upset because she doesn't want me to help," I complain, wanting to punch a hole in the drywall, but refraining since I do not wish to get in more trouble.

Melody's skin glows in the barely lit room. She has such strength, such grace and like the axes I am drawn to her, like a honeybee to a flower. Her presence drowns me… in a good way.

"You are her child," Melody begins. "It is in her nature to protect you."

"What about Ando?" I ask, grinding my teeth. "He's younger and smaller than me. I'm the eldest, but he's going to fight with Mom tonight. It's not fair."

"You are human, my dear," she restates the obvious.

"I know that," I complain, crumpling the sheer curtain in my hands. "I want to help."

"Marina only wants to keep you safe," Melody continues. "Due to current circumstances, Ando can do more than you. It does not mean that she does not have faith in your abilities."

"I guess," I respond, realizing that she is right.

Melody grins.

"When you have children of your own, you will understand," the Muse states as she smiles warmly.

"May I ask you a question?" I sit on the edge of my bed.

"Of course," she grins, taking my place near the window.

"If I plead with Gaia, will she return my powers to me?"

The Muse shrugs for the first time that I can recall.

"Melody?"

"Yes, dearest?" She studies the sky and frowns.

"I understand why I am being punished," I sigh. "I misused my powers and people got hurt."

Melody nods.

"But how much *'punishment'* can one person take?" I demand as the first teardrop falls. "How much physical and mental anguish can I take before it kills me?"

"Do not dismay, my beautiful great-granddaughter," Melody comforts. "I see wondrous things in your future."

"As a Siren or as a human?" I question with a hope-filled heart.

Melody smirks.

"What kind of great-grandmother would I be if I gave away the ending?" she playfully teases.

Her comment makes me giggle.

"So, there is hope for me?" I soak up her soothing energy.

"Do you remember the story of Pandora's Box?" She counters my question with a question of her own, just like Mom.

Enthusiastically, I nod.

"Pandora opened a magical box that held all of the world's plagues and all of humanity suffered for it," I summarize the gist of it. "Not such an uplifting story, especially when I could be Pandora's twin."

Melody shakes her head and laughs.

"Do you remember what was left in the box when all of the plagues were released?" Melody quizzes with an endearing expression.

I think for a moment and then it comes to me.

I smile too.

"Hope!"

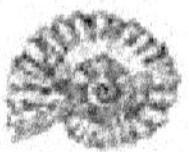

Taking a nap sounded like a good idea at the time. Tired from my 'flashback', I cuddled Ando's teddy bear, Alfredo, and fell fast asleep. Unfortunately, instead of waking more refreshed and energetic, I am even more exhausted than before.

This time, I wake to scratching at the wooden barrier that covers the broken window. Glancing in that direction, I squint to focus, but I cannot see anything outside because of the plywood. This also makes my room way too dark.

"Why didn't I take Ando's flashlight?" I whisper to myself, easing up to a standing position. "Isn't there meant to be a full moon tonight?"

Then I hear them from outside... close outside, perhaps right behind the wood.

"Are you sleepy, baby Siren?" a croaky voice questions as I slowly walk to the window.

"Or do you need to nappy-nap some more?" another higher-pitched voice replies.

Filled with dread, I stop in midstride.

"Wisteria?" I whisper, already realizing who has come for me. "Dahlia, is that you?"

"Baby Siren's ankle is better," a different voice responds.

"Baby Siren put our sisters in the ground!" one of them hisses. "Naughty, Baby Siren!"

"Get out of here or I'll put *you* in the ground!" I threaten at the top of my lungs, hearing my own teeth chattering.

"Evil, wicked Siren-baby!" they all proclaim at once.

Not wanting to stick around to see what they will do next; I race downstairs to the kitchen. Panic-stricken and shaking with fear, I search the house for Mom and Ando, but they are nowhere to be found.

"Ando!" I yell, beating back a wave of tears and the nausea that accompanies it. "Mom?"

Suddenly, my mind drifts to Melody.

"Melody!" I bellow, the single word getting caught in my throat.

"Left you, they have?" a voice I do not recognize startles me and I slowly turn.

Behind me stands the most intimidating pair of Mermaids I have ever seen. The first is at least six-feet-tall with long stringy platinum hair, and eyes as dark as the obsidian charm I wear around my neck. Beside her stands another, but she is nearly my height with a similar build to mine, just thinner and more athletic than I am.

"No one to protect you from the bumpy grumpy things," the taller one sneers, licking her chapped lips as she rakes me up, then down, then up again.

"Maybe I should put *you* in the ground, you dog-faced moron," I insult, wanting to seem fiercer than I actually am.

What I wouldn't do to have my Siren powers back.

"Get out or I'll—"

"Or you'll do what, Selena?" The smaller one uses my name which throws me further off guard. "Stab us with this?"

The snarky Mermaid holds up my quiver of arrows and snaps them into several pieces, throwing the remnants onto the ground at my feet.

"Or maybe you'll, shine this bright light in our faces," she guesses, holding up the LED flashlight. That she throws against the wall, and I watch as it shatters into a hundred little pieces.

Damn it! Now, I'm screwed!

"Not so brave without your mother and brother, are you?" the petite Mermaid ribs, moving closer. "Everyone loves you, don't they, Selena?"

Huh?

"All the girls want to be your friends, and all the boys want to date you, protect you… *love you*," the small one recaps.

Why does she seem so familiar?

"W-who are y-you?" I stutter as I take a step backward and inadvertently bump into the cabinet.

"W-ho are y-you?" the Mermaid copies me then laughs.

I know this thing! I just can't tell from where.

"Ever since you moved to my island you've been nothing but a pain in my ass," the Mermaid scorns. "Always taking what's mine. Always being where you're not supposed to be."

"I don't even know you," I blurt, getting tired of her rant. "You people attacked us!"

"You people?" she shouts, her eyes narrowing. "My people have suffered by your hands for eons and now it's time to change that."

"I don't understand what you mean," I say, looking around for a way out of this room. "I'm almost seventeen. I haven't been around for eons."

"Your kind! Your kind! Your kind!" Her less articulate companion decides to assist in the Selena-bashing. "Your kind stole! Your kind bring pain! Your kind bring death!"

"*'To follow a Siren is to follow death,'*" the more intelligent Mermaid quotes. "I didn't figure it out until a few weeks ago. What you were. How you could do what you could do."

Nervously, I step backwards and bump into the edge of the countertop with my butt. I immediately realize which drawer I am leaning against, the one with the knives; large, pointy, dangerously sharp knives that would give me a fighting chance against these '*things.*'

"Do what?" I ask, calculating if I can make it to the backdoor before they can catch me and rip my head off.

"Sing so beautifully," she says with a jealous glare. "Steal the Winter Solo from me... steal *Andrew* from me."

My chest tightens and my palms start to sweat.

Dear Heavenly Father!

"Amy?" I whisper, narrowing my eyes.

"Duh." The teen Mermaid grins, showing her jagged teeth.

"How... *when... What in the hell!*" I gasp. "You're a... *Mermaid?*"

"Surprise!" she yells with a serial killer smile that reminds me of Jack Nicholson in *The Shining* (another movie I should never have watched alone at night).

"How is this possible?" I grill, too shocked to plan my escape.

"It wasn't until the homecoming dance that things started *'happening'* to me," Amy reveals, her features softening for the moment.

"I don't understand," I repeat, stalling for time.

"When you saved me, your scales scraped me and the venom they carry intermingled with my blood," she informs, recalling the incident I will never forget. "As you probably already know, it made me immune to your witchy ways for a short period of time, but it didn't stop there."

"But I—" In a blink of an eye, the furious femme fatale backhands my cheek, shocking me into pained silence.

"*Shhh!*" she hisses. "I'm talking!"

Reeling from the blow, I reply with only a nod, taking a step sideways away from the violent teen and the utensil drawer that holds the knives.

Amy smiles, but it does not reach her cold, dead, black eyes.

"But then something else happened," my nemesis confesses as she wags her boney finger at me. "I started craving raw seafood, my skin started to get more sensitive to sunlight, and lots of other things that I couldn't explain started happening."

"Oh," I manage to say as my brain returns to my lack of a game plan. "That must have been scary."

"Scary?" She laughs like a maniac. "Scary doesn't come close to what I've been through!"

Like a caged animal, she starts to pace, her translucent skin hinting of the blue veins running below.

Then she stops and turns to glare at me.

"My hair started falling out, my eyes kept turning black… I felt like complete crap!" she shouts while stomping her bare feet.

"I'm sorry," I whisper, and I honestly do feel sorry for her. No one, not even her, deserves that.

"My father got so worried that he took me to a specialist on the mainland to undergo tests." The distraught teenager makes a noise that sounds like a whimper but then pulls herself together. "When they couldn't find any explanations, we came back home."

"How did you find out that you're *this*?" I counter, pointing to her and her friend.

Amy clicks her talons together.

Great! She's got talons too.

"It's a funny story actually." She smiles and it is completely unnerving. "My mother died when I was a little girl, my father claimed it was cancer. Turns out she was a Mermaid. Isn't that a hoot?"

"Bu-but how did she have you?" I ask in a jumbled rush.

Amy glares at me like I am stupid, and right now I feel incredibly stupid.

"She pretended to be human." Her eyes swirl to their normal icy-blue then quickly back to black. "She seduced my father, got married and… *Here I Am!*"

My eyebrow arches to my hairline.

"Your father didn't know what she was?" I question, sheepishly, feeling sympathy toward the little rodent that contributed to half of her DNA.

Again, Amy glares at me.

"Did your stepfather know that your mother was a Siren?" she belittles with annoyance along with an emotion that I cannot put my finger on.

"Not at first," I grumble to myself. "Not until last year, the same time as you."

For a long moment, Amy stands contemplating my admission. Her face contorts, her eyes appear to well with tears, but she immediately returns to herself.

"Back to what I was saying," she coos.

"Go right ahead," I encourage, actually wanting to hear the rest of her account.

"According to my mother's diary… "

Perfect! Does every single supernatural being own a diary… journal… whatever?

"… she was being pursued by these two Siren-bitches," the teen, whatever she is now, stares at me. "According to her diary, she was looking for a quick meal, came across some old dude and his granddaughter fishing near one of the little islands in the harbor—"

My eyes widen.

"You mean… *Nicole*?" I gasp, feeling nauseous. "*Nicole Wong?*"

Amy grins.

"That's the one!" she proclaims as she sharpens her talons against each other. The sound it makes is similar to fingernails being scraped down a chalkboard.

"Your mother was going to *eat* Nicole?" I question, hoping I did not hear her correctly.

"Yeah!" she yells. "So what?! We got to eat too!"

"And you don't see anything wrong with that?" I move two tiny steps toward the backdoor. This time I feel the drawer tug on my shirt.

"Fish gotta swim… birds gotta fly," she sings it like a song, a really strange and morbid song. "Mermaids gotta eat."

Her counterpart immediately starts chuckling.

"You've got some serious mental health issues," I sneer, slowly reaching behind my back, opening the drawer and reaching inside. Searching around, I find Mom's large cleaver; the one she uses when she wants to cut through bone easily. It usually takes only one good swing to sever a chicken or beef bone. I figure Mermaid flesh should not be a problem.

"If you're wondering where your mother and kid brother are, they've already gone down to the cove," Amy divulges, calmly, walking towards me. "I had one of my lackeys lure them down there. Mermaids aren't the greatest thinkers. They're more into *'smash-and-grab jobs'*, but I'm changing all that."

"Why did you *lure* them down there?" I grill, keeping her distracted.

"Because your mom's a super-Siren and so is your little bro," she moans with irritation. "Do you know how many of my family members they've killed in the past few days?"

I shake my head as I tighten my grip on the cleaver's handle.

"Too many to count, that's how many!" the teen yells, face turning even paler, if that is possible.

"I'm sorry," I apologize, not meaning it.

"And you, little Miss Perfect," she growls as she stands only a couple of inches away. "You've done your fair share of spreading carnage."

"It was self-defense," I reply, ready to swing at her head.

"Enough!" The larger Mermaid finally jumps in and pushes Amy out of the way. "Kill her!"

"Forsythia! No!" Amy barks and tries to seize her, but the irate larger-than-life Mermaid grabs me and starts to choke, choke me until I start to feel my eyeballs ready to pop out of their sockets. Taking a chance, I swing the cleaver but only manage to cut the thing's forearm that is currently squeezing the life out of me. Then suddenly, she stops, releases me, and steps away. Amy takes the opportunity to lunge but is surprised when she stops in midair and hovers a few feet off of the floor, arms and legs swinging, mouth sputtering obscenities that would make a seasoned sailor blush.

"What's going on?" Amy screams at the top of her lungs.

"Selena?" I hear Melody's voice from out on the balcony. "Stop goofing off and come with me."

I grin as I walk past the two immobile Mermaids.

"That's so cool!" I smile as I rush outside to meet Melody. "How long can you hold them like that?"

"I have to keep them in my sightline, or they will return to normal," Melody admits.

"I'll say it again." I grin. "That is so freaking cool!"

"No time for small talk," Melody reprimands. "Your mother and brother need your assistance. Where is your bow and arrows?"

I frown.

"Smashed," I reply, looking down at my feet.

"No time to waste, Selena," she reminds. "Hurry! And Selena?"

"Yes?"

"You are not just a Siren," she smiles. "You are so much more than you realize."

"I don't understand," I huff, wrapping my oxygen deprived mind around her statement.

"True power comes from within," she continues. "Remember your Aria, remember your love of family and of humanity. Love is your greatest strength."

Pushing her words from my brain for the moment, I race out of the house and down the steps not fully understanding Melody's advice. I am *not* a Siren anymore. I do not have the ability to control men through song or have access to super strength or night vision. I cannot call on my battle scales to avoid getting hurt during an attack. Unfortunately, I am also cut off from my family telepathically and the silence is killing me.

I am not a heroine. I am just me.

Just Selena.

And with any luck, I pray that will be enough.

It is too dark. There is a full moon somewhere in the sky, but it is covered completely by clouds. I guess this is Mom's doing. After all, Sirens can see in the dark. However, so can Mermaids. I, on the other hand, cannot see anything at all.

Trying to be surefooted, I take small steps all the while checking the surface of where my feet are landing. Hopefully, it will not be Mermaids who kill me. Truth be told, I would rather meet my maker by slipping and cracking my skull open here. At least that would be a quick death. Amy, on the other hand, would relish the act of torturing me before administering the harshest of deaths.

I wish I had my Siren powers right now. The first thing I would do is shine some freaking moonlight down on the shoreline. Can Mermaids control the weather? If I survive tonight, I will make sure to find out.

As if a genie has somehow decided to grant my wish, the wind begins to blow harder and successfully clears away the clouds.

Much better!

It takes all of my willpower not to call out for Mom and Ando. Strategy is our mother's forte, so I know that she has all of her bases covered, but you never know what sort of trickery these Mermaids have up their proverbial sleeves. I would not put anything past them, especially with Amy supposedly leading their factions.

"Lena." Ando startles me from the base of the rocks. "Have you seen Mommy?"

"No," I whisper, searching the surface of the cove. "I thought she would be with you."

"We got separated when the Mermaids attacked," he pants, and I notice the long bright-red talon marks on his face and neck. "There's a lot of them."

"Quantify a lot," I request, helping him out of the water.

"Huh?" he pouts. "What does quantify mean?"

"It means *'how many are there'*," I clarify, feeling annoyed at our situation.

Before he can respond, we hear the first set of screeches and wails coming from beneath the waves. The only way to describe it is loud and scary. It reminds me of hundreds of orcas attacking hundreds of great white sharks. Even a Siren should not be in the water right now.

"What is that?" Ando stands with the axe grasped tightly at his side.

"I don't know," I murmur, feeling like a bullseye out in the open like this.

"Do you think Mommy is okay?" His eyes flash with concern.

Gently, I rest my hand on his shoulder for comfort, for him, and for me.

"I hope so," I reply then turn to get a better view of the horizon.

It is almost sunrise. Mermaids are extremely sensitive to sunlight. Hopefully, they will retreat and give us a chance to recuperate. Then again, perhaps not.

"Lena, what's that?" Ando asks, pointing. "Over there?"

I squint to see what the shape is floating on the surface.

"Damn it! It's Mom!" I hear the words leave my mouth and instantly feel sick.

Without another word, Ando dives back into the water and disappears almost immediately only to resurface next to Mom's limp body. Unfortunately, she is not moving, which is not a good sign. In the water, my brother is utterly in control and even manages to get Mom to the shore still holding his axe.

"Is she alright?" I pull her heavy body out of the water like a sack of grain.

"I don't know," Ando answers in a panic, wiping the salt water from his face.

Off kilter, my mind begins to race.

"Is she breathing?" he grills as I examine her.

I smile.

"She's breathing," I declare with relief. "They must have just knocked her out."

Ando smiles too.

"Let's get her back to the house," my brother suggests rigidly as he holds her upper body while I carry her legs, but on our way to the steps, glowing bodies begin to emerge from the sea. They cannot stand because of their tails, but they crawl determined to get to us. They remind me of maggots writhing and slithering on top of a piece of rotting flesh. Their transparent bodies are covered in slashes and oozing wounds, and I smile knowing that Ando and Mom created the carnage.

"There you are!" I hear Amy's voice from near the steps. "I thought you got away."

Ando gasps as his eyes widen in shock.

"Is that A-Amy?" he stammers with surprise.

"Yes, it is," I grumble, halting my advance.

"She's a Mermaid?" he spits it out like the words are bitter.

"I sure am, baby Siren," she giggles.

"What did you do to Melody?" I probe as she walks closer.

"Oh, that old broad with the magic?" Amy sniffs. "We have magic too or is that bit of information not in your grandfather's journal?"

Ando's eyes widen even more.

"She knows about—"

"Yes," I interrupt before he can finish.

"How?" he grumbles.

"Nicole," I remind.

"Shut up! Just shut up!" Amy bellows making us jump. "I'm so sick of hearing your voices!"

Boldly, I step forward, tired of being afraid.

"Why are you doing this, Amy?" I question, staring into her cold, dead eyes.

"You stole Andrew from me!" she screeches, and the sound echoes off of the surrounding cliffs.

Annoyed, my eyebrows hitch to my hairline, and my right foot starts to tap on its own. If it were actually possible to feel blood boiling, I would be experiencing that sensation right now. This has got to stop. Living in fear is not my cup of tea. I would rather her kill me now and get it over with. No more.

"Andrew never belonged to you, you slut," I harass, knowing she has a short fuse. "He did everything in his power to avoid you!"

"That's a lie!" Amy snarls, taking a step forward. "We belong together!"

Defiantly, I put my hands on my hips.

"Why?" I taunt, determined to stand my ground, no matter what. "Because you say so?"

Then I feel it.

Suddenly, the hairs on my arms and legs are standing on end and not due to fear. My palms have stopped sweating, and I feel my blood actually heating inside of my blood vessels. For a moment, I swear I hear the sound of the sea increasing and I think I hear Ando wishing that our mother would wake up.

An intense pain doubles me over, but I endure it. Inside, I feel my heartbeat steady, my muscles harden, and for a brief second, I hear the call of the sea. It is comforting. It is welcoming. And it calls me home.

Holy Crap!

Dear Father!

Are my powers coming back?

Taken aback, the teen Mermaid just glares at me, speechless for the moment.

"It has always been *you* pursuing him, never *him* pursuing you," I remind smugly, coming to a standing position. "If he wanted you, he knew that he could have you seven ways to Sunday because you made it quite clear that you were ready, willing and able."

Still, she stares at me with her mouth gaping.

"So, you have to say to yourself: why didn't he want me?" I continue jabbing, not caring if she attacks or not.

"Shut up!" Amy screams as she claws at her own skin. "Shut your filthy mouth!"

But I cannot. I can feel my heartbeat accelerating to a gallop and suddenly I want to fight. I need to fight, fight until my knuckles swell and bleed. This is how I felt when I was a Siren.

Powerful.

Magical.

Unstoppable!

"Big bad Amy can't handle the truth," I snicker, feeling empowered, the fury of my Siren blood fueling my courage. "I suggest you leave while you still can."

At last, Amy smiles. It is forced and her lips are trembling, but she manages a smile, nonetheless. However, at this moment, I am not afraid.

"And who's going to make me leave?" the teen mocks. "You?"

Feeling sassy, I give her my most brilliant smile.

"You bet your transparent ass," I mock back with a sarcastic tone that surprises even me.

Losing what is left of her composure, Amy starts to close the distance between us, when Ando steps forward, clutched in his hands is Heracles; the axe he now claims as his own. Amy halts her steps and watches the blade glisten under the waning moonlight.

"Stay where you are, Amy!" he yells with the force of a grown man. "Or I'll chop your ugly head off!"

"Don't worry, Ando." She grins appearing unaffected, showing her shark-like teeth. "I'll make it quick and relatively painless."

Unafraid, he takes another step forward, clutching his axe as if he is Paul Bunyan and Amy is a piece of timber.

"I said, leave her alone!" he barks another warning and stubbornly stands his ground.

To my surprise, Amy remains in place. Her face contorted with rage and her eyes locked onto my brother. All I can do is stare at the both of them.

"That's not very nice," the teen hisses. "I've changed my mind. I'll kill you first, baby Siren."

I'll be damned if I let her touch one hair on my brother's head.

"Stop!" I bellow, the sound like anvils slamming together. The harshness of it causes both Ando and Amy to halt in their tracks. Neither of them can take their eyes off of me. "Touch him and I will kill you."

"I'd like to see you try," Amy suddenly seems perkier. "You're human now. I can smell it on you… right now."

"If you're so certain of that, then make your move," I growl and for some reason I think about calling in a storm, and overhead one cloud begins to roll in from the east. It is small, but ominous. With one thought, I order the lightning to strike and it… *Happens!*

From the cloud, the first bolt of lightning strikes the churning sea while a second hits the ground where we are standing. The rocky surface begins to tremble then pitch, then slowly steadies itself. The sky is brighter, but in the distance another lone storm cloud is moving in. Unaware of what is happening, we continue to stare as this one stops directly above Amy and her companion's head. This time, lightning strikes a foot away from their bare feet, making them simultaneously scream and jump.

Amy's face turns even whiter, if that is even possible.

"How did you d-do that?" Amy stutters, looking horrified.

"Does it matter?" I hear Ligeia's voice behind me as she climbs out of the rough sea holding several severed limbs, of which she throws at Amy's cohort's feet, making them yelp in fear. My aunt stands before her unyielding like Zeus himself. Her red tresses blowing behind her like multihued flames, eyes brighter than jewels, but there is something different about her.

Then I realize what it is.

She is *not* naked. Surprisingly, her scales are artfully arranged like a short toga efficiently covering all of her private parts. The improvised clothing makes her even more stunning and more human in appearance.

"Who are you?" Amy questions, smart enough to take a step backward.

"She's your worst nightmare." Ando smirks, giving Ligeia a thumbs up which she returns.

"Kill red-Siren!" Forsythia releases a shrill battle cry and runs toward Ligeia, but our aunt quickly turns to the side, swipes at the Mermaid with her talons fully extended and we witness Forsythia's head detach from her still moving body.

Realizing her predicament, Amy starts to shake.

"That was my favorite minion!" The teen throws a fit. "You fish-bitch!"

"That is not polite." Leukosia exits the sea carrying the dead body of another Mermaid over her shoulder like a sack of potatoes. Like her sister, she wears her scales in a similar fashion except her toga is down to her knees whereas Ligeia's is at mid-thigh. "Now, be a good little Mermaid and slither home."

"Which one are you?" Amy's lips are trembling now.

"Where are my manners?" Our regal, blonde aunt bows low. "I am Leukosia, and you are?"

"A-Amy… Amy J-Jacobs," the Mermaid stutters her response, looking around in a daze.

Leukosia turns to me and smiles.

"That is an odd name for a Mermaid," My mentor frowns. "Is it not, sister?"

Tia Ligeia nods in agreement.

"They are normally named after flowers and plants and other such nonsense," Ligeia scoffs, brazenly.

You can see the fury in Amy's face as she stares at the aunts then back at me. Then she looks down at our feet where our mother still lays unconscious.

"Oh no," she taunts, ignoring Ligeia and Leukosia for the moment. "Poor Mama Siren is dead."

"She's not dead!" Ando shouts.

His outburst amuses Amy.

"But she will be very shortly," she bullies, increasing the length of her already long talons.

Boldly, the teen takes a step towards Mom determined to keep her promise, but she is startled by a third voice.

"Touch one hair on her head and I'll kill you myself." The familiar masculine voice makes us all turn around.

Ando and I stand speechless as the person comes out of the shadows and into view. He is tall with dark hair, caramel-colored skin, and hypnotic hazel-brown eyes. His wavy hair hangs slightly over his eyes showing that he has not had a haircut in months. He also desperately needs a shave, but it does not take away from his handsomeness.

"Don't I get a hello?" He smiles lovingly at both of us.

My brother and I both speak at once.

"Daddy?"

CHAPTER SIXTEEN

We stand, speechless, unable to blink for fear that the man standing before us will disappear.

It is as if all the stars, in all the heavens, in all the lands, suddenly and inexplicitly align at the right moment, of the right hour, of the right day, of the right month, of the right year.

In retrospect, I would have to liken it to reincarnation or some other such miracle. It is not something that happens often and I certainly never thought that it could happen to me. Selena Antonius Thermopolis Marquez, daughter of a Siren, granddaughter/niece of *The Three*, great-granddaughter of Melpomene the Muse, current human, etc.

I am numb… I truly am.

All I can do is stare at him and wonder if it is all just a glorious dream.

Confused, Amy glares at Dad, then at us, then back to Dad. At this point, he is not smiling but studying our teenage foe. And although he does not say a word, the vibe that is coming from him speaks volumes. In a nutshell, he looks dangerous.

"Dr. Marquez?" Amy probes with trembling lips. "I thought you were dead?"

Our father smiles, but it does not reach his eyes.

"So did I," he replies without emotion.

"Daddy?" Ando questions on the verge of tears. "Is that really you?"

"It is, *mi amor*." David winks.

"I saw you die," I blurt, tears starting to well. "I wasn't imagining it. You were dead."

"It is a long story, sweetheart," he counters, and the sound of his voice pushes me over the edge to the point that I start to choke on my sobs.

Instinctively, Ando takes my hand as we both run toward Dad, hugging him tightly as he wraps his strong arms around us. It is a sensation that I cannot describe in words. If I was still a Siren, I would be singing right now. Singing to the birds. Singing to the world.

"I've missed you two." David's tears begin to fall too. "So much."

Unmoved by our reunion, Amy turns back to me wearing a scowl of epic proportions.

"You lead a charmed life, Selena Marquez," she almost spits the words at me.

Pfft!

Well… maybe my luck is changing for the better.

"I'm glad one of us thinks so." I smirk, glaring at her, afraid of letting my guard down for fear of retaliation. I would not put it past her to strike when all of my family members are around just to make a point. She is evil and I am certain that it would give her great joy to end my life even if she died in the process.

"Enough chit-chat, ladies," Dad speaks, his Spanish accent stronger than I remember it. "Get your cronies out of here, Amy. It's been a long time since I've seen my family."

Without missing a beat, Amy smiles at him and does a quick curtsy then lets out one of those banshee-like, eardrum-popping shrieks. The surviving Mermaids crawl back to the edge and slip silently into the sea, leaving the fallen where they lay. All around us are broken bodies strewn around like so many bags of trash.

Again, Amy turns to me and surprises me even more. Before our eyes, her stringy platinum hair begins to soften and thicken until it returns to its natural golden blonde. Her eyes reduce to their regular size as her irises lighten until they are the soft azure blue that I am used to. The transparency of her skin solidifies and becomes denser, returning to her naturally pale human complexion, even her freckles return.

Unencumbered, she stands defiantly before us, hands on hips wearing nothing but an evil grin. Unlike her, I glance around at the carnage, ignoring my stomach as it begins to churn. We cannot just leave them here to rot. It would not only be immoral, but in poor taste.

"What about the bodies?" I ask, filled with concern. "We can't just leave them there."

Ligeia and Leukosia smile ruefully.

"Wait," they say together as they hold hands and close their eyes.

No sooner than they begin their strange ritual, the horizon begins to lighten. Shadows flee to dark places and are replaced by glowing prisms of sunlight. It happens more quickly than usual, but it happens all the same, and as we bear witness to the dawning of a brand-new day, something incredible happens.

"Are the sisters calling on the sun *early*?" I grill my brother who looks just as stupefied as I do.

All he can do is shrug.

"Look!" Ando shouts pointing at the deceased Mermaids littering the rocks. "They're burning!"

And they are burning!

Heavenly Father! They are burning like autumn leaves on a funeral pyre!

As we continue to watch, the flames rise higher spitting particles bathed in burnished golds, burgundies, and midnight-blues then rapidly subside until hardly an ember remains, but that is not the end. Oh no! It is not the end at all. Then what remains redistributes and lightens until it transforms into the silvery seafoam that appears on the crest of magnificent waves.

"It's true!" I gasp. "It's really true!"

The sisters appear vindicated.

"Children of the sea return to the sea," they say with a humble bow to the fallen Mermaid clan.

"This isn't over, Selena," Amy purrs then runs and swan-dives into the water with the rest of her remaining brethren.

Who would have thought that Amy would be the leader of a clan of inbred Mermaids?

Certainly not me!

Ugg!

But that is a problem for another day.

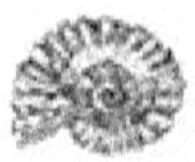

It takes a while for Mom to wake-up, but when she does, we already have her back in bed with several of Ligeia and Leukosia's scales healing her more severe wounds. Thankfully, her battle scales did their job well and protected her major organs. Everything else should be healed in a few hours. When she finally opens her eyes, the entire family is staring at her, all except David who is in another room.

"Ouch!" Mom squeaks, rubbing the large kumquat-sized bump on her forehead. "What happened? Did we win?"

"You are getting soft in your old age," Tia Ligeia speaks first not even attempting to hide her frown. "We retrieved your axe from the bottom of the cove. It was irresponsible of you to leave it lying around."

"I didn't *leave* it, I got attacked by twenty crazed Mermaids, and it got knocked out of my hand," Mom states flatly, ignoring Ligeia's stern stare.

"It still should not have happened." The red head sulks and folds her arms across her chest defiantly.

"I'm sorry," Mom scoffs, holding her left side. "Next time, I'll look after it better."

"See that you do," Ligeia responds with a harrumph, clearly not recognizing Mom's sarcasm.

"Living among the humans has dulled your senses," Tia Leukosia scolds next. "You need to spend more time in the sea, Marina. Tomorrow, we shall spar."

"Thanks, Tia," Mom smirks. "Nice to see you too. Did we win?"

"We won the battle," Tia Ligeia tells it like it is. "Not necessarily the war."

"Thank you, Tia, for sugar-coating it for me," Mom groans in pain, propping up on her side to search for another pillow.

"Are you okay, Mommy?" Ando asks as he gives her a gentle hug. "You were sleeping for a really long time."

"I'll be fine, son," she says, kissing his cheek. "Don't you worry anymore."

With difficulty, Mom manages to prop herself up to a seated position.

"What's with the togas?" The quickly healing Siren giggles, staring at the *dressed* Sirens.

"A *friend* of ours took offense to our nakedness," they both answer at once. "So, we improvised."

Mom gives an approving thumbs up.

"You look very fashionable," Mom compliments.

The aunts glance down at their *'clothing'* with pleased grins.

"Thank you!" They answer as one.

"How long was I out?" My mother reaches for the glass of water we put on the adjacent nightstand.

"Three incredibly long hours," David informs as he steps into the room freshly shaved and showered. His hair is still down to his shoulders and resembles *Tarzan's*, but other than that he looks amazing.

"David!" Mom yells as she jumps out of bed and into her husband's awaiting arms. "You're home!"

They hold each other close, so close that no light can pass between their bodies.

"I couldn't stay away any longer," he confesses, kissing her sweetly, uncaring of who is watching.

"We can vouch for that," the aunts say in unison. "He threatened to set Paradiso on fire if we did not let him come home."

I chuckle. That does sound like David!

The harmony of their intertwining voices is music to my ears. I did not realize how much I have missed them until right now. Maybe my luck truly is changing.

"He is extremely stubborn for a human," Ligeia answers with a grimace. "He should have stayed on Paradiso for a little while longer."

"Wait," Mom states, taking a step back. "I thought you cured him."

"Mom?" I ask. "Did you know that Dad was still alive?"

Mom just stands there looking guilty.

"Did Ando know too?" I add, glancing at my brother.

Ando looks down at his feet verifying his guilt.

"You told Ando that Dad was alive, but you didn't tell me?" I accuse on the brink of tears.

"No! Dear Father, no!" Mom proclaims as she takes a step towards me.

"Then how does he know?" I quiz, pointing at my brother who is still staring at his sneakers. "And I don't?"

"I saw Daddy in a dream," Ando admits, looking at me at last. "I saw him with the aunts on Paradiso. I saw when they healed him with the venom from their scales. I saw everything, Lena, but I didn't know if it was real or not."

Ando tries to take my hand, but I move it.

"Don't be mad at me, Lena," he begs. "I'm sorry."

All I can do is just stare at them.

"I've been blaming myself for weeks for Dad's death," I say with a sniffle. "For weeks and nobody bothered to tell me that he *wasn't* dead."

"Selena," Tia Leukosia speaks up. "Your stepfather did have a heart attack and he did almost die—"

David raises his hand.

"Technically, I was clinically dead for three minutes," he states, boastfully, as if it is something to be proud of.

"That doesn't make me feel better," I grunt and then I smile and hug him again.

"At first, Marina did not know we had saved him," Leukosia reaffirms. "It was not until a few days ago that we informed her."

"We did not want to get her hopes up if we failed," they say as one. "We knew she could not lose him twice."

"Is that why you've been so peppy?" I turn to my mother.

Slowly, she nods and I notice that they are holding hands. I smile even though I do not want to. I smile because we have our David back.

"So, what are the consequences?" I boldly probe, turning to the aunts. "I've learned the hard way that there are always consequences."

The aunts look at me, but do not answer. This time David does.

"*The Calling* took a lot out of me," he explains, still holding on to Mom's hand. "Both physically and mentally."

"In what way?" I grill as I sit on their bed, awaiting the bad news.

"Being the vessel for all of those powers: *The Three*, your brother, and Melody, put a great deal of strain on my body. Too much strain for a mortal. The only thing that saved me was—"

My stepfather suddenly stops and averts his eyes, just like Ando does when he is hiding something, something big.

"Please continue," I urge waiting for the big surprise. "What saved you?"

David closes his eyes and takes a deep breath.

"Remember when I asked you to bring me samples of the water in The Siren Grotto?"

I stare at him, almost afraid to answer.

"Yesss," I reply, drawing out the word.

"I was conducting experiments with it," he admits, meekly.

"What sort of experiments?" I probe, pressing my fingertips to my temples.

"I was… injecting myself with it," he responds, almost too rapidly to comprehend.

Almost.

"David!" Mom gasps. "Are you crazy or just plain stupid?"

"Why would you do that?" I lay my hand over my stomach.

"I wanted to see Paradiso with my own eyes, but you all were so adamant that the particles in the grotto would kill me," he stops to take a much-needed breath. "But then I examined it logically. When people are vaccinated, they receive minute quantities of the same virus that they want to be immune to."

"Yeah," I respond, looking at my mother's sallow face.

David smiles.

"I figured I could do the same thing," he confesses. "I could inject small quantities of it into my bloodstream to build up immunity to it."

He pauses.

"And it worked!" he exclaims triumphantly.

"But?" I add.

"But… what?" he asks, pretending that it is all so simple.

"Tell us the consequence," I order, folding my arms across my chest and refusing to back down.

"The particles did the trick," he says without a smile. "A little too well."

"What does that mean?" Mom interrogates as she studies his expression.

Gently, he takes both of her hands in his and tenderly kisses them, his eyes never leaving hers. In this moment, I honestly see them. Not just as Mom and Dad, but as Marina and David, two souls who have found each other once again, in sickness and in health, not even till death do they part. Not even Death could keep them apart. They were destined to meet, fall in love and create the next generation of… *whatever* Ando and I are or will be.

"If the particles weren't in my system, I wouldn't have survived," he finally comes clean.

"I don't understand," Mom groans as she turns to the aunts for more data.

"In order for your husband to stay alive, he must have daily doses of the water in the Siren Grotto," Tia Leukosia discloses without heat.

"If he misses just one day of injections," Ligeia adds. "He will cease to exist."

"You mean he'll die, for good." Ando's voice is shaky.

"That is correct," the aunts say as one.

"But don't worry." David perks up. "I'm working on a serum to alleviate having to take multiple doses a day."

"Is that possible?" I question, feeling hopeful.

"Anything is possible." Dad grins. "My family is living proof of that."

I have never been so happy. I have never seen my family so happy. Even the aunts have decided to stay with us, on land, for a few days. Not only to make sure that the Mermaids do not return, but to spend time as a family. If I were to guess, they have probably grown used to that warm human factor. I am also positive that caring for David all these weeks has stirred unfamiliar maternal urges. Being near Melody probably also had a similar effect on them.

I wonder where Melody has disappeared to. Amy had mentioned something about Mermaids having their own magic. I guess they did something to her astral projection, but then again that was only a projection of Melody not the real one. Deep in my soul, I am sure she is safe, regardless of where she is right now.

"How's brunch?" Mom grins from ear to ear as all six of us sit around the dining table eating and chatting.

Mom has gone all out on the brunch spread. There are platters piled high with golden slices of French toast, mounds of steaming sausages, perfectly cooked hash-browned potatoes, served with sticky-sweet maple syrup and creamy honey-butter. A jug of freshly squeezed orange juice also sets on the table. Our mother has truly outdone herself.

"Does it taste alright?" Mom grills, hesitating to smile as she looks at her family eating together.

"It's delicious, *mi esposa bonita*." Dad grins, and wags his eyebrows suggestively, making us all giggle, all except the aunts who are taking tiny, mouse-like bites of their French toast. Unlike the rest of us, who are gobbling it up like we have not eaten in days.

"It's really yummy," Ando informs the table as he reaches for another sausage link. "May I have another?"

"You've eaten three pieces." I smirk. "You're a pig."

The enthusiastic boy laughs.

"Oink! Oink!" my brother responds, crinkling up his nose into a snout.

"Ok, you two," Dad interrupts our joking. "Eat up! The food is getting cold."

"Listen to your father," Mom urges without heat.

Ando and I look at each other and smile.

"What are *these*?" Ligeia and Leukosia both ask as they stab their perspective sausage links with the tines of their forks. They are both wearing grimaces as they inspect the cylindrical shaped pieces of pork products.

"Those are delicious," Dad responds with a smile. "Taste it. You might like it."

"What animal are they made from?" Ligeia continues to stare at her plate.

"They're made from pork," I testify simply. "Which comes from pigs."

"What else?" Leukosia questions, picking one link up with her fingers and wiggling it in the air like a worm she is about to put on a fishing hook.

Wanting to be helpful, I race around the corner and read the back of the package the meat came in. The ingredients are fairly straightforward except for—

Hmm!

"The ingredients please," both sisters insist at once, making me nervous.

"Well… umm… " I try to find the words but cannot.

"Lena, what's in them?" Ando urges.

At last, I steady myself and just say it.

"Pork… "

"We know that." Mom smirks. "What are the rest of the ingredients?"

"Are you sure you want to know?" I ask with one hand on my hip.

"Tell us!" Every person at the table orders at once.

"There's water, of course, corn syrup, some salt, pork broth with natural flavorings, dextrose," I continue while everyone is staring at me.

"Is there more?" Ando giggles.

"Kind of." I blush.

"We would like to know the rest." The aunts speak as one, putting me on the spot.

"There is also lemon juice powder, natural flavors, BHA, propyl gallate, citric acid and collagen casing." I finish, taking a much-needed breath.

"These extra ingredients are acceptable in the food supply?" Leukosia probes with a disgusted look.

"What are they used for?" Ligeia states flatly.

"They help to preserve the freshness, taste and color along with keeping it more appealing visually," David answers, purposely adding more complicated terms.

"We see." They both frown.

"Some of the same ingredients are in Doritos and Hostess products." My stepfather adds with a grin knowing that they love, love, *LOVE*, those pantry staples.

That convinces them!

Excitedly, they glance at each other and then at Dad and finally back to their sausages. Everyone at the table can tell that they are mentally debating the best course of action for this *'sausage problem'*. When it appears that all hope is lost, they each stab it with their forks, take a bite and begin to chew.

"How is it?" Mom asks, trying to hide her smile with her napkin.

There is no response given as they continue to taste it.

"It is... *chewy*," they answer together.

"Anything else?" I also try to hide my grin with my hand.

"It is a bit *greasy*," they continue, staring at each other.

"But do you like it?" Ando exclaims as he eats his own piece of sausage.

There is a long pause.

"We think it will take another bite to determine our opinion," the aunts announce as they reach for their other half of breakfast meat to continue further 'taste testing'.

Family! You gotta love 'em!

CHAPTER SEVENTEEN

An entire week has gone by and nothing remotely fishy has occurred, but that does not matter: Dad is back in our lives, and it is awesome. In fact, things have picked up right where they left off and it is as though the *'tragedy'* had never happened. For instance, David has already returned to work (part-time at least), and Dorinda is overjoyed, of course, as well as all of the Ocean World's sea life.

To my mother's delight, her husband has checked-off several items on her 'honey-do' list like fixing the broken windows and cleanup any lingering bloodstains on the hardwood floors, along with other odds-and-ends that need mending.

"What should we do today?" Mom probes as she lies on the couch with her feet propped up on Dad's lap. Contentedly, she listens to the softly falling rain while we watch *Tom and Jerry* cartoons on cable.

Ando looks over his shoulder from his lounging position on an extra-large floor pillow we recently purchased from the home decorating store.   Mom only got one since it was the last. Hopefully the rest of the shipment will be here in a few days, but in the meanwhile, Ando and I have been taking turns with this one. Today, it technically belongs to Ando.

"We could go to the movies?" Ando shares his suggestion as he bites into a celery stalk stuffed with cream cheese. "The new comic-book action movie is out."

"Good suggestion, buddy," Dad replies, giving a warm smile and a wink as he snacks on a ripe Granny Smith apple. "What do you want to do today, Selena?"

I glance over, not sure what I want to do. All I have been doing lately is fighting off bad guys, now that there is a lull in that; I am not sure what to do with myself.

"Anything is fine with me," I respond, feeling tired, but not tired enough to take a nap.

"If we go to the movies, you could invite Nicole and Jenny," Dad suggests, ignorant of the fact that Nicole's parents forbade her to be friends with me, and Jenny has not called me for the entire week.

I frown as Mom and Ando quickly catch Dad up to date about Nicole's possession, Mr. and Mrs. Wong being attacked, Mrs. Wong's kidnapping, and all the rest of the drama that he has missed. When all is told, he sits for a moment with his mouth hanging open from shock before he finally responds.

"Wow!" Dad exclaims. "I've certainly missed a lot."

I smile.

"I'm basically a social pariah." I chuckle under my breath, recalling when I was younger and thought it was a *'social piranha'*. I had fish on the brain even back then. "My best friends hate me; Andrew is still in Alaska with his dad, Mike—"

I practically jump out of my seated position on the floor beside my brother.

"Mike is back in town!" I squeal.

"He is?" Ando beams, making bird-like dancing motions with his arms and neck.

"I forgot about the text he sent me last week saying that basketball camp was almost finished, and he couldn't wait to be back home!" I express with excitement. "He got back yesterday!"

"We should go to the movies then to Mike's parents' pizza place for dinner," Ando suggests, smiling like an adorable lunatic.

"Maybe he'd like to go to the movies with us?" Mom puts the idea out there.

"I'll check," I say, pulling my cellphone out of my pocket and hitting the preprogrammed number from the contact list.

The whole family sits up to eavesdrops, but I do not mind if I get to see at least one of my friends. Mike is usually the first one to volunteer to go to the movies. Like me, he is a movie junky. It also helps that he is addicted to movie snacks.

"MT's Pizza Parlor, how can I help you?" I recognize Mrs. Taylor's voice over the line.

"Hi, Mrs. Taylor!" I greet her with a smile. "This is Selena, Selena Marquez, I met you a while back—"

"Selena! Of course, sweetheart!" Mrs. Taylor sweetly greets back. "It's been a long time. How have you been?"

"I've been… great!" I fib with my fingers crossed.

"What can I do for you, Selena?" she questions cheerfully. "Do you need a pie?"

"There are two things; can we reserve a table for dinner tonight around six or six-thirty?" I ask.

"No worries, I'll have a table for you guys no matter what time you come in."

I blush.

"Thank you!" I grin. "The second thing is, may I please talk to Mike?"

"I'm sorry, sweetie, but Mike went to the movies with Nicole and Jenny," she informs then pauses. "I assumed you were going with them."

"Umm… no… I was… umm… busy, could you please cancel that table for me?" I ask, feeling a knot in my stomach.

"Sure, sweetie." Mrs. Taylor hesitates. "Is everything alright?"

"Yes, ma'am," I lie again, now feeling a headache coming on. "I forgot that we have a previous engagement. I'm sorry."

"No worries, Selena," Mrs. Taylor replies with her same sunny disposition. "If things change give me a call back."

I smile.

"I will," I counter, feeling the growing lump in my throat and the tears welling. "Say hello to Mr. Taylor for me."

"Please say *'hello'* to your folks for me and your brother," she says back then softly hangs up.

Forlorn and depressed, I lean back onto my brother's floor pillow and cover my face with my arms.

"Mike's at the movies with Nicole and Jenny," I say to the room in general.

"They didn't ask you to go with them?" Mom sits up wearing her sad puppy eyes which makes me feel worse.

"Do you still want to go to the movies?" Dad questions with his disappointed expression.

"You all can go." I smile, but inside I feel like crying. "I think I'll stay home and read."

Dad sits up.

"Do you know what I really want to do?" he announces to all of us at once.

"What, Daddy?" My brother sits up too.

"I haven't been on a picnic in ages," my stepfather says, winking at me. "The last one we had was on Ischia, remember? During that outdoor concert."

We all nod and smile.

"But it's raining," I reply with a pouty lip, looking outside at the falling raindrops.

"That's okay." Mom grins. "We'll have an indoor picnic."

Ando beams.

"Can we set up the tent?" he pleads with a face that cannot be declined due to its cuteness factor.

"But of course," Dad answers using a French accent. "Ando and I will take care of the menu, and the girls can set up the tent."

Mom chuckles but covers her mouth to hide it.

"We'll find a movie to watch during our picnic," Mom adds with a smile.

"Sounds great!" Dad scoops Ando up into his arms and spins him around until he is dizzy.

"Where's the tent?" I soak up my family's enthusiasm.

"In the garage." Dad beams. "It's on the second shelf near the generator."

"Get going, soldiers!" Mom salutes.

With a much lighter heart, Mom and I head to the garage to retrieve the small popup tent that Ando and I used to pitch in the backyard in Ohio, while the guys march into the kitchen to prepare our food.

I have to admit the boys did a terrific job with the meal, which brings me to the conclusion that they should always do the cooking and the cleaning. Not all of the time. Perhaps just five days out of the week and on rainy days like today.

"Mmm," I moan as I take another bite of the grilled ham and cheese sandwich. "This is amazing!"

"Thanks, Lena," Ando responds with a mouthful of sandwich.

Mom and Dad are sitting with us on the blue and white checkered plastic picnic tablecloth on the living room floor, directly in front of the pitched tent. The food is neatly arranged in the middle and is easily accessed by everyone. Dad and Ando were determined to make everything perfect.

"May I have more tomato soup?" I ask, passing my bowl to David who ladles another serving into my vessel.

"Certainly." Dad grins. "Anyone else needs a refill?"

"I do!" Ando clamors. "I do!"

"What about you, honey?" Dad turns to Mom.

"No, thank you," she announces, holding her stomach. "No more for me."

"Is your stomach still bothering you?" our father questions with concern.

"I'm fine," our mother chuckles as she gently touches his cheek. "It's probably from all of the excitement."

Tuning out their spousal banter, I notice that the entire living room smells of hot soup and gooey sandwiches. I have already eaten two sandwiches, and I am about to start on my second bowl of soup. I must admit, they truly did a superb job on the food.

"What's for dessert?" I wipe my mouth with my paper napkin.

Ando claps.

"Guess!" he replies jubilantly, the outer area around his lips stained with soup.

"Umm," I sound, pretending to think hard. "Ice cream?"

"Nope!" he exclaims. "Try again."

Mom guesses next.

"Is it cake with some type of pudding-like filling?"

"Wrong! One last try," he announces with a grin.

We think one last time.

"Is it pie?" Dad jumps in.

Ando gives David a look and shakes his head.

"Daddy, you can't guess," my brother informs with an eye roll. "You already know what it is."

"Shucks!" The patriarch of our family states, energetically. "I forgot."

Ando giggles then uncovers his dessert masterpiece which looks like…

"Ando?" I query, studying the glass bowl of something colorful. "What is that?"

"You wanna guess?" He grins. "You'll never guess."

"I believe you," I grumble under my breath as I stare at the lava-lamp looking dessert.

"Mommy, do you know what it is?" my brother inquires, grinning mischievously.

"Umm… I'll need a few minutes, son," Mom replies as she scratches her chin.

Completely lost at what it could be, the Siren and I whisper amongst ourselves as we examine the dish from every angle. I cannot speak for my mother, but I am unable to make heads nor tails of it.

On one side, it looks like yellow cake with some sort of gummy fruit particles. From the other, it resembles a blueberry pie smashed with multicolored marshmallow bits… maybe. Then when you examine it from the top, it resembles melted vanilla ice cream covered with a cereal topping.

Inevitably, my brain starts to hurt, but I do not let that dissuade me from guessing.

I am just about to take another stab at it when my cellphone rings. Excited that it might be Jenny, Mike or possibly Nicole, I answer on the third ring.

"Hello Jenny?" I say, forgetting to look at the caller identification.

"I was missing you." The familiar teen voice speaks, and my knees go weak. "Is this a bad time?"

Andrew!

Immediately, my cheeks redden.

"Your timing is perfect," I compliment, trying not to blush anymore, but my parents and brother are already making sappy faces at me.

"I'm going to take this call in the other room," I announce to everyone, who have now started making kissing faces. "One moment, Andrew."

"Hi, Andrew!" Mom, Dad, and Ando call out loudly so my *boyfriend* can hear them.

Yes!

He officially asked me to be his girlfriend!

A few days ago, he called to check on me, and I broke down and told him everything that was happening including my stepfather's return, the Wong family unfriending us, the Mermaid infestation (which, of course, Amy had to be the highlight), all of my bad luck, plus— heaven help me—I even confessed about kissing Ares. To my surprise, he forgave me for crushing on the God of War but made me promise that now that we have made our relationship 'official', there would be no more of that.

Have I mentioned lately how much I love this guy? Well, I do!

"What are you guys up to tonight?" Andrew chuckles.

As if answering, the rain beats harder on the wood protecting the broken windowpane in the kitchen, the one that one of Amy's recruits broke just for the hell of it.

"It's storming right now, so we decided to have an indoor picnic," I explain. "Dad and Ando made the food and Mom and I pitched the tent."

There is a brief pause before he adds:

"I thought it was raining?"

"The tent is in the living room." I blush and grin at the same time.

"My mom and I used to do that too," he admits with a smile in his voice.

Wanting him to hear the storm, I unlock the back door and stand under the awning that shades a small portion of the back balcony. To my delight, the rain smells strong with a combination of salt and cut grass. Somehow it soothes me.

"I'm sorry for interrupting," Andrew apologizes, unnecessarily.

"Don't worry about it." I beam. "We were just guessing what Ando made for dessert. It's a big mess of, *'stuff'.*"

"That must be the recipe I taught him," Andrew jokes.

"Is that so?" I smirk, getting a kick out of his playfulness.

"I'm an expert at making stuff." He laughs, causing me to laugh too.

"Was there a reason for this lovely call, Mr. Barnett?" I ask, twirling a curl around my index finger.

"Actually, there is a reason, Miss Marquez," he reveals then pauses.

"Really?" I quiz with surprise. "What is it?"

"Well… "

He pauses for a brief moment which makes me nervous.

"What would you like for your birthday?" he questions, seriously. "I didn't want to guess and mess it up."

Happy tears begin to well, but not because I am sad. I have never had a boyfriend before, and the idea of having such an amazing one just overwhelms me. *Andrew* is amazing!

"With all of the craziness going on, I completely forgot about my birthday," I confess, sheepishly.

"Are you having a party?" he questions, genuinely interested.

"Who would I invite?" I blurt. "None of my friends are talking to me besides you."

"You only turn seventeen once," he reminds.

"I'll think about how I want, or if I want to celebrate it, okay?" I reply, firmly.

"Sounds good," he responds. "Now, back to my original question. What would you like for your birthday?

"I will love anything you give me," I say with a sincere smile.

"C'mon." The teen chuckles. "Can you please give me a suggestion?"

"Give me something from your heart and I will definitely love it." I blush again, wishing he were here with me.

"Don't get mad at me if I don't get you the right thing," he warns with a smile in his voice.

"I won't," I giggle. "I promise."

"Ok." He exhales a held breath. "That makes me feel better."

"How is the lost tribe of Inuit doing?" I inquire, genuinely interested, as well as wanting to change the uncomfortable subject of a birthday celebration without my best friends.

At the beginning of the summer, Andrew and his father stumbled upon an indigenous tribe of Native Americans deep in the heart of Alaska. According to Andrew's dad, the tribe has been secluded, by choice, from the rest of civilization for a very long time. They live following ancient customs and procedures. From what Andrew has said, the villagers still worship their ancient deities, including a female goddess that has protected them for centuries.

"They're well," Andrew replies then gets tightlipped. "I can't go into any real detail."

"I understand." I nod, even though he could not see me.

"One day soon, I'll tell you everything," he promises, but he seems distracted.

"I look forward to it." I chuckle, looking out at the sea wondering why it has been so calm even with the storm.

Strange.

"When are you coming home?" I ask, suddenly feeling anxious.

"The day before your birthday," he responds with a smile in his deep voice.

"My birthday is in a couple of days." I grin and my heartbeat quickens from his news.

Andrew chuckles too.

"I know, silly."

Feeling playful, I stick my tongue out at the phone.

"I know that you know," I poke fun at him.

Again, my *boyfriend* takes a pause.

"It was nice hearing your voice," Andrew flirts, making me blush.

"May I call you tomorrow?" I question with a hopeful heart.

"You better," he says sweetly, making my palms perspire.

"Lena!" Ando unexpectantly yells from the living room. *"Dessert is melting! Hurry up!"*

"I'll be right there!" I yell back and I can hear Andrew laughing on the other end even though he is using his hand to cover the speaker.

"I've got to go," I reply with hesitation, not wanting to end our conversation.

Andrew snickers.

"I heard," he states, jovially. "We'll talk soon."

"Be safe among the Inuit," I remind, jokingly.

"You be safe among the Mermaids," he jokes back.

"Andrew?" I force myself to stay calm.

"Yes, Selena?"

"I love you," I say for the first time, nervously biting my lower lip. "You know that… don't you?"

He pauses momentarily.

"I do."

All in all, it could not have been a nicer day.

CHAPTER EIGHTEEN

All of this pressure!

I cannot take all of this pressure! Maybe if I say it out loud, they might take pity on me.

Ok! Here goes!

"I want a chocolate cake with chocolate frosting and chocolate mousse as the filling," I announce it as fast as I can.

"But not everyone likes so much chocolate," Mom utters her concern, but I decide to ignore her.

"It's her birthday, Mommy." Ando sticks up for me, and I give him a high-five.

"Daddy? What do you think about the chocolate cake overload?" Mom asks her husband, and we all turn to glare at David who is looking off into space. "David?"

Finally, he snaps out of it.

"Umm… chocolate sounds terrific to me." He smiles weakly.

"Are you feeling okay?" Mom interrogates with a concerned expression.

"Yeah." The cagey scientist grins, leaning against the counter. "We still haven't found a venue."

"I think we should have it here." I smile, wanting the cozy environment of being at home. "I don't have that many friends and the ones that I do have aren't speaking to me."

"That might change," Mom adds, trying to cheer me up.

"Even if it did, we have more than enough space." I grin, hoping to make her feel not so sad for me.

"Okay," Mom beams. "Home sounds like a great idea."

"What about food?" Ando questions as he snacks on a carrot.

Both Mom and I smile.

"Let's keep it simple," Mom interjects.

"Can we have a barbeque?" I exclaim, recalling Mom's incredible grilling skills.

"Barbeque! Barbeque!" Ando cheers like a sports fan gone wild.

"We can grill hot dogs and burgers," I continue. "And we can make your famous potato salad and baked beans."

"Any appetizers?" Mom asks, but she already knows what I am going to say.

Before I can say what I want, Ando jumps in.

"Lena wants deviled eggs, pimento-cheese finger sandwiches, spinach-artichoke dip and stuffed mushrooms," my brother states with a giant grin.

I laugh.

"You know me so well, baby bro," I praise, giving him another high-five.

"I'll add that to the menu." Mom chuckles, writing it down on her notepad.

"What else do we need?" Ando asks, deep in thought as if it is his party and not mine.

"What would you like for drinks?" Mom glances up.

"I think lemonade and iced tea would be perfect," I reply with enthusiasm.

"Should we have a themed-party?" Mom questions.

"I've always wanted a barn/country theme under the stars with bales of hay, picnic tables with checkered tablecloths, and cool string lights illuminating everything." I describe the vision in my mind. "Mason jars for drinks, corn-on-the-cob, and music! All of my favorite songs to dance to!"

Mom wears a frown.

"I'm not a Siren," I remind. "If I sing, no one will act crazy."

"That sounds fun!" Ando states eagerly, going to the fridge for another cold carrot.

"That was easy," Mom confesses with a chuckle, looking at her notes. "What do you think, David?"

"Huh?" Dad responds, but he does not seem like himself.

Then I remember.

"Dad hasn't taken his medicine today!" I announce, speed walking to his office and retrieving the clear bottle marked: **Siren Grotto H20 Sample** along with a clean syringe and a prepacked alcohol wipe.

"Th-thanks, Marina," Dad stutters, forehead sweaty.

"It's Selena, Dad," I correct, gently.

He barely smiles, just stares at me, lips turning blue and hands starting to shake. Before he can take the syringe from my hand, he falls to the ground and begins to convulse.

"Take my temperature, Selena," Dad whispers with trembling lips.

"Now?!" I shout in complete despair.

"I need the data to be as specific as possible." He coughs and wheezes at the same time.

Quickly, I run to his office and retrieve the tympanic membrane thermometer from his desk. As fast as my feet can carry me, I burst into the kitchen, kneel beside him and place it gently in his ear. After a few seconds, I check, but before I can read off the degrees, I realize that he is foaming at the mouth.

"Dad!" I scream, resting his head on my lap so he does not slam it into the tiles.

"I'm alright," he fibs and points to the thermometer. "What's the reading?"

Panic-stricken, I try to focus on the task at hand instead of how close to death my stepdad appears.

"Your temperature has shot up to one-hundred and six!" I tell, feeling my heartbeat accelerate.

David closes his eyes and stops talking.

This can't be good!

"David?" Mom screeches in full panic mode. "Check his pulse!"

Quickly, I locate one of his carotid arteries at the side of the neck and gently place two fingers there until I feel his pulse.

"Mom, his pulse is weak," I announce on the verge of tears.

"Where's the needle?!" Mom cries, frantically.

"Right here!" I reply, holding it out to her.

With trembling hands, she snatches the needle and fills it with two cubic centimeters of grotto water. Next, she makes sure there are no air bubbles just like David showed her. Seeing that she has got her hands full prepping the medicine and also trying to keep my stepfather still, I rip open the alcohol pad and wipe clean an area on his upper left arm.

Ando is about to cry, so I give him a task to do to get him out of the room.

"Ando," I order. "Go upstairs and get a washcloth for me."

"Okay," he says, speeding out of the room.

"Wet it!" I shout after him.

"Okay!" he shouts back.

As soon as he leaves, Mom injects David with the liquid and after a few seconds the shaking stops, his temperature returns to normal, and the foaming ceases.

"Marina?" Dad sputters the name as he takes a deep breath. "Selena?"

"We're both here," we answer as one.

Blindly, he reaches for us.

"I can't see," he groans with tears in his eyes.

My heart begins to race.

"How could you forget to take your medicine?" Mom's tears begin streaming down her face.

"I was doing an ex-experiment," Dad confesses, an experiment that I was a part of, but I am not crazy enough to confess to it right now.

"What?!" Mom bellows, slapping him on the arm where she just injected.

"Ouch!" David bolts into an upright position, covering the injured area with his hand. "You saved me just to kill me?"

"Looks like!" Mom snarls and pushes him away.

"Why?" he counters, slowly sitting straighter, bracing for another punch.

"Why were you conducting an experiment?" Mom questions with hurt in her eyes.

Just then Ando returns with the washcloth in his hand. Sadly, he looks at Dad who is rapidly returning to his normal self.

"Are you okay?" Ando exclaims, glancing from parent to parent.

"I'm fine, son," Dad informs with a semi-cheerful disposition.

"Answer my question, David," Mom growls as she taps her foot.

Dad sighs with frustration.

"I have to see how long a specific amount of medicine lasts," David informs in his scientific tone.

"You are unbelievable!" my mother insults, lashing out. "Experimenting is what got you into trouble in the first place!"

Dad's eyes widen.

"If I hadn't been *'experimenting'* we would never have been able to save Selena!" he shouts right back.

At his proclamation, Mom shuts her mouth, instantly realizing that he is more than accurate. If David had not been injecting himself with grotto water, he would not have been able to enter Paradiso. He was the only one who was not a Siren and therefore the only one who could pass through the barrier that I had erected.

"Please, stop," I sigh, feeling the weight of what has happened on my shoulders. "We all know that I am the one to blame for all of this."

"We all do things that we regret, Selena," Dad comforts sincerely. "But risking my life to save yours is something I would do over and over again until the end of time."

I smile even though I feel horrible.

"What's the upside to this?" Mom questions, looking at Dad from the top of his head to the soles of his feet.

My stepfather smiles, takes her hand and turns to leave the house.

"Follow me and you'll find out." He smirks like the Cheshire cat from *Alice in Wonderland*.

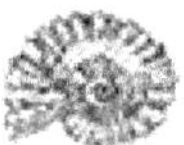

We all follow Dad down to the rocky shoreline wondering what he has to show us. Mom has a look of complete annoyance, Ando just wants to go swimming, and I keep remembering Mermaid bodies covering the ground. All in all, we do not look like a happy procession.

"David, what are we doing down here?" Mom huffs and pouts as she stops at the bottom of the steps, almost causing a pileup, then notices the aunts bobbing in the surf near the cove entrance.

"I want to show you all something." He grins as he takes off his T-shirt and stands wearing only his swimming shorts.

"What do you think you're doing?" Mom growls, angrily. "You're not going in there!"

"Could you please just trust me." David sighs and takes her near the edge where the sea slams against the rocky coastline and creates the most beautiful mist.

"I don't know if I can—" Mom begins, but Dad cuts her off.

"Marina, I know that you're scared about all of this, but I guarantee that it is worth it when you see what I can do," her husband implores with a twinkle in his eyes.

"What are you able to do?" Mom demands, glaring at him.

Momentarily ignoring her protest, Dad kisses her cheek.

"Watch," he says then immediately jumps into the agitating sea.

"Oh no!" Mom screams. "David!"

Immediately, our mother starts to undress, but wanting to see what happens, I stop her. David may be cavalier when it comes to many things, but not to placing himself in reckless endangerment or willingly placing the wellbeing of his family in jeopardy. No matter what, he will always stay safe for us.

"How long has he been down there?" Mom questions with fear-filled eyes.

Uneasily, I glance at my watch.

"About a minute," as I say this, David emerges wearing a huge smile.

"Time me, now" he requests then disappears again.

One-minute turns to five then turns to fifteen and then…

"I'm going after him." Mom frowns and is about to jump in when Ligeia and Leukosia exit the sea and sit at the edge of the shoreline with their feet dangling in the water.

"Wait," they order together. "Give him a chance."

Against her better judgement, Mom waits. Her foot is tapping the entire time. Soon she starts to pace and bite her fingernails.

"How long has it been now?" my mother questions, her face a sickly green hue.

"It's been thirty minutes," Ando replies, searching the surface for any sign of our father.

Suddenly, David's body breaches the water. He looks thrilled and able to last even longer. Seeing Mom's stunned expression, he exits the sea and sits beside the aunts.

"I've actually stayed submerged for close to forty minutes," he educates, gleefully.

"That's extremely impressive." Mom actually exhales her held breath and gives him a full smile.

Next, he reaches for a small rock that is near him. Joyfully, he holds it up for us to see it.

"Look at what I can do." Dad beams as he gives the rock a squeeze and it breaks into almost powder.

Ando, Mom and I can only stare with our mouths open.

"No comments?" He chuckles as he stands and brushes off his palms. "I was hoping for some sort of reaction."

"How did this happen?" Mom gasps, needing to sit down.

"Apparently, it is one of the side effects from the grotto water." Leukosia smiles brightly.

Mom stares, stunned.

"And super strength is a part of the effect too?" she blurts, not knowing which way is up.

"This is a blessing," David speaks up. "Now, you don't have to worry about me so much. Can't you see? I'm not a burden anymore."

My mother stares at him with her mouth open.

"You were never a burden." The Siren pouts, her eyes welling with tears. "You're my husband and I love you."

"That didn't come out right," Dad groans, feeling guilty.

"David, show her what else you can do," the sisters encourage aloud.

My stepfather smiles like a little boy but says nothing.

"I'm not upset with you, David. Well, that's not completely true—" my mother announces to the wind I suppose. "Well of course, I know you didn't mean for this to happen."

Then, quite unexpectantly, my mother stomps her right foot and growls.

"I don't wanna discuss this anymore," she sighs, throwing both arms above her head in a show of exasperation.

So weird!

"Mom?" I question, glancing around the area. "Who are you talking to?"

"Your father," Mom replies, nodding in Dad's direction.

"No, I don't want you to feel like that... " Mom states rather loudly. "*Because...* that's why!"

"Mom?" I snap at the top of my voice.

"What?" she snaps back then quickly apologizes. "No! I'm not being difficult. *You're* being difficult!"

Oh no!

My mother has finally lost her ever loving Siren mind!

"Mommy—" my brother tries to disrupt her rant but is cut off.

"Son, I am talking to your father," she announces rather loudly. "Can't you hear him—"

"He's not saying anything," I interrupt, glancing at David who has been silent for the last several minutes.

Expectedly, Ando laughs and claps his hands.

"I can hear Daddy too!" he exclaims, and squeals like a piglet. "He's inside of my head!"

"So can we," the Aunts grin.

It is then I realize what is happening.

"Dad, can you communicate telepathically?" I utter, completely dumbstruck.

David blushes.

"It appears so."

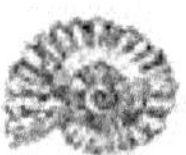

The surprises keep coming and coming and my brain is fried because of it. Dad is more of a Siren than I am. Naturally, he does not have gills, but he can hold his breath for up to fifty minutes, when he concentrates. Without a doubt, he has the strength of a Siren, and to top it all off; he can communicate with the rest of the family using his mind. All I can do is stand on the sidelines, watch and try not to get in the way.

"Lena, what are you doing out here?" Ando probes as he steps out onto the back balcony.

"Just watching the stars." I sigh sadly, inhaling the sweet night air.

"By yourself?" His eyes are narrow, and I feel a lecture looming.

"Yup!" I respond, looking up towards the heavens at Orion's Belt.

"Can I sit with you?" he asks, already pulling up a lounge chair and making himself comfortable.

I giggle.

"Would it matter if I had said *'no'*?" I tease like sisters often do.

He only grins and hands me a bowl of freshly cut strawberries with two scoops of vanilla ice cream and a drizzle of chocolate sauce.

"Thanks!" I gleam, gladly taking the bowl.

"Mom told me to give this to you," he informs as he gazes up at the stars too.

Unwilling to let it go to waste, I take a healthy bite enjoying as the ice cream melts on my tongue. To my left, my brother glances around the balcony and I know what he is thinking. Not because I can read his mind, but because I know how my little brother thinks.

"Aren't you afraid of Mermaids attacking you out here by yourself?" He keeps a watchful eye out.

To tell the truth, I have thought about it… thought about getting attacked way too much.

"No, I don't think they will bother us for a while." I grin. "Not after the beating the family gave them. Amy will wait until her numbers are higher or maybe… "

Ando smiles at me.

"Why are you smiling at me like that?" I grill, blushing.

"You're good at that," he compliments.

"Good at what?" I question as my mind jumps to other things.

"Battle strategies and knowing what people are going to do." The insightful boy grins. "You remind me of Mom."

I really turn red then.

"Soooo… " he starts. "You got your powers back?"

"Temporarily." I give a loud exhale. "It left as soon as it came back."

"How did that happen?" he queries, avoiding eye contact.

At a loss, I shrug.

"I'm not sure," I answer, truthfully. "It was probably adrenaline."

"Do you miss it?" Ando quizzes as he turns to face me.

"Miss what?" I pretend not to understand his question.

"You know." He pouts.

"You mean being a Siren?" I answer, looking at the dark horizon and enjoying the song of the sea as it serenades the moon.

"Yeah," he sighs. "Don't you miss being in the sea?"

"I definitely don't miss the pull it has on me," I confess, honestly. "But I miss the feeling of peace that it gave me."

"Is that all?" he continues, grabbing my bowl of ice cream and berries and taking a huge spoonful.

"I miss being able to talk to the animals," I confess, starting to feel depressed.

"Did I tell you that Whistler, the dolphin, has a wife now?" Ando makes a funny face.

I shake my head as I try not to laugh at my brother's reaction.

"No, you didn't tell me that he got married," I inform, wanting to hear more.

"He's gonna be a dad soon." He grimaces and takes another bite of my dessert.

"Is he excited?" I ask, feeling happier.

Ando nods.

"Tell him congratulations for me," I beg with a broad grin.

"I will," Ando promises.

"Can you believe that Daddy has superpowers?" he queries, wiping dripping ice cream from his chin with his palm then wiping it on the front of his t-shirt.

I cannot help but laugh at the little boy who is actively eating all of my dessert.

"I think it's cool that he isn't helpless anymore," I say without heat. "I imagine it would be hard for a man like our father not to be able to protect his family."

"What do you mean, Lena?"

"Dad is old fashioned," I explain. "He takes pride in being a good provider and protector."

Ando nods in agreement.

"Mommy's not happy," my sibling reminds, licking the spoon.

I shrug.

"It will take time to get used to it," I respond, clearing the week's events from my mind. "But she's happy to have him back in our lives. We all are."

"Yeah," Ando agrees, twirling the spoon in his hand.

More at ease, I turn toward the heavens again. It is impossible not to notice that the stars are bright this evening. Their faraway flickers have no trouble illuminating the dark cloudless canvas while the moon—although crescent in shape—is just as impressive. If I were as artistic as Mom and Ando, I would want to create a painting of it to preserve its beauty forever.

Seeing nature at its best, I feel the need to confess.

"Believe it or not, I miss your voice in my head," I reveal with a grin and stick my tongue out at him. "I miss my powers too. I feel lost without them."

"Really?"

"Really," I admit with a heavy heart.

"I thought you wanted to be human?" he states, blankly.

"I thought I did," I reply, humbly, feeling the tightening in my chest once more.

"Lena?"

"Yeah?" I grin, closing my eyes, enjoying my brother's company.

"Do you want to be a Siren again or do you want to keep being human?"

It does not take me long to answer. In fact, I have been thinking about it for quite some time. It is an easy question. Easier than I thought it would be.

"I miss being a Siren… very much," I mumble, taking his warm hand in mine.

Smiling, he leans back in his seat and continues eating my dessert.

"Good," he sighs.

I turn to him, now utterly bewildered by his one-word response.

"Why?" I ask, studying that far away glimmer in his clear eyes. "Do you know something that I don't?"

He smiles with that mysterious smile that he inherited from his father.

"Maybe…"

CHAPTER NINETEEN

Everything seems to be in order. I hope. The house is neat and tidy. The appetizers are arranged methodically on party trays. Dad is manning the grill with the expertise of a highly trained chef. Mom, Ando, and I have decorated both inside and outside to resemble a cozy country home; all set for a shindig of epic proportions. Even the aunts have promised to make a cameo appearance later tonight.

"Did you send out the invitations?" I interrogate, my anxiety level at an all-time high.

"I did." Mom laughs and gives me a reassuring pat on the back. "Stop worrying. You'll get frown-lines."

I smile.

"Sirens don't get frown-lines, remember?" I tease, then parry. "Hmm… Since I'm not a Siren, maybe I can get them now?"

"Semantics." Mom giggles as she sets a clear glass vase filled with daisies in the center of the buffet table. "Everything is ready. All we need are the guests."

Wearily, I frown.

"I don't think anyone will show up," I reply, sadly.

"Have faith," Melody encourages from behind, scaring the daylights out of us both.

"Don't do that!" I yelp, clutching my chest. "Can you wear a bell around your neck, please?"

Melody giggles.

"I am sorry." The stunning Muse grins in her astral form. "I just wanted to wish you a good night and happy birthday, my darling, Selena."

"You're not staying?" I extend my bottom lip. "It won't be much of a party without you."

Melody winks.

"I will be back later when the party goers have left," she promises. "I would not want your friends having heart attacks due to seeing me like *this*."

The all-powerful being waves her hands over her non-corporeal form.

"You're right." I grin and blush at the same time. "See you later."

"Have fun, my dear," Melody wishes, blowing me a kiss as she fades into nothing.

Just as she fades out, the doorbell rings.

"Oh my gosh!" I bluster. "Who do you think that is?"

"I don't know." Mom smiles. "You should probably go answer it."

I nod, smooth my curls and take a deep breath.

"Here I go," I declare, feeling anxious.

"Good luck!" Mom grins. "You look gorgeous."

"Are you sure?" I ask for the tenth time in ten minutes.

Looking down at my ensemble, I sigh.

When I was in my closet searching for an outfit, this seemed plausible. I wanted to look 'more mature' after all, so I chose a black and white floral sundress that reaches the tops of my knees and a pair of two-inch black heels. It is a little bit dressier than I am used to, but it still has a laid-back casual vibe about it. This is my first time wearing it and it feels so weird in comparison to my jeans which I want to be buried in.

"I don't feel like myself in this." I pout. "Are you sure I don't look like a dork?"

"You look just fine." Mom gives me a wink of approval.

The doorbell rings again.

"If you don't answer the door, whoever it is will leave," Mom reminds with a chuckle.

"True." I giggle.

Taking a deep breath to steady my nerves, I creep to the front door. On pins and needles, I tiptoe to reach the peephole.

"It's Jenny!" I shout, forgetting that she could hear me.

As imagined, she looks beautiful wearing the same black cocktail-length dress that she wore for the homecoming dance. Her hair is in a stylish up-do, and she has just a smidgeon of make-up on. She looks just like a fashion model.

With shaking hands, I tug open the door and hug her before she can protest. We stand in the doorway for a long minute as I continue to squeeze her body tight.

"It's nice to see you too." Jenny snickers and gently pushes me away. "I love you too, darling, but breathing was becoming an issue."

"Thank you for coming to my birthday party!" I beam with a moronic expression. "I was getting worried that absolutely no one would show up."

Jenny smiles.

"Are you kiddin'," she says with a playful wink. "I wouldn't miss this for the world."

"Come in, Jenny," Mom calls from the living room. "The party is in here, not out there."

"Yes, please get your butt in here," I respond, pulling her inside and closing the door behind her.

As soon as the door shuts, the doorbell rings again.

"I'll get it," I inform my first guest. "Help yourself to some appetizers."

Jenny nods.

"Where should I put this?" she asks, holding up a birthday-themed gift bag.

"There's a table in the next room," I say, turning to answer the door. "You can't miss it."

Jenny nods and disappears into the formal dining room. Nervously, I smooth my dress and take another deep breath. Maybe tonight will not be a disaster after all.

Again, I peek out of the peephole, just in case Mermaids decide to crash my party. Although I do not think that they would be so polite as to ring the doorbell.

"Mike!" I scream like a crazed fan. "You're here!"

Casually cool, Mike looks great in a black, button-down dress shirt, dark jeans, and sneakers. His hair is neatly cropped, but stylish, and of course, he smells terrific. It is difficult not to ogle him.

"Live and in person!" He beams with a sweet smile.

"Did you miss me?" I hear myself quiz.

"Did you miss me?" he questions back.

"Not really," I joke.

"So not cool." The brilliant athlete pouts, pretending to be offended.

"I missed you, you big dork!" I jibe, straining my neck to look up at him.

Mike laughs with that endearing laugh of his and picks me up in a bear-hug, completely lifting me off of the floor. He has grown at least an inch or two since the beginning of summer vacation. I am certain he is over six-four now. His shoulders are broader, and his muscles have muscles. Fortunately, he still reminds me of a great big teddy bear.

"Happy Birthday, woman!" he growls and smiles at the same time. "How did you manage to get prettier over the summer?"

I blush and shake my head.

"Stop that!" I chastise without heat. "Get in here!"

"Oh wow!" The teen whistles low as he takes in the room's decorations. "It looks sensational in here. It's like being in a real barn, but without the smell of cows."

"Thank you," I say, making him put me back down. "Make yourself comfortable. The gift table is in the dining room along with the appetizers. Jenny is in there too."

Mike's eyes light up.

"The Jen-ster is back!" He smiles, evilly. "I've got to go and harass that girl. She didn't return any of my calls over the summer."

I laugh.

"Have fun!" I giggle.

When the doorbell rings again, I am still in the same spot.

"Dr. Khan! Miss Khan!" I exclaim excitedly. "So glad you could make it! Please, come on in!"

"You look gorgeous, and all grown up!" Dr. Khan praises, making my cheeks heat.

"Selena, I've missed you!" Miss Khan hugs me tightly.

"How was India?" I question, fascinated that she got to visit somewhere so exotic.

"Hot!" she jokes, giving me a vibrant smile.

"Please, come inside," I add, welcomingly. "Mom is in the kitchen and Dad is on the back deck grilling."

"I can't believe that you're seventeen already," Dr. Khan purrs, looking me over. "Time is racing by."

I grin knowing exactly what she means, but before I can respond there is a knock at the door.

"I'll get that," I state, eager to know who the next guest will be. "Make yourself at home."

Woot! People are actually coming to my party! Things are looking up!

"Thanks so much for com—" I stop in midsentence at the person standing in front of me.

"Hello, beautiful." Andrew sighs and blushes at the same time.

"Andrew!" I exclaim, jumping into his arms and kissing him, forgetting that his mother is standing beside us. "I'm so sorry, Ms. Barnett."

Andrew's mother giggles.

"It's no problem." Ms. Barnett blushes. "I didn't see *much*."

"Mom," Andrew chastises, blushing too. "Please don't embarrass me."

"Come in, come in," I insist taking them both by the hand. "Refreshments are in the dining room which is right through there."

I point and release their hands, but Andrew immediately grabs it again.

"Mom, can you please take this with you," he asks, handing the large present he is holding to his mother.

"Don't be too long, you two," Ms. Barnett teases. "Happy birthday, Selena!"

"Thanks a lot, Ms. Barnett." I giggle, giving her son's hand a squeeze.

Before his mother is fully out of the room, Andrew pulls me close. He smells just as I remember, incredible mixed with male-heavenliness. He has also grown taller and might be just an inch shorter than Mike now. His eyes are greener, and his dark hair is as black as mine. There is something about his mannerisms too. He seems more comfortable and confident.

"I've missed you so much," he tells, kissing my cheek, his gaze locked onto mine.

"I'm glad you're home," I gush, inhaling his familiar scent.

Dear Father! He is even more stunning than I remember. I'm definitely hooked!

"Me too." My boyfriend smiles, leading me into the dining room to see our friends. "Selena?"

"Yes?" I swoon, loving having him this close.

"I need to talk to you about something," he says flatly. "Something important."

"Alright," I respond. "Is after the party okay?"

He nods his approval and gives me another kiss, but this time on my forehead. *Wow!* I cannot believe that he is so tall now.

"The appetizers are in the dining room, so we should find Jenny and Mike there too," I coo, not caring who hears.

Andrew snickers.

As we turn the corner, we see Mike and Jenny chatting while snacking on the homemade appetizers. Mike, as usual, has a plate piled with a little of everything. Jenny, seemingly daintier, also has a full plate, but not as high. They both smile when they see us.

"Selena!" Mike exclaims with excitement. "These deviled eggs are delicious. Better than my mom's. Just don't tell her I said that."

"Mums the word." I smirk.

"How was camp?" Andrew joins in, giving his best friend a playful punch to the abdomen.

"It was intense," Mike confides then takes a sip of his lemonade. "We were up at the crack of dawn and in bed by nine at night. I hurt in places I never knew existed."

"How was it in Alaska?" Jenny questions with a huge grin then takes a bite of one of her stuffed mushrooms.

Andrew scratches his head.

"It's gorgeous terrain," he says with a far-off look in his dreamy eyes. "I miss it already."

"Well, I'm glad you're here," I remind whole-heartedly, giving him a quick peck to the cheek.

"What about you, Red?" Mike inquires, elbowing Jenny on the arm. "How was the Emerald Isle?"

"Lovely and green," Jenny begins and manages to tell us all about her three-month stay starting from the moment she landed in Dublin to the flight back to Isla Flora. No detail is left uncovered.

"… and that's why my cousin, Liam, wears a patch," she finishes in classic-Jenny form making us all stare with our mouths open.

After a few seconds of processing, we all laugh.

Same old Jenny!

"I can't believe you are a model," Mike teases, mischievously. "Are all the Irish seeing-impaired?"

"So not funny." Jenny blushes then jab him in the ribs.

"I mean, who likes red hair and freckles?" Mike continues even after Jenny's face reddens in warning. "Or tall and skinny?"

"I'm not that skinny anymore," Jenny whines and pinches his arm hard making him yelp.

"Cut it out!" Mike shouts, rubbing the hurt area.

"You cut it out!" Jenny retaliates.

Fortunately, Mom steps into the room holding a stack of napkins and disposable plates.

"Dinner is ready," she announces with a welcoming smile. "You guys can catch-up later."

"Yes, Mrs. Marquez," they all reply as one.

"Let me help you with those," Mike offers as he takes the items my mother is carrying.

"Thank you, Michael," Mom grins. "You are quite the gentleman."

"I'll make sure to tell my mom," he replies, blushing even more.

Mike turns a soft shade of burgundy as he follows my mother out of the room.

"Did your mom do something different with her hair?" Andrew drools, so I hit him on the shoulder.

"No." I laugh. "It's the same as it always is."

"It looks… fuller… bouncier." The teen blushes, earning him a punch to the gut, if he had a gut.

Sirens have it made; I shake my head.

"You have nothing to worry about," Andrew adds, taking my hand in his.

"What do you mean?" I question, letting him lead me through the house to the back door.

"Your mom is a Siren, so people will always see her as gorgeous," he explains. "Even though technically she *is* pure perfection."

"*Wow!* This is so not where I thought you were going with this," I huff, trying to pull my hand out of his, but he only holds it tighter.

"What I was trying to say… is that… you make this impossible to get out, woman… " he rambles like I sometimes do. "I know that I'm in love with you, *You*, Selena Marquez, the person *not* the Siren."

"How can you tell?" I counter, sincerely interested in his theory.

"What people feel for Sirens is obsession," he clarifies, obviously he has contemplated about the subject often.

"Obsession?" I repeat, not liking the sound of that.

"A wise woman once told me that only the purest of hearts can truly fall in love with a Siren," he expands his explanation.

"Who told you that?" I grill, suddenly feeling jealous.

"One of the female elders of the Inuit tribe," he confesses.

"You told them about *me… us… Sirens*?" I question as my stomach pitches like a small boat on a stormy sea.

"No, I didn't talk about you specifically," he promises. "We were having a *hypothetical* discussion about myths and folklore in modern society. The subject of Sirens just came up."

"Sounds deep," I state under my breath. "What did you say about Sirens in general?"

"I posed the question: *'What if Sirens existed in modern society and, if so, what would be the ramifications?'*."

I chuckle.

"When did you get to be so profound?" I joke.

"I've always been profound," he replies, good-humoredly. "I just don't usually show it."

"What exactly were you trying to figure out? In English please." I jibe.

"I wanted to know if true love is possible with an entity that is capable of *simulating* love," he tells as he halts in mid-step right before we reach the door which leads to the deck where our friends and family are getting food.

"And what was her response?" I interrogate, intrigued by his conversation about *'hypothetical'* Sirens.

He grins before he speaks.

"Because you're human now, none of my feelings are artificial," he emphasizes.

"You were worried about me putting the whammy on you?" I probe, feeling like a heel.

"Wouldn't you be?" he queries, sincerely.

"I guess so," I whisper, wanting this discussion to end.

"She asked me a lot of questions and we talked a lot," he informs cheerfully.

"About what?"

"About how I feel about you," he states, flatly.

I look away, not wanting to know the truth in case it is not in my favor.

"What was the conclusion?" I whisper.

"I really *am* in love with you," he blurts like I should have already known the answer.

I look at him unable to respond.

"Do you know how I know that it's true love and not obsession?" he questions, touching my cheek.

I shrug, still avoiding his gaze.

"Because my heart still skips a beat when I think about you even when we are far apart." The teen smiles as he pushes a stray strand of hair behind my ear. "My palms get all clammy right before I hold your hand, and my mouth goes dry when I know I'm going to talk to you.

That's how I know."

"I never thought about it that way," I admit, feeling sheepish.

"Lena! Andrew!" Ando barks, staring at us with a peculiar look on his face. "The food is gonna get cold. *Jeez!"*

"Be right there, Andover," Andrew jibes.

"Hurry up!" my brother blusters. "If we eat fast, we can start on the cake!"

"We'll be right there!" I say, giving a warning growl.

Nervously, I turn back to my companion.

"So, you love me?" I grin.

"Mostly." He chuckles earning him a playful slap. "What about you? Is it real for you?"

I am about to answer when Ando returns.

"Mom says to move it or lose it," he states firmly then turns and walks away. "I'm tired of guarding your burger. I'm hungry too."

"To be continued," Andrew says with a wink.

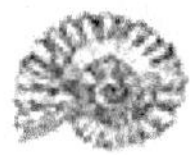

The rest of the evening was wonderful. The DJ that David hired is fun and has the latest music, plus he plays everything from the eighties through the nineties. He deftly mixes contemporary tunes with group dances like The Electric Slide and The Cupid Shuffle. To my amazement, everyone is dancing including the parents and David's co-workers. Even my brother is getting his groove-on with all of the ladies.

"Time to cut the cake!" Dad declares, wrangling everyone into the formal dining room.

"You need a partner to cut the cake with," Dr. Khan mischievously provokes over the crowd.

"I'm her partner," Andrew speaks up, taking my hand again.

"Okay!" Dr. Khan grins. "And a handsome partner at that." She winks and everyone chuckles.

"This cake is definitely chocolate." Andrew grins, staring at the three layered, chocolate tower of lusciousness decorated with white and dark chocolate curls.

"It's got chocolate mousse in between each layer," I boast with a devilish grin and salivating tongue.

Impatiently, I wait for everyone to sing Happy Birthday which makes me turn red. Afterward, Andrew and I pose for pictures, smiling, all the while hating all of the attention. Then it is time to cut the incredible cake. Carefully, we use a sharp knife and slice the first piece.

"Feed her the first bite," Dorinda requests over the crowd.

"Umm," I say as my face heats. "Do we have to do that?"

"It's tradition," Miss Khan reinforces, clapping with delight.

"Fine, we'll do it," I reply, meekly, wanting to hide under a rock.

Andrew grins as he feeds me the first forkful of cake and then I reciprocate.

"Kiss her!" someone yells, making me almost choke on what is in my mouth.

"Yeah! Go ahead and kiss her!" another voice that I do not recognize shouts over the din.

Before I can protest, Andrew bends and kisses me innocently on the lips causing the whole crowd to *ooh* and *ahh*.

"That is so sweet," I hear the voice and recognize it immediately.

Slowly, I turn to face the direction that it came from and there, right next to a stack of hay is Amy and her father. She is lovely in a silver knee-length dress and matching shoes. Her hair is straight, sleek, and down to her tiny waist and wearing far too much make-up.

"You two make the cutest couple." Amy sneers. "Go on with your cake-eating ceremony. I didn't mean to interrupt."

"What's she doing here?" Jenny probes, looking over her shoulder at the uninvited guest.

"Happy birthday, Selena." Amy leers as she slowly approaches. "Hello handsome."

As if I am not here, she rakes my boyfriend with her eyes from head to toe then back again. Andrew, growing more uncomfortable by the minute, simply avoids her gaze.

"Why in the world are you with her?" she grills, running one of her expertly manicured fingers down Andrew's cobalt-blue dress shirt. "She's so beneath you and me."

Immediately, he grabs her wrist, but she easily pulls her arm away.

"Leave, Amy," I order beneath my breath, not wanting to cause a scene. "You weren't invited."

"I figured my invitation got lost in the mail." The young Mermaid grins, slowly walking around Andrew and I as if she is a stalking shark and we are the fat seals.

"What are you doing here, Amy?" Ms. Barnett appears out of nowhere.

Amy glares at Andrew's mother who glares right back.

"I wasn't expecting riffraff at this shindig. Dogs belong outside, Selena," Amy snarls. "Didn't your mother teach you that?"

"Amy!" Mr. Jacobs rushes over. "I forbid you to cause a scene."

"But Daddy, I'm behaving, cross my heart," she glowers. "I was just making small talk with my friends."

"Hello, Stuart," Ms. Barnett greets without a smile.

"Hello, Andrea." Mr. Jacobs lowers his head.

"Are we done with the pleasantries?" Amy blusters, taking Andrew's hand. "I'd like to dance."

Calmly, Andrew pulls away.

"Get out of here, Amy," the teenager states as he stares coldly at the disturbed young woman… Mermaid… *whatever*.

"I've missed you," she purrs, touching his lapel. "Have you missed me?"

"Amy we're leaving!" Mr. Jacobs commands, taking his daughter by the hand and heading toward the front door, but she breaks free and turns back to my date.

"Dump this skank and I'll make it worth your while," she proposes then suggestively licks her lips.

Ashen and stunned, Mr. Jacobs turns to my parents who appear just as surprised at the dramatic scene playing out in front of the entire birthday party.

"David… Marina, I am so very sorry," the horrified father apologizes on his daughter's behalf. "I'll take care of this at home."

Andrew bends to whisper in her ear and when he finishes, Amy slaps his face and storms out, leaving us all staring after her. Mr. Jacobs apologizes once more and then races after his snooty child. Somehow, I feel sorry for him.

"Leave it to Amy to always be the center of attention," I joke, unable to think of how else to handle the situation.

The guests stare at me then at each other, and to my relief, begin discussing the incident amongst each other.

"Here, have a slice," Andrew replies, handing me a piece of cake.

Needing to forget the whole thing, I take a bite of cake and try to push the incident out of my head.

Even after Amy crashed my party, everyone still ended the evening on a happy note. They all complimented the festive décor, the beautiful location overlooking the Caribbean, the exquisite food, and, of course, the mouth-watering cake.

"It was a wonderful party," Miss Khan and her mother say at once.

"I'm glad you could make it," Mom expresses her goodbyes, and sends them off with hugs and a plate of leftovers.

"I have not danced so much in ages," Ms. Barnett states, following The Khans. "Thanks so much for inviting me."

"We've got to get together more often, Andrea," Mom answers honestly as she hugs Andrew's mom, who just happens to be her boss.

"I'm going to hold you to that." The reserved editor blushes.

"Where's Andrew?" Mom looks around.

Ms. Barnett shakes her head.

"We drove separately," she informs with a roll of her expressive, emerald-green eyes, eyes exactly like Andrew's.

"Separately?" I repeat, bewildered.

"Roger, his dad, bought him a used car for helping him out this summer." Ms. Barnett grins. "Nothing fancy, but it is clean, inexpensive and dependable."

My hands both go to my waist and perch there as my right foot starts to tap.

"He hasn't left yet, has he?" I ask, suddenly feeling slighted. "We were supposed to talk about something important."

"I'm sure he's still here." Ms. Barnett smiles warmly. "He and Mike are probably near what's left of the food."

Unexpectedly, Mom leans toward her boss.

"Andrea, what was the deal between you and Amy?" Mom questions, so no one else will overhear.

"She doesn't like me very much," her manager says pushing her glasses back onto her nose bridge. "Her mother and I didn't get along either."

"You knew her mother?" I gulp, knowing that the late Mr. Jacobs was a merciless killer.

Does she know about Amy's mother being a Mermaid? A Mermaid who liked to snack on children? Jeez! I hope not!

"Rose, Amy's mother, and I didn't have much in common," Ms. Barnett educates our small group.

"So… you were friends with the Jacob's?" I blurt, finding that interesting.

"We were friends for many years until—"

"Until, what?" Mom and I both ask at once.

Nervously, Andrea glances at her watch.

"It's getting late," she whispers. "I'll see you at the office on Monday, Marina?"

"Absolutely," Mom agrees as she gives the woman a friendly hug. "Drive safely."

Ms. Barnett waves and rushes to her car.

"That was interesting," Mom reflects, tapping her bottom lip.

"Extremely." I giggle, doing the same.

"Mrs. Marquez, Selena, thank you so much for a great evening," Jenny thanks, giving us both hugs and kisses on the cheek. "I've got to get going. I don't want my grandparents to worry."

"Of course." Gently, my mother hugs her and thanks her for coming. "Take your time, alright?"

Jenny nods.

"I'll talk to you tomorrow," my friend tells as she hugs me once more.

"Sounds good to me." I smile, waving as she leaves.

"I've got to go too," Mike informs, carrying a covered plate with food. "I had a great time."

"Thank you so much for coming!" I hug his waist as he kisses me on the top of the head.

"Talk to you soon." Mike smiles and heads out.

Then I feel a tap on my shoulder.

"May I bother you for a moment?" Andrew nervously grins.

"Sure," I reply, taking his outstretched hand. "What's up?"

"Come with me." He leads me to the now empty balcony with the present that he brought held tightly in his free hand.

"Open it," he orders without looking at me.

"Okay." My face heats as I tear off the festive wrapping paper.

"Save the card for later," he pleads, appearing anxious.

"Should I be worried?" I jibe, pleading with the butterflies to stop flapping in my stomach.

Confidently, he shakes his head.

"Be careful," he warns. "It's breakable."

Carefully, I unwrap the rectangular shaped box and unwind the item from the multiple layers of bubble-wrap to reveal a twelve-inch totem pole. It is the most intricate and ingenious totem pole that I have ever seen, and I have seen a lot of them since David once lived in Alaska and was completely intrigued by them.

The base of this particular totem depicts the sea with its crashing waves, painted in a vivid aquamarine highlighted by stark-white seafoam. The second layer shows a lovely woman emerging from the waves with hair as black as midnight. The third section shows three women who resemble my aunts and grandmother, Parthenope, their eyes the same mesmerizing hue of the waves. In the next section, there is an exotic island that could pass for Paradiso or Isla Flora. Finally, at the top of the totem pole is a dark-haired woman with outstretched wings flying toward the moon.

Also, the scent of the wood is so familiar.

"What type of wood is this?" I ask, sniffing it again.

Andrew thinks for a moment before answering.

"Sedna carved it from a block of western red cedar," he reveals, rubbing the nape of his neck.

"Sedna," I repeat, liking the way it sounds. "Made this?"

Andrew nods.

"This is incredible!" I gasp, examining it from all sides. "The colors that she used are so vibrant and rich."

"Sedna, the elder that I was telling you about, hand-carved this for me for you," he explains.

"I love it!" I gush, holding the totem in one hand and hugging him with the other. "I'll take good care of it! I promise. I know just where to put it."

"Do you really like it?" He blushes.

"I really do!" I sigh happily. "This totem pole is breathtaking." I beam.

"Are you sure you didn't tell her about my ancestry?" I quiz.

"Nope." He smiles. "But she said that the wood spoke to her, and this is what came from it."

Overwhelmed by the generous gesture, I kiss him tenderly and lay my head against his chest. His heart is beating wildly as if he has just run a tiresome race. For some reason, it soothes me.

"Thank you for my gift." I smile, inhaling his scent. "I love it almost as much as I love you, Mr. Barnett."

And I mean that from the bottom of my heart.

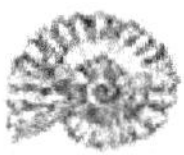

No matter how hard I try, I cannot take my eyes off it. The totem that Andrew gave me somehow speaks to my soul. It shows my family line in such a beautiful, elegant way. Every time I look at it, I beam.

Tap! Tap! Tap!

"What the hell?" I mumble to myself as I look around.

The room is quiet and there are no other sounds coming from the rest of the house. Ando is in bed completely worn out from the party. Mom and Dad turned in right after our guests left. The only one still awake is me.

Tap! Tap!

"What is that sound?"

I lunge from the bed, grab my mother's mace and dash to the window. It is dark outside with no sign of the moon. The little light that it gave off earlier is now hidden by thick storm clouds. In the distance, I can hear the muffled cracks of lightning along with the low booms of thunder that follow.

"Who's throwing pebbles at my window?!" I chastise aloud, trying to locate the culprit. "F-Y-I: I'm armed, dangerous, and so tired of *this*!"

Tap! Tap! Tap!

At last, my eyes adjust to the dark and I see her, Nicole, waving at me from down below. Her hair is in a neat bun, and she is dressed in jeans and a shirt. Her feet are bare and in her hands is a neatly wrapped gift.

She motions for me to come down, and I hesitate for only a few seconds. Before I can stop myself, I am running downstairs with the can of mace still in my hand toward the front door. Making sure to turn off the alarm, I quietly close the door behind me and run around to the back of the house. Standing waiting for me in the same place is Nicole.

"What are you doing here?" I whisper, stopping a few feet away. "Are you possessed by Mermaids again?"

She immediately pinches me.

"Nope!" I laugh. "It's still you."

The teen looks at me with weepy eyes.

"I'm sorry that I couldn't come to your party," she apologizes. "My parents wouldn't let me."

"I understand." I grin, clasping my hands together. "Do they know that you're here now?"

She pauses and has the good sense to look guilty.

"Not really," she divulges as she stares at her toes. "I stole a car."

"What?" I blurt then lower my voice. "Have you lost your mind?"

"Not really *stole* per say," she clarifies, biting her bottom lip. "More like I *borrowed* my brothers' Jeep."

"*Nicole!*" I exclaim in a harsh whisper. "You are nuts! Your brothers are going to have a conniption!"

"I know, but I wanted to give you this before your birthday was over." She grins and hands me the small, jewelry box shaped gift.

Worried for her, I glance at my watch. According to the display, it is eleven-fifty-five at night. Five more minutes and the day I was born will be over.

"Thank you," I reply, tears welling. "You didn't have to get me anything."

"I wanted to." She beams. "Open it!"

The sparkling silver wrapping paper is so delicate that I hate tearing it; however, Nicole loses patience and rips it off for me. Astonished by the kind gesture, my hands start to shake, and it takes more effort to remove the lid from the white box. When I finally get it open, what I see makes the tears fall.

"It's a locket!" I screech then slap my hand over my mouth.

"*Shh!*" Nicole reprimands. "You're going to wake everyone."

"I can't believe that you got this for me." I sniffle, holding back the sobs that want to follow. "It must have cost a small fortune."

"I've been working more hours at my parents' grocery store." My estranged friend giggles. "I convinced my dad that I needed to earn some extra cash."

"I don't know what to say." I grin until my face hurts.

"I'm glad you like it." Nicole nervously plays with her fingers. "Look inside of it."

Obediently, I do as she requests. Inside of the locket is a tiny picture of the six of us: Jenny, Mike, Andrew, Nicole, Ando and me.

I recognize the photo immediately.

"This is the picture we took in front of the movie theatre that night after the swim meet." I chuckle, wiping the tears away.

"Keep it close to your heart," she orders with a sniffle. "That way we will always be together… no matter what."

Suddenly, Nicole's watch beeps.

"It's midnight," she advises. "Your birthday is officially over."

I grin as I add the silver locket to the rest of my charms. It sparkles even in the dark. So does Nicole's smile.

"I have to go soon." The young woman grimaces. "I don't want my parents to find out that I snuck out of the house."

"Do you want some cake before you leave?" I stall her with sweets knowing that they are her weakness.

It does not take long for her to nod.

"Wait right here," I order, running to the house. "I'll be right back."

Shortly after, I return with the remainder of the birthday cake and two forks. I also found a small plate with the last of the deviled eggs and stuffed mushrooms. I searched for the pimento cheese finger sandwiches, but they were nowhere to be found. Under my arm, I have a bottle of water in case Nicole has to wash the evidence off of her mouth. When she eats chocolate, she can turn into a little piglet.

Silently, we sit on the grass, and I wait as Nicole takes her first bite of cake. Her eyes instantly close and she moans in ecstasy. When she finishes chewing, she can barely speak.

"This is better than seeing Mike in his swim trunks," she moans again, taking another bite.

"You crack me up," I sputter, unable to stop myself.

"Ok, tell me everything that's happened since the last time we saw each other," Nicole pleads. "But talk slowly so I can enjoy this cake."

I smile.

"Amy crashed my party," I reveal.

"Get out!" The shocked high schooler proclaims, slapping my thigh.

"I swear!" I cross my heart and hope to die.

"Tell me more," Nicole encourages, continuing to nom.

"Well, remember when Amy and I jumped off the balcony at the homecoming dance?"

"Yeah," she responds, reaching for a deviled egg.

"Wait! Scratch that!" I wave my hands around my head like I am swatting at insects.

"Ooo-kay," Nicole replies with a smirk.

"You'll never guess what I found out," I reply, taking a stuffed mushroom off the plate.

"What did you find out?" she asks, the deviled egg hovering near her open mouth.

I hesitate, debating whether or not to tell her about Amy or her mom.

"Spill it, Selena," she orders as she takes a bite of the hearty treat. "Oh my gosh! Does this have *crabmeat* in it?"

I nod.

I should say it quickly before I chicken out.

"Amy is a Mermaid, and it wasn't a giant fish that pulled you out of your grandfather's boat when you were a little girl… it was Nicole's mom, Rose! You were going to be her lunch!"

Nicole begins to choke on the egg. Gently, I pat her back and then open the bottled water so she could clear her throat. Speechless, Nicole sits on the grass with her mouth wide open.

Thankfully, there are no flying bugs out tonight. I would not want her to swallow one.

"Did you hear what I said about Amy?" I ask, biting my lip.

Nicole nods.

"What about her mom?"

My best friend nods again and this time closes her mouth.

"Did you understand the part about her wanting to *eat* you?" I ask. "Nod if you are still with me."

Slowly, she nods as she takes another sip of water.

"Did all of this information make your brain explode?" I dig for clarification.

Nicole nods again and lets out a long exhale.

"I'm sorry," I apologize, feeling contrite. "But I wanted you to know that it was *Amy* controlling you and it was *Amy's mother* who tried to kill you."

"But your Aunt Leukosia saved me," Nicole responds, blinking often as though she is still trying to process all of this.

"Yes." I smile. "My Aunt Leukosia saved you."

"What happened to Amy's mother?"

I swallow hard not wanting to say it out loud.

"Tell me, Selena," Nicole urges. "I might as well know it all."

"In order to protect you." I pause feeling awkward. "My aunts had to… *kill* Amy's mom."

Nicole stops drinking.

"Mr. Jacobs told everyone that she drowned," Nicole replies without emotion.

Well, technically she did.

The teen contemplates my statement, but all I can do is watch her.

"At least now I know why Amy possessed *me*," Nicole mumbles under her breath. "She blames me for what happened to her mom."

"It's her mother's fault for trying to freaking eat you!" I snap, unexpectedly feeling that all too familiar power surging inside of me, and for a brief second my Siren-vision switches on.

Startled, I cover my eyes.

"What's wrong?"

"Nothing," I fib as it passes. "Just an eyelash or dirt."

"Have I ever told you that Amy and I used to be friends in kindergarten?" Nicole admits meekly.

I shake my head and hand her the slice of cake she was munching on.

"A couple of times, I even spent the night at her house, and she stayed at my house a few times too," Nicole says it like it is a secret.

"What happened?"

"I'm not sure." Nicole blinks as if emerging from a strange dream. "One day, she came to school and told me that her mother said we couldn't be friends anymore."

"Why?" I ask, feeling sad for both girls.

"Amy never told me why," Nicole answers with weepy eyes. "That was the last time we talked… except if we absolutely had to because of school."

"So weird." I give my friend a much-needed hug.

Nicole literally shakes it off which makes me laugh.

"No more sad talk," my best friend announces, wiping her eyes. "Tell me more about the party."

I blush.

"Okay… you'll never guess what Andrew got me for my birthday… "

CHAPTER TWENTY

Monday morning arrives on padded paws, but I try to ignore it and focus on the positives. I have my health. My skin is clear for the moment. I found two dollars in change under the couch cushions and my hair looks extra shiny this morning. All in all, it is a great start to the day, until my brother bursts into my room without knocking.

"Happy Labor Day, Lena!" He giggles and throws himself down on my neatly made bed. "Tomorrow is the first day of school!"

Ugg!

"Why are you so happy about that?" I frown and push him off of the bed while I smooth out the wrinkles he caused, and re-fluff the pillows.

"I love school!" He beams. "I'm going to be a first grader this year."

"Whoop-tee-do!" I mock, grabbing my scuba gear and sunblock.

"Aren't you excited?"

"Do I look excited?" I growl, sliding my feet into my sandals.

"Where are you going?" he questions as I leave the room, race down the stairs, and exit the house.

"For a dive," I say excitedly, pushing the thought of starting school out of my head.

Ando stares at me.

"You're going by yourself?" he asks with concern.

"Yes, I'm going *alone*." I emphasize the word alone.

"You're not a good swimmer," he reminds, further irritating me.

"That's why I'm using scuba gear," I respond sarcastically, holding the items up toward the sky.

"I'm telling Mom and Dad," he threatens as he gives me a harsh look.

"Go ahead," I poke, wanting him to give me some privacy.

"I will," he counters, heading back to the house, stomping his little feet.

"Hey!" I call after him.

"What?" he grunts, turning to face me.

"Mom and Dad went to the store to get us school supplies." I grin. "They won't be back for a while."

Ando does a baby growl at me.

"You can't go swimming by yourself!" he yells. "I'll tell the aunts!"

"They took a leisurely swim to Jost Van Dyke to check on a school of marlin." I smirk, knowing that I have won this battle of wits. "They will be gone for a few days."

He pauses for a moment.

"Where's Jost Van Dyke?"

"It's one of the main islands in the British Virgin Islands," I educate, proud that I know that fact. "It's not too far from here."

"Then I'm going with you," he says, following me again.

"No," I rebuke, shaking my head. "I don't need you to babysit me. I'm older than you."

"But you're human," Ando retells as if I have forgotten.

"That's why I'm using scuba gear... made for humans... by humans," I scoff and stomp down the rocky steps.

"Let me put on my swimming trunks," he requests as he runs back into the house. "Wait for me!"

"Pff!" I snicker, continuing down to the shoreline, grumbling. "Who does he think he is? My guardian?"

The water is quite calm today with barely any movement. *Great!* Better for me. I can catch a quick swim and be back before my parents are the wiser. Getting Ando to keep his trap closed is simple. All I have to do is bribe him with action figures or toy cars.

Problem solved!

Hastily, I put on the scuba gear over my bathing suit and lowered myself into the sea. The water is tranquil and at the perfect temperature. Overhead, the gulls are squawking at a school of flying fish racing across the surface toward the open ocean. For a moment, I actually feel jealous.

As my body submerges, I see everything with new eyes. Among the long tangles of seaweed that grow out of the sandy floor, tiny carefree silver fish play hide-and-seek between their forest-green leaves as the slowly moving currents make the plants dance in place. In the distance, all I see is blue in multiple shades, dark and light mingling together in perfect harmony. I miss this so much.

Then I feel the first tug. Then the second; finally, my flippers are ripped off of my feet.

What the hell is going on!

Terrified at what I might see, but really needing to see what has me, I decide to look down anyway.

Staring back at me is Andrew, his hair black as night, eyes green as emeralds, but his skin is slightly translucent, and he has a soft inner glow that radiates all around him. He smiles and I notice that his once perfect teeth are now sharper and resemble shark's teeth. Then I look at the side of his neck.

Gills! Dear Father! He has gills! The man that I love has… gills?

As fast as I can, I paddle my way back to the surface, bursting out of the sea like a submarine performing an emergency blow. Horrified, I punch him right in the nose not caring if I break it or not.

"Ouch! Damn it, Selena!" he bellows. "That hurt!"

Unable to process what I am seeing; I slap him several times in the head and face and even get a few scratches in. All I can think of is that Amy sent him to kill me. I am so stupid believing someone as perfect as Andrew would want to be with me, and not only that—

He's a fish-boy!

Effortlessly, he grabs my wrists and holds them still. He stares at me with glossy, tear-filled eyes, eyes that burn right through my soul. How can he still have that effect on me?

"Selena!" he states firmly. "I'm not going to hurt you. Amy didn't send me, and I need you to be still."

Stunned, I continue to stare at my boyfriend who is effortlessly treading water beside me and then I feel it. Something brushes against my legs, and I scream. I scream so loud that my throat starts to hurt.

Gross! Not that!

"Don't freak out," Andrew declares calmly.

"Something touched me!" I proclaim in a state of panic. "What was that?"

He blushes.

"Look down," he requests, and I oblige.

What I see makes me hyperventilate.

"It's a tail!" I snap, losing my mind. "You have a tail? My God! *You have a tail!"*

"Keep your voice down… please," he begs. "Ando will hear you."

No words form in my brain. All of my senses shut down and if I cannot control it, I am going to lose my lunch right here… right now.

"What the hell is going on?" I say at last, staring at the stranger in front of me.

Andrew blushes even more then tries to hold my hands, but I yank them away.

"We need to talk," he says in a rush of words, looking toward the shore.

"Ya think!" I practically growl. "Are you a freaking Mermaid?"

He frowns.

"Actually, females are called Mermaids," he educates, giving a weak smile. "I'm a Merman."

"A Merman?" I groan, feeling my temples throbbing. "I think I'm going to be sick."

"Selena!" Ando's voice startles me from the shore. "I told you to wait for me!"

"Wait, Ando!" I yell, turning back to Andrew, but to my surprise he is gone, and I am left alone trying to figure out what crazy nightmare realm I am trapped in.

When I turn back, Ando is beside me.

"What's wrong?" he questions, wiping saltwater from his eyes.

"Nothing," I fib, glancing around the cove for any sign of my boyfriend.

"Are you ready to go diving?" He grins.

"Uh huh," I respond, scratching my head.

"Maybe, we can catch some lobsters for dinner," my brother insists.

My face heats even though the water is at a mild temperature.

"Let's go!" Ando exclaims, oblivious to what has recently occurred. "Race you to the bottom!"

I nod but let him start without me. Right now, my head is filled with all sorts of contradicting thoughts, all about my Andrew. The athletic teen who is also smart and funny.

This cannot be good.

Not good at all.

The End?

(I think not!)

EPILOGUE

By the time our parents return home, Ando and I already have dinner waiting: pan-fried pork chops with mashed potatoes and steamed green beans. My brother chose the menu after I complained about eating seafood… again.

"We made dinner!" Ando and I both yell as Mom rushes past us into her room, slamming both her bedroom door and then the bathroom door behind her.

Dad follows carrying several bags of school supplies that he dumps on the couch. The bags contain every item imaginable: ballpoint pens, number two pencils, an assortment of art supplies and paper, lots and lots of paper: construction paper, printer paper, graph paper, notebook paper… paper galore!

"This must have cost you guys a small fortune," I mock, lightheartedly.

"You made dinner?" Dad grins, ignoring my comment as he sniffs the air like a hound tracking a raw steak. "Have I told you lately that I love you?"

We both laugh.

"What's the matter with Mom?" I probe, taking one of the bags and rummaging through it.

"She hasn't been feeling well," Dad answers, staring at the closed door that leads to their bedroom.

"Should we make her a plate?" I ask, staring at the door too.

Dad nods.

"That sounds like a good idea," he agrees, taking off his sneakers. "We'll leave it in the microwave. Hopefully, she'll eat it later."

"Let's eat then," I say feeling extremely hungry.

"After you." Dad follows us into the kitchen.

Pretending to be Mom, I bring the containers of food to the table and place them in the middle. It all smells really... *off*... like it has all spoiled.

"What's wrong?" Ando inquires. "Why are you making a funny face?"

"I don't know," I respond, fighting off the overwhelming need to vomit.

"You're sweating," Dad apprises, pointing to my forehead. "It's cool in here."

Without thinking, I run my hand over my forehead and then wipe the perspiration onto my shirt like Ando would. I am just about to excuse myself, when my mother trudges into the kitchen holding her stomach and looking incredibly green.

"Honey?" Dad stands and helps her sit in the empty seat beside him. "Are you still feeling ill?"

Mom nods, her brow is sweaty too.

"Mommy, what's wrong?" Ando looks like he is about to cry.

Our mother just stares at all of us with this weird expression.

"Marina, please say something," Dad begs with a harsh Spanish lilt to his voice. "Tell us what's going on."

Mom smiles and blushes at the same time as she holds up the pregnancy test with the blue plus sign on the stick.

"I'm pregnant!" she exclaims excitedly, clapping her hands like Ando would, beaming from ear to ear.

What the f—!

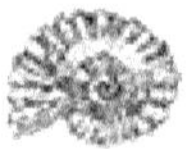

To say that today has been surprising is an understatement. Undoubtedly, I am still in shock from seeing Andrew as a Merman and now my mom claims that she is pregnant. Well, that put everyone in a bad mood, everyone except my parents who are jumping for joy and already discussing baby names. Unfortunately, not only was dinner ruined because everyone else was too shocked to eat, but now another factor has been introduced into our already complicated familial equation.

Ando also took it pretty hard, even though he is pretending to be happy. Who can blame him? He is about to lose his position as the baby of the family. Now, he will have competition for everyone's affections. Fortunately, I am safe. I am the eldest child and will always have that rank.

"Ando, are you done yet?" I ask as I pound on the bathroom door.

"I am now," he finally responds as he throws open the door and stomps down the hallway to his room.

"Do you want to talk about it?" I call after him.

"No!" he huffs and slams his door shut.

"Fine then," I sulk, feeling abandoned. "I'm just your big sister. It's okay to shut me out."

Brat!

The bathroom is sort of chilly tonight. I am not sure why, considering Ando was in here for almost ten minutes using up all of the hot water. I do not know why he is suddenly so angry with me. I did nothing. It was our father who planted his flag on Mt.

Olympus when we were in Capri during summer break. If my brother wants to blame someone, blame Dad.

Oh well! I shrug. *He'll come around eventually.*

Quickly, I strip down to my birthday suit and jump into the pre-warmed shower. Not wanting to waste any more water, I grab the bar of soap and start to lather up. As is my custom, I start from the face and work my way down until all of my bits are properly and thoroughly clean. Then I rinse really well…

Wait!

As the water rinses off all of the suds, I happen to notice them… tiny, pin-sized shaped purplish bruises between my fingers and toes. Probably hallucinating, I examine them again, turns out they are real. The same marks were there before when I started showing the Siren traits.

Please be a sign!

Well, isn't this a fortuitous change of events?

Maybe, the Earth has decided that I have suffered enough.

Maybe, I have proven that I can make good decisions and still be a Siren.

I cross my fingers and say a silent prayer, knowing fully well that anything can happen.

Especially in this family!

ABOUT THE AUTHOR

 Alisa K. Michaels, an American author and schoolteacher, lives with her husband in the South-Eastern United States. Michaels is a Rollins College Alumna having degrees both in English and Secondary Education.

She brings to her authorship her experiences growing up on a beautiful, tropical island paradise in the U.S. Virgin Islands before coming to the mainland in her youth. She draws from those experiences to create her fantastical vision.

Alisa K. Michaels is a proud mother of three grown daughters, and a closet monster named Bucky.